A PINCH OF LUCK

HANNAH PHILLIPS

Book Cover by Addie Reid

Illustrations by Kye Auri

https://hannahphillipsauthor.weebly.com/

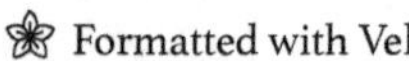 Formatted with Vellum

To all my spoonies.
You are seen, and you can make it through this.
You'll always have a person to turn to in me.

TRIGGER WARNINGS:

Throughout reading, you will come across these triggers. If you need a break from reading, need to put the book down, or put the book down before you start, feel free. Your mental health comes first.

This book was written with a lot of my own experiences. Please know that the entire book is written with the utmost care; I've had multiple people read and help me make this book the best it can be.

Please also know that every individual has a different experience when it comes to their disabilities. Someone else's FND (functional neurological disorder) is most likely different than mine and Clover's. Everyone has a different road when it comes to getting diagnosed and medicated; even if they may have the same disability as Clover (or any other person or fictional character) does not mean their experience is the same.

Mild Cursing
Hospital Visits
Medical Problems

Medical Trauma
Flaws of US Healthcare
Mental Health Struggles
Death of a Parent (off page)
Injury and Illness of a family member (off page)

All my love,
Hannah

NOTE ON AI

No Artificial Intelligence was used in the creation of this novel, or any art on or in the book.

Due to the rise of Artificial Intelligence (AI), authors are being targeted for using emdashes and stylized punctuation, among other techniques. Hannah Phillips, as well as most fiction authors, have been using these techniques for years; long before AI was being used to write.

Thousands upon thousands of authors works were downloaded illegally to train these AI systems— without the author or publisher's prior knowledge. They were also not compensated.

Please know that AI imitates authors' works, not the other way around.

Thank you.

1

———

I don't know what I was thinking. I wheel myself through the airport slowly, drowsy even after sleeping nine of the eleven hour flight. I'm still tired despite the smooth flight.

I wasn't planning on coming to England after being diagnosed with FND (Functional Neurological Disorder). Waking up without feeling in your legs, not being able to fully know they're there until being able to see them, changes everything about your life, except apparently, your dreams. I thought about staying closer to home, but ultimately didn't want to give up on my dreams. When would I have an opportunity like this again? My parents supported my decision wholeheartedly.

I groan as I cut another corner too close, knocking me and my chair off kilter. We haven't gotten around to getting me a custom wheelchair, as we have been more concentrated on getting me to England before classes start. I'm exhausted and I can't wait to get to my dorm and fall asleep.

There's a man standing in front of me holding a sign that says "Clover Dixon". I sigh, relieved, at least this part is working how it should. When I wheel up to him, he looks down at me and blinks, "I don't think you're who I'm looking for."

"You sure?" I ask, "Cause my name is Clover Dixon and I requested a car."

"Oh please, there's no way a girl in a wheelchair came overseas for school without a chaperone." I blink at him, feeling the rush of spiteful energy reinvigorate me. To start, I'm not a girl; I'm nonbinary. Secondly; people in wheelchairs aren't restricted to staying at home.

"I told you," I say again, this time more firmly, "my name is Clover Dixon, and I'm going to school in Newcastle. Now that we've got that settled, can you please drive me to my dorm so I can sleep?"

Why did his one sentence give me more motivation to do this than anything that my parents said? I roll my eyes at his blank stare.

He nods once and I roll forward, opening the back door of the car and tossing my carry-on and my backpack in. I stand up, fold the chair and sit down.

"You mind being a dear and tossing that in the back? Gently, or else you owe me a new chair," I say sweetly before slamming the door shut in his face. He deserves it after how he treated me.

WE DROVE for half an hour before getting to campus. Neither of us said anything during the drive. At least I didn't, as, I had my headphones on listening to music. I didn't want to deal with anymore of this idiot's bullshit. I know I'm a wheelchair user, but it doesn't mean I should be treated any differently.

He pulls up to Tyne Hall, one wheel propped up on the

sidewalk. I groan internally, his careless parking is going to make this much harder for me.

He immediately gets out of the car, yanking my wheelchair out of the trunk of the car aggressively. I roll my eyes as I get my bags together and get out of the car. The driver's tapping his foot impatiently, like he's annoyed with me and my chair.

The moment I'm on the sidewalk, the driver gets back in hastily and takes off without another word.

I load my bags onto the back of my chair and sit down. I turn to get a closer look at the hall, and freeze. There are four stairs to get through the main entrance.

I turn around and rustle through my bag, frantically trying to find the information packet that I was sent. Once I find it, I pull it out of my backpack and flip through it. The moment I see it, I dial the help number for Tyne Hall.

"Hello, Tyne Hall, how can I help you?" A pleasant voice trills through my phone.

"Hi," I say, trying my best to be pleasant as well, "Is there an accessible entrance to get into the hall?"

"Accessible?" she asks. *I have a bad feeling about this...*

"Yes, accessible, as in can I get into the building as a wheel-chair user?"

"Oh, umm... the inside of the building was built to be accessible but I don't think there's any way for wheelchair users to get in."

"Well... that's not good," I sigh to myself, trying not to push my frustration in her direction— I know it's not her fault.

"Are you assigned to this dorm?" She asks after a few seconds, realization hitting her.

"Yup," I tell her, looking down at the paper again like it's magically going to change to an accessible dorm, "Dorm room... 124."

I remember researching the university, and their dorms

after my symptoms started. I had already accepted their offer to go to school here; when I called housing and admissions I was assured that I would have an accessible dorm.

"I'm sorry, I don't think there's anything I can do to help you with this. If there's anything you can think of, I will help you as best as I can."

"Actually, I think there is something you could do to help me..."

"I'M SORRY, there aren't any more accessible dorms available," is the only thing I've been told over the past hour. I'm still sitting outside Tyne Hall, since I've got nowhere else to go while trying to get this figured out.

I put my head in my hands after hanging up my seventh call. I'm in a foreign country, alone, and without somewhere to stay. What a great way to start my first day in England.

I want to text my friends Adria and Caitlyn, but it's the middle of the night back home. I shake my head, there's no way I'll be able to sleep in my chair on the street. I desperately need to figure something out.

Someone catches my eye across the street. He's sitting at a cafe, drinking something— probably tea if he's British. He's been watching me for awhile. He's hot, but if he's a stalker I don't want anything to do with him.

We make eye contact and he smiles at me. I smile back, unable to resist. He raises an eyebrow at me, concern seems to etch his features. Obviously he's noticed me like I've noticed him.

He stands up and puts his drink down, holding eye contact with me. He holds up one finger in a 'one second' gesture.

Before I know it, he's back. He crosses the street, walking

in my direction. I flinch a bit as I notice he's coming directly towards me. There's nothing I can do to stop this interaction. I shift my chair so the handles are to the back of the building and put my rolling suitcase in front of my legs, instinctively.

He gets to me and smiles. Now that I'm closer, I can tell that he's close to my age with dark hair and dark eyes. Dark eyes are said to be the most boring, but his eyes are so deep and expressive. I've never seen anything like them.

"Is everything alright?" He asks, expression laced with concern. He has a British accent.

"Oh, yeah, everything's fine," I say, doing my best to sound convincing.

"Are you sure? I've seen you dial at least three different people frantically. Do you go here, then? Is this your dorm?"

"Do *you* go here?" I shoot his words back at him.

"Yeah, I'm in the archaeology program."

"That's cool, I'm in the classical studies program." I share, feeling more comfortable now that we've started talking.

"I'm Kaid, by the way," he introduces himself, holding his hand out to me.

"Clover."

"So..." he pauses awkwardly, as if trying to decide how he wants to say his next sentence. "Now that we're a bit acquainted, are you comfortable telling me about what's going on here?"

"I can't get into my dorm," I shrug, trying to hold back my tears. This isn't the time for tears. "I don't have anywhere to stay tonight."

He looks to Tyne Hall, then back to my wheelchair, then to Tyne Hall again and finally to my face.

"You know," he starts, shifting back and forth on the balls of his feet nervously.

"I have an flat with a spare room... it's on the first floor and all hardwood."

"I'm shocked that room hasn't been taken," I study him intently.

He shrugs, "I haven't really been looking for anyone, I don't need to have a roommate."

"Really?"

"The room's yours if you want it."

"I don't have much money," I tell him. If he has a spare room and hasn't given it away yet, he probably has money. Lots of it.

"We can worry about that later," he shrugs, "Please come, at least for tonight. If you don't want to stay after tonight, I'll help you find a new place."

"Are you sure?" I can't resist asking.

"Of course I'm sure, I wouldn't ask if I wasn't. Now, what do you say?"

"You know what?" I sigh, "Why not."

2

K aid's apartment is absolutely amazing. He did say it was wheelchair accessible, but I was skeptical at first. Turns out he was right, and it's even better than I could've imagined.

The place is massive, with windows along the back wall, a garden and a balcony.

"Nice place," I tell him as I fully roll in. I'm awestruck with the apartment.

"Thanks," he smiles, "I'll show you to your room. I'm sure you've had a long day."

I exhale, so thankful to not have to talk to anyone anymore.

He leads me down a wide hallway and to the first room. I roll into the room, and turn to Kaid.

"Thank you," I tell him, "For everything."

"If you need it, the bathroom is at the end of the hall. Have a good night." He smiles at me warmly, closing the door softly behind him as he leaves.

I wheel over to the bed, pushing the covers to the side, locking my chair and transferring onto the bed.

A LOUD KNOCK echoes around my room, waking me from my deep slumber.

"What?" I mumble to myself, my voice still groggy from sleep. All the memories from yesterday come rushing back to me.

Another knock echoes, and I raise my voice as I tell him to "Come in."

"Good morning, Miss Clover," he says as he opens my door and comes into my room. He stays on the opposite side of the room, holding a tray of food.

"What time is it?" I mutter, pulling myself up a bit to see him. I rub at my eyes, trying to see a bit clearer.

"It's almost noon. You seemed tired, so I let you sleep," he shrugs.

"It's almost noon?" I immediately sit up, my lower back screaming in pain. *Right, my body doesn't work that way anymore.* "I have so much to do!"

"Well, the first priority is to get you rested."

"I figured the first priority was to get me rooted into this timezone," I grumble, transferring into my chair. I sigh to myself as I realize that I'm wearing the same clothes that I was wearing yesterday.

"We'll worry about that tomorrow."

"My classes start tomorrow." I roll towards the hallway, trying to get to the bathroom. I turn back towards him, as he continues talking.

"No classes start tomorrow, I assure you," he says. "You should eat something before you start worrying."

"Too late," I grumble, and roll down the hall.

"You need to eat," Kaid's leaning against the kitchen counter, scrolling on his phone as I roll into the main area of the apartment.

"I'll eat later, I need to find somewhere to stay."

"There's nowhere else to stay, everything's booked. I figured that would be your first stop, so I checked. You're more than welcome to look again if you want," he tells me gently.

"Fine, I'll eat." I

"Come on, we can eat in the kitchen," he says, walking down the hallway. I roll behind him slowly, my body still sore from the uncomfortable plane seat I was stuck in yesterday.

In the kitchen, there's a whole array of food. No wonder he wanted me to come to the kitchen, he made so much food. He made every sort of breakfast food one could imagine.

"Now don't expect this everyday…" he trails off as he sits down next to me. "I was craving a little bit of everything."

"Why don't I believe you?" I ask as I start filling my plate up with the food he made. He chuckles, not answering me as he fills his plate up.

"You can stay here as long as you'd like," he tells me, changing the subject. "I truly am sorry that there isn't anywhere else for you to go. I'll help you find somewhere to stay, but I can almost guarantee that there won't be anything open until spring semester starts."

I sigh, suddenly not feeling hungry. I really want to talk to Caitlyn and Adria, but I can't right now.

"Thanks," I tell him, stabbing my pancake more times than necessary.

"You need to stop stressing," he says quietly, reaching a hand out towards me. He doesn't touch me, though, just rests his hand above my shoulder and waits for me to nod before putting his hand down to comfort me. *At least he's polite. If I have to be stuck here, at least I have someone nice with me.*

"How about we go out today? Get your mind off of everything, and have you get to know Newcastle," he offers, taking a bite of bacon.

"Sure, why not," I say. If I'm going to be stuck here, I might as well get to know Kaid. Here's hoping that the two of us can become friends.

After breakfast, I make my way back to my room. The room is completely void of my belongings except for the backpack and carry-on I flew with. Everything else is probably at Tyne Hall still— most of my stuff was shipped here. I make a note on my phone to call someone to get my stuff transferred. I try to do it now, but they're closed on Sundays. *Of course they are.*

Kaid didn't tell me what time he wanted to leave; so I check the current time is in Lockwoods Lake, the small town that my best friends still live in. Unfortunately it's early enough that they probably aren't awake yet. I would feel terrible if I woke them up, even if it was for a valid reason.

A knock sounds at my door. "Hey, are you almost ready?" Kaid stands in my open doorway, leaning against the doorframe. "I figured I would show you around the general area, and head to campus for a bit so we can scope out your schedule."

"You really thrive on organization, don't you?" I chuckle, transferring myself back into my chair from my bed.

"I do not," he says too quickly.

I laugh.

"May I push you?" He asks, gesturing to the handles of my chair. Once I nod, he puts his hands down and pushes me out of my room, making sure to turn the light off.

"What do you say to a round of twenty questions?" I suggest, wringing my hands together. If we're going to be living together, we should probably get to know each other.

"Sounds great to me," he says, steering me out the front door of the apartment. We make our way through the lobby and then we're outside.

I was so stressed last night, after everything that occurred, that I didn't actually get the chance to look around Newcastle. It's absolutely beautiful, buildings both old and new surrounding the street we're on, a gorgeous blue sky with bright white clouds. I know that I'm looking at the same sky that I looked at in Lockwoods Lake, but it's so much brighter and more beautiful here.

"Here's my first question," Kaid says as he wheels me down the street, making sure that he doesn't hit any severe bumps. I've never had someone so considerate while driving my chair before. Heck, I'm barely this considerate with myself.

"What's your go to coffee shop order?" He asks.

"Huh, I thought you were going to say 'what's your favorite color?'"

"Nah, that's too basic."

"Teal isn't basic," I argue.

"Teal isn't basic," he agrees, "but at least my question is relevant."

"Relevant to what?"

He doesn't answer, only helps me up a curb and guides my chair towards a building. The building is small, but looks homey.

"What's your go to coffee shop order?" He repeats as he opens the door to the building, gesturing for me to roll in.

"Chai latte," I tell him as the smell of coffee overwhelms me. The small building is a coffee shop, a very small coffee shop. It looks like a small business that modified the first level of a house. It's beautiful.

"Chai latte it is," Kaid announces as he walks into the shop behind me. The door closes behind him and he rolls me up to the counter.

Before I have the chance to say anything, Kaid starts to order. "A large chai latte, and a large vanilla latte," he tells the barista behind the counter. They nod, writing the order on some paper cups.

Kaid pulls his card out of his wallet, and I immediately exclaim "Wait a minute—"

"Nope," he says, apparently knowing what I'm about to say. "You've gone through enough these past twenty four hours, let me buy you a singular latte."

"You don't need to do that," I insist, "you've already offered me a place to stay, and that's more than enough."

"Too bad," he says, swiping his card on the machine, "I like spoiling my friends."

"You already consider me your friend?" I ask as we move off to the side to wait for our drinks.

He shrugs shyly, "Why not."

Our lattes are put on the counter, and I immediately grab it and take a sip, burning my tongue."Oww," I winced, fanning my mouth with my hands.

"Well at least I can check off that you'll drink your latte the second you get it even if it's boiling hot," Kain teases as he grabs his latte as well.

I put my drink into the cup holder attached to the side of my chair. I then hold my hand out, silently telling Kaid to hand me his drink so he can push my chair still.

He hands me his drink and we make our way out of the coffee shop.

"Your go," he tells me, the door slamming shut behind us.

"What's your favorite color?"

"Please tell me you're kidding."

"Of course not! Color preferences are incredibly important."

"But so basic, God, Miss. Clover, don't you have a better question?" I cringe as he says 'Miss Clover', and he doesn't notice. It's probably too late now to correct him on my pronouns, so I don't bother saying anything.

"Okay, fine," I argue back, "Why are you so basic in getting a vanilla latte?"

"Please tell me you're joking."

"Nope," I pop the 'p'.

"Vanilla lattes aren't basic! Most cafes don't sell them here!"

"Seriously?" I ask, shocked, "Vanilla lattes are the most basic thing back in America."

"Huh," he muses.

He guides us down the street until we reach what I'm assuming is the Main Street. There are small businesses scattered everywhere now, compared to being surrounded by houses and apartment complexes before.

There's so much to see and do, and I'm glad that I have Kaid to show me around. I would've been overwhelmed by myself otherwise.

"Where to first?" I ask, trying not to turn all the way around in my chair as I rush to read business signs as we pass.

"I was thinking we could stop at a convenience store or bookstore."

"I'm always down for a bookstore," I tell him, getting more excited by the second.

"I figured you'd be excited by that." I can hear the smile in his tone. We cross the street, and he stops my chair in front of an older building.

"Don't worry," he says as I open my mouth to talk, "I know

it doesn't look accessible, but there's a back entrance. You'll find that if you go up to the front door, it's nowhere as aesthetically pleasing as the back."

"Really?" I turn around to look at him skeptically.

"Really. One of the owners is a wheelchair user, they wanted to make it so that wheelchair users have the better experience compared to able-bodied people for once."

"Hurry up, we need to go in!"

He wheels me up to the back door, and hits the button to open it. The door opens immediately and Kaid steps back from my chair.

"I'll let you take it from here," he tells me, giving me space to roll myself into the building.

He's right. The wheelchair entrance is so incredibly gorgeous and aesthetically pleasing. There are fairy lights strewn across the bookshelves, being the primary light in the space. The shelves are all dark, and I immediately feel calm wash over me. I can see this being a place I come back to visit frequently.

I roll around the store, waving at the clerk reading behind the checkout counter, as I look through the shelves. Nothing's really peaking my interest until I come across the classics shelf.

My hand twitches as I see a special edition of *Sense and Sensibility* by Jane Austen, my favorite book of all time. My hand reaches out before I can think about it, grazing the faux leather spine.

I've been wanting to reread it, so I might as well buy it, right? I pick it up and examine it closer. This is the book of my dreams.

"You find something?" I jump in my seat, not realizing someone was there. I turn around to see a smiling Kaid.

"O-oh umm, I'm not sure," I stutter, looking back down at the book in my hands.

He raises an eyebrow at me, an amused look on his face. "So, are you going to buy it?"

"Yes," I say with finality, not letting myself look at the price tag. I make my way to the checkout, Kaid behind me with a few books in hand.

3

———

My first day of school starts with me falling out of my bed. I groan, I've really got to get used to bed sizes here. It's a few centimeters difference, but it's a bigger pain than expected.

I grab my chair and pull it towards me. I use the mattress to hoist myself upright before transferring into my chair.

My alarm hasn't gone off yet, but it's close enough to time that I might as well get up. There's no way can just go back to sleep, anyways, I'm too anxious.

"Good morning, Miss Clover," Kaid says, walking past my room. I leave the door open while I'm sleeping, just in case I need to go to the bathroom or something. I cringe at him saying 'Miss' but there's nothing that I can do about it now.

"Morning, Kaid," I say, to get my mind off of him misgendering me. He doesn't know, so it isn't his fault. It's actually mine for not saying anything sooner.

"Ready for your first day?" he asks, adjusting his shirt.

"I think so," I nod. I wheel to my closet and grab my clothes out. It's been a few days since we went out to that bookstore, and since then we've gotten into a routine of sorts and have gotten to know each other better. The rest of my things have also been delivered from Tyne Hall which makes everything easier.

"I can drive you, if you want," he offers, "I'm heading in the same direction."

"I thought you didn't have classes today?" I turn around and look at him confused.

"I looked at my schedule wrong," he pulls his shirt a bit more aggressively than before, "apparently I have an eight am class." I look at the clock, it's seven thirty.

I raise an eyebrow, "Shouldn't you be heading towards campus then?"

"I'm just waiting to see if you need a ride," I look at him, wide eyed. I just woke up, and he needs to be out the door within the next five minutes if he wants to be there on time. My class isn't until nine, but the car is the easiest and most reliable way for me to travel. You never know if wheelchairs can get on the trains, it's always been hit or miss. I've been too scared to try.

"Give me five minutes," I tell him, slamming the door in a rush before I start to get ready for the day. Thankfully I had planned out the exact steps needed for me to get out the door, and can get fully ready quicker than I'd usually be able to.

WE MANAGE to get to Newcastle University on time for Kaid's class. He rushes out of the car, barely getting the chance to say 'bye' to me, right as the car gets put into park. I chuckle to myself, not being able to resist.

I get out of the car slowly, using the car to hold myself up as I make my way to the trunk of Kaid's SUV. Kaid has said a thousand times that I would never have to take my chair out of the back by myself, saying that he'd always be there to help me. I don't blame him for needing to go to class, and accidentally forgetting to help me. It happens. I had to do this by myself anytime I wanted to go anywhere back home. It's not that big of a deal.

I open the back hatch of the SUV and slowly pull the chair out, using my upper body to keep us both steady. I slowly push the chair down, not letting it fall or touch my legs. I push the folded chair open, put the cushion down and sit down, letting out a deep breath as I do. I always forget how much effort it is to get my chair out.

"Oh my god, Clover, I'm so sorry!" I hear someone yell as I close the trunk and lock the car. I turn in my chair and see Kaid running towards me.

"What are you doing?" I yell back at him, "Go to class!"

"I'm so sorry I forgot to set your chair up," he said, panting with exertion.

"You're fine, I've got it, no problem."

"You shouldn't have to!" he exclaims, sounding annoyed at himself, "I should've helped you."

"I told you, it's fine," I insist, "You're going to be late for class, you need to go!"

"Fine," he surrenders, turning around and rushing back towards the school.

I roll my eyes, and put my headphones in. My arms aren't used to pushing myself everywhere yet, so having music playing helps me divert my concentration from the pain.

I start rolling myself slowly towards the library, taking my time. On the way, I watch the hustle and bustle of students trying to get to class on time. I honestly don't know who would want to take an eight am class.

Once I get to the library, I settle at a table on the first floor not wanting to bother with finding an elevator. I open my computer and begin looking through the syllabi from my classes, wanting to get ahead. I got here on a scholarship, and I am not about to lose it.

I GET to my first class of the day ten minutes early. I gave myself plenty of time to get there, figuring I would struggle to find it. Luckily, it was much easier than I thought it would be. I immediately set up my computer with the professor's slides, as only being able to sit in the back of lecture halls makes it a lot harder to see slides, and my notebook before grabbing my book to start reading.

I pull my old, annotated copy of *Sense and Sensibility* out of my bag and put it on my desk to read. It's a comfort book for me, and it felt right starting a reread on my first day of my Classical Studies degree. The minute I started it for the first time years ago, I knew it was going to be a favorite, and started annotating, putting all my thoughts into the pages. Since then, I've reread it countless times, always finding new things to annotate. This book is one of my most prized possessions, housing my deepest thoughts and feelings.

Class starts, and I immediately get engulfed in the professor's lecture. Having a morning class was far from my first choice but this class, "Jane Austen's Impact", which was only available at this time, promised a trip to visit her home in Hampshire at the end of the semester. Who could say no to that?

The door to the lecture hall creaks open about ten minutes into the lecture. If I wasn't stuck in the back of the hall, I probably wouldn't have heard it. Plus, it probably wouldn't have distracted me from my notes.

Of course, whoever is late to the lecture decides that the best place for them to sit is next to me. I suppress my groan, and continue scribbling notes.

"What did I miss?" they lean over and whisper to me. I let out a sigh, quiet enough that they can't hear me and scratch out "turn your airdrop on" on a scrap piece of paper and pass it to them. Luckily enough for them, I'm in a giving mood. Maybe it's because it's my first day here, and I want to make friends, or maybe I'm feeling generous. Either way, I pass the paper to them.

They turn their AirDrop on, and I send the presentation their way. They immediately start writing their own notes, and I immediately feel better about helping them. They might have been late, but it's clear that they care about the class too. Seems like we might actually end up being similar enough to be friends. I'll have to find out after class. I divert my attention back to the professor and frantically write notes.

After class ends, I look over to my right at the person who slipped into class late. They look like a female around my age, but I don't want to assume anything. They have shiny black hair that falls to their mid back, olive-toned skin, and the most beautiful chocolate brown eyes.

"Thank you so much for sending me the presentation, you really saved my ass," she exclaims turning to look at me.

"It's no problem," I tell her, "My name's Clover, xe/xem pronouns."

"Zahra, she/her," she smiles at me. "I was considering asking to borrow notes from the first ten minutes of the lecture, but I missed it and that's my fault."

"I can send you the notes," I say before I can think about it again. I just have this feeling about Zahra, that if I play my cards right, we're going to be good friends.

"Oh, I knew you were the right person to sit by," she says happily, "I had this feeling about you."

"Aww, thanks," I smile. I write my phone number and email on another scrap of paper and slide it over to Zahra. "Reach out to me later, and I'll send you the notes."

"Maybe we could be study buddies?" she offers. "The prof said that she would assign partners if we didn't have them, and since we're sharing notes maybe we could be study buddies too?"

"Oh I forgot about that," I mutter to myself, "In that case, here's my phone number." I scribble down my phone number quickly and she laughs.

"Thanks again for the help," she says, "English isn't really my speciality, but Jane Austen was my Mom's favorite."

"Was?"

"O-oh, umm..."

"Shit, sorry, you don't have to answer that if you don't want to."

"No, it's fine, I just didn't expect you to notice that. She passed away few months ago. By that point, I had already declared my major, definitely not English, but a spot opened in this class and it felt like fate. So I took it, for my Mom," she says softly, not looking up at me.

"I'll help you if you need it," I say softly, my hand hovering over hers. I don't want to touch her if she's not comfortable, but I still want her to know I'm there for her.

She looks up at me finally and smiles gently, "Thanks Clover."

I change the topic after a few seconds of awkward silence, figuring that we'd both appreciate the distraction.

"You didn't really miss much," I assure her, "It was mostly

just syllabus stuff, and it's nothing you can't find on the actual paper."

"Oh good," she sounds genuinely relieved, "My alarm didn't go off this morning, and I wasn't about to miss this class." Now that she says that, I notice that she seems a bit disheveled.

"Don't worry about it," I smile, and she smiles back.

4

"**K**aid?" I call as I roll into his apartment. I wasn't able to find him after my class, so I had to make my own way home. It didn't really bother me, it just took me a bit longer than I expected. My arms are exhausted now, I'm so excited to get to my room and to lay flat on my back.

Nobody answers, and I shrug to myself. I roll into the apartment the rest of the way, closing the door behind me. The apartment doesn't seem empty, like it is. I mean, Kaid would answer if I called, right?

I roll into the living room, and deposit my backpack from my handlebars onto the couch. Something falls and I immediately turn around to see what it is. One of the throw pillows is now off of the couch, the pillow was all the way on the couch. How is it on the floor now?

I roll towards the back of the couch, not going to be able to go lay down without knowing what's going on.

I hear something shuffle from behind the couch and I immediately wheel over to see. I guess this is how I die. I'm pretty sure this is how most characters in horror movies die.

"What the hell are you doing?" Kaid exclaims from behind the couch.

"What the hell are you doing?" I exclaim back, my heart beating erratically in my chest. *What the hell is he doing, hiding behind the couch?*

"What are you doing here, I thought your class didn't end until noon?"

"It's one thirty," I deadpan, "Why are you hiding behind the couch?"

"I like sitting here sometimes..." he says after a few seconds of hesitation.

"What?"

"I like sitting behind the couch, and journalling. I feel like I'm away from the world back here."

"I yelled for you when I got home!"

"I didn't hear anything! I swear, it's a lot more isolated back here than you would expect."

"Oh whatever," I roll my eyes, and roll my chair back, "If you need me, I'll be in my room laying down."

"Okay...?"

"I'll see you for dinner," I holler over my shoulder as I make my way to my room.

"What's your favorite movie?" Kaid asks me at dinner a few hours later.

"I don't know," I look up him, confused. "Why are you asking about movies?"

He shrugs, "I figured we could have a movie night tonight."

"It's a school night."

"We're in college now, Miss Clover, we can do whatever we want."

"I don't know..."

"Come on, Clover, do something fun for once."

"What? I'm fun," I huff, feigning offense.

"Okay, I'll bite," he leans back in his chair and raises an eyebrow at me, "What do you do that's fun?"

"I... umm... read a lot."

"Okay, reading could be considered fun, but you only read classics. Classics aren't fun. Classics make me feel like I'm being forced to read for school."

"Classics aren't boring!" I exclaim, appalled.

"They are for me," he shrugs, "Now, what's your favorite movie?"

"*Sense and Sensibility*— the version..."

"Please tell me you're joking."

"What now?" I exclaim, leaning over the table more, "I answered your question!"

"I'm not about to watch a classic Jane Austen movie," he tells me plainly, "We're going to watch *The Princess Bride*, and that's that."

"Okay fine," I roll my eyes. I divert my attention back to my dinner, shoveling food down my throat. Kaid is so good at cooking, I would pay him good money— (if I had good money)— to make me dinner every night. In my opinion, he'd be better suited as a cook than as an archaeologist like he's studying to be.

After we finish eating dinner, Kaid sets up the couch for him to watch a movie while I clean the dishes. I'd much rather do the dishes than cook, and he'd rather cook than do dishes so we have the perfect arrangement.

"Come on," he laments, as I start to go down the hall to my room. He pats the spot on the couch next to him, "It's time for us to watch *The Princess Bride*,"

"I have classes tomorrow," I tell him, yet again.

"So? I do too," he says nonchalantly, "Come on, Clover, live your life to the fullest."

"It feels like you're trying to convince me to go to a club or something, not watch a movie."

"Ew, I would never try to make you go to a club. I hate clubs. And alcohol."

"Great, I'm glad we have the same opinion."

"I'm not trying to make you leave the apartment, just to sit on the couch and watch T.V for a few hours, it's really not that big of a deal. I want to hang out with my roomieee," he holds the last word out, and for a few seconds I wonder if he's going to keep going until I say 'yes'.

"You know what?" I sigh under my breath, "Let me go grab a blanket from my room, and then I'll be there."

"Yes!" He exclaims excitedly, falling into the couch in excitement.

I go to my room and grab my blanket like I told Kaid I would and then make my way back into the living room. Kaid has made a little area for me to sit, making sure that I had a spot for my legs to be propped up. I don't know how he knew that I'm most comfortable with my legs propped up, but obviously he's noticed how I tend to sit when I'm not in my chair.

There are also pillows making a little barrier around me, either for making sure I stay upright or to make sure that Kaid and I don't touch. I can't decide which is more likely, but I'll never say no to having a bunch of pillows surrounding me on a big comfortable couch.

"Do you want me to help you?" He offers, like he always does when I need to transfer into or out of my chair. I'm about to say no, but when I try and get out, I struggle. I must've pushed a bit too hard earlier, wheeling myself back from school.

"Yes, please," I say quietly, feeling embarrassed by needing the help. I don't let myself make eye contact with him as he stands up from his spot on the couch and holds his arm for me to grab onto as I stand out of my chair.

"I read online that nighttime is harder for people with chronic illnesses," he tells me as I sit down on the couch.

He doesn't immediately leave, mentally debating with himself about something. "I mean, I don't know exactly what chronic conditions you have, and I don't want to ask. But I do want to try and help you as much as possible."

A strong blush forms on my face at his words, I don't think anyone's cared this much about me outside of Caitlyn and Adria.

"Well, I have a chronic condition called Functional Neurological Disorder-" I stop as I see Kaid on his phone, "What are you doing?"

"I'm googling it."

"You know, 'googling' isn't an official word," I sigh, "do you want me to continue or not?"

"Can't you keep going while I research this?"

"No, because that means that I'll end up having to repeat it."

"Okay okay, let me finish typing this out before I forget it, and then I'll put my full attention on you. Promise."

He quickly types out whatever he was typing on his phone before putting it down on the couch next to him. He then gives me his full attention.

"Okay, Functional Neurological Disorder," he says. "Hit me."

I chuckle, and look down at my hands. I never like talking about my experience with FND, as it's kind of triggering for me. But I feel like Kaid deserves to know after everything he's does for me. I feel like we're going to be close one day anyways, might as well tell him now instead of delaying the inevitable.

"Well FND- sorry that's the acronym for Functional Neuro Disorder-"

"Stop worrying about it, I got the acronym. Calm down," he puts a hand on my knee and freezes, like he didn't think before his hand moved. He leaves his hand there, though, and rubs small circles gently to calm me down.

"Thanks," I say softly, and move on, "FND is a really weird illness, and is different for every person who has it. I mean, for me I woke up on a random July morning and my legs were numb. For others—"

"I'm sorry— can you repeat what you just said?"

"I woke up on a random July morning and my legs were numb?"

"Yeah that."

"What about it?"

"I need a second to process this, I mean seriously. You just woke up one day and your legs were numb?" I nod. "Damn, that sounds absolutely terrifying."

"Yeah, no doubt," I mutter, "I can't walk very well, and it hurts so much that I don't bother if I'm able to use my chair."

"Damn, talk about life flipping upside down,"

"Exactly," I nod. "As I was saying, everyone has a different experience with FND, some people can walk with or without mobility aids, some people can't even get out of their beds."

"Crazy."

"For real, sometimes I think that doctors diagnose FND because they don't have anything else to diagnose."

"Huh, I can see why you would think that," Kaid says, his other arm reaching over my shoulder. He pulls me closer to him and rubs his hand on my shoulder.

"Do you want to watch *The Princess Bride* now?" He asks, out of the blue.

"What?" I look at him confused. "Do I want to watch *The Princess Bride* now?"

"That's what I said," he clarifies, "I figured we don't want to talk about FND all night. I don't want to accidentally stress you out or something, so I figured we could do what we intended to do now."

"Good idea," I let out a breath. "Let's watch the movie."

5

____

"If you're not sitting next to your partner, now's the time for you to move next to them. I guarantee you're going to want to sit with them throughout the semester," Professor Kingston announces as everyone floods into the classroom.

Zahra and I are already settled in the back of the classroom. I'm pretty sure we're the only ones who have a partner for this project, the rest of the class is scrambling around changing seats and finding partners.

"It's nine o'clock on this lovely Wednesday morning," she announces, "Sit down, sit down everyone, so we can now explore the lovely world of Jane Austen."

Everyone rushes to sit in the closest seat to them. I've never seen a class listen to instruction so well. Is this how school is in the UK? Or is everyone reacting this way because Professor Kingston is attractive? It could go either way.

"Jane Austen, born in 1775, died at 45 in 1817," she says, clicking a button to switch the slide on her slideshow. "She wrote six complete novels in her life, two of which were published after her death, one of which you are going to do research on, and now that we've gotten past the boring part we can get to the interesting parts."

She clicks the slide again and there are six boxes, one for each of Austen's novels.

"*Pride and Prejudice, Sense and Sensibility, Emma, Persuasion, Northanger Abbey, and Mansfield Park.* These are the six most known Austen novels, and these would be the easiest for you to do your project on. There are multiple more, but since they aren't as popular it'll be harder to find information on them. Austen herself stated that she didn't believe that her novels were relevant or would be in the future, let alone two hundred years from publication. Isn't that fascinating?" she continues, pointing to each box as she talks.

I look over to Zahra and she nods, obviously agreeing to choosing one of the six novels. I'm not sure if it's going to be first come first serve on picking out novels, so I grab a post-it note from my bag and scribble *Sense and Sensibility* on it. I slide it over to Zahra who barely glances at it before nodding to me.

"This is a larger class, so I don't mind if more than one group has the same book." I sigh in relief at her words, "But I do want to know by the end of class, so talk it out with your partner and I'll be around."

The class immediately starts chattering around us, figuring out what book they are going to research.

"You want to do *Sense and Sensibility*?" Zahra asks, turning her chair towards me, "Why?"

"It's my favorite book," I tell her, "Did your Mom have a favorite Austen?" Zahra doesn't know it, but if her mom had a favorite book, I'd immediately forfeit my choice.

"Actually, it was *Sense and Sensibility*," she says softly, "I'm glad you love that book too, now we don't have to fight over what book to do for the project."

"I would've immediately relinquished it to you."

"Appreciate it."

"Of course."

"So what do we need to do for this project?"

"It's a really loose presentation, actually," I mutter as I skim through the requirements on my computer screen. "You need to do a presentation- no slideshows- about your book of choice, describing how people have interpreted the story over time."

"So it could literally be anything."

"Exactly."

"There's a lot of adaptations, there's even a Bollywood version, we could do our project on that."

"When you say a lot...?"

"I mean eight, some movies some tv shows, from all different cultures."

"We could watch them all in time order, and then do our presentation from there."

"Sounds good to me."

"I'll make a list and send it to you later."

"Oh wait, I still need to text you so you have my number," Zahra pulls her phone out of her pocket and types something on it before putting it down. I feel my phone buzz in my pocket, and set a mental reminder to save her contact later.

I pull my computer closer to me and start typing in an attempt to get a list of all of the *Sense and Sensibility* adaptations. *Sense and Sensibility* always gets me incredibly motivated, I don't know why. Everyone I ever talk to says that Austen is boring, but to me her and her books are the most interesting topic.

"Hello," Professor Kingston comes up to me and Zahra, "I figured I would start back here, you two seemed pretty excited about the project."

chair from the hospital, I don't have the means to get a better one."

"I think we need to eventually get you a better chair."

"That probably won't be able to happen until I get back to the states."

"Wait, what do you mean by that?" Zahra asks confused.

"Turn left here, and then it's the second building on the right," I tell her. "I'm actually an exchange student, I got accepted before I became disabled and started using the wheelchair, but I decided to come regardless."

"I'm glad you're here," she says softly as we make our way to the apartment building. Conversation trails off as we go to the apartment.

I unlock the door and gently toss it open. The door stays open, making it much easier for me to wheel into the apartment.

"Hey, what's up?" I hear Kaid holler from the living room most likely. Zahra freezes, immediately grasping the handlebars of my wheelchair and yanking back.

"What?" I turn my head to look at her confused, "That's just my room- oh I forgot to tell you about Kaid, didn't I?"

"Yup, you did."

"Shit, sorry," I cringe, "Kaid is my roommate, I wouldn't be here still if it weren't for him."

"Wow, he really must be special."

"I'd say so." I say quietly enough that Zahra can't hear me.

She lets go of the push handles, probably forgetting she was still holding on, and I wheel myself into the living room.

"Hey Kaid," I say as he comes into my sight, "This is my friend, Zahra, we're working on a project together for my Jane Austen class. I hope you don't mind that I invited her over."

"Oh, I don't mind at all," he says flippantly, "any friend of Clover's is a friend of mine, it's nice to meet you Zahra."

"Nice to meet you too," she says.

"Are you two planning on working in your room, or in here?"

"Umm... it depends on if I can find the first TV show," I look at Zahra, who shrugs. "We're probably going to start in my room, so I can take my bags off my chair, and then go from there."

"Sounds good to me."

6

———

"**A**h ha!" I declare excitedly a few hours later. I've been searching for a way to watch all of the *Sense and Sensibility* adaptations, for mine and Zahra's presentation, and it's been a struggle to say the least.

There are so many different interpretations, starting as early as 1971, going through so many different cultures. It's great, but also extremely difficult to find copies to watch.

"What's all the excitement about?" Kaid asks, coming up to my doorway and leaning on it.

"I finally got my hands on the Bollywood *Sense and Sensibility*," I tell him, pumping my fist.

"There's a Bollywood *Sense and Sensibility*?" He asks skeptically, "Now this, I wanna see."

"Me too," I tell him, "That's why I've been trying to find a copy of it to watch."

"You know, I could have helped you with finding copies. I have friends in the trade."

"How do you have so many connections? I barely have two friends here."

"You're also an exchange student, and have barely been

here for a week," he says softly, coming into the room the rest of the way.

"Good point,"

"I was thinking, though, that we could hang out this weekend," he suggests, sitting on the desk chair I moved to the corner of the room. He had it in the room when I first moved in, and I didn't need it, so I shoved it to the corner. I guess it's now Kaid's chair to sit in when he visits my room.

"Hang out?" I repeat.

"That's what I said, yeah."

"What were you thinking of doing?"

"Well there's this really cool science center in the city."

"I haven't been to one of those in years!" I exclaim excitedly, "That sounds so much fun!"

"I'm glad you think so, especially since I already bought tickets," he rubs the back of his head, "for some reason I thought I had already asked you, bought the tickets, and then realized," he trails off. I laugh, that sounds like something he would do.

THE WEEKEND COMES QUICKLY. Kaid and I have been chattering about our trip all week in excitement, and the day has finally come.

"Let's go!" Kaid bellows excitedly, as I roll into the living room.

"I need food," I grumble, still half asleep. Excited, but half asleep. It's a good thing that Kaid's driving today. And always, because I would definitely cause an accident, getting confused on which lane to drive in.

"Oh yeah, that's probably important," he concedes. He

paces around the kitchen for a second, checking cabinets, "We can just swing through McDonald's or something."

"Please tell me you're joking," I grumble, rolling into the kitchen. I open a lower cabinet, and grab a granola bar. This is exactly what I need right now.

"Can I have one?" I throw one at his head before he finishes his question, and before I process his words. He told me that he played sports as a kid, he should be able to catch it.

"Ow!" he exclaims, a split second later. *Oops, apparently I underestimated him.*

"Sorry."

"No you're not."

"Yeah, you're right."

"Gee, thanks."

"We should probably get going," I tell him as I toss my granola bar wrapper in the trash.

"Oh right!" He drops the topic immediately and walks over behind me. He puts his hands on my push bars and leans over the back of the chair to put his head on top of mine. "Let's head out, as long as you're ready."

"I'm ready, let's go!"

"Wow, this reminds me of home," I say, taking in my surroundings as Kaid rolls me into the science center. He just checked us in and got our wristbands, and we now have free rein of the area.

"Well that was the last thing I expected you to say," he chuckles.

"I have a museum like this somewhat close to my place back in the States," I reminisce, half ignoring his words, "I used to go all the time with my family before I moved."

"Moved here?"

"No, before I moved to Lockwoods Lake before my junior year. Now that I'm thinking about it, I really need to text my friends and set up a time for us to talk again..."

"What the heck is a 'junior year'?" Kaid asks confused.

"Year, umm, 11."

"Americans and all of their weird slang," Kaid mutters under his breath quietly. I probably wasn't supposed to hear it, but I nod my head in response anyways.

"Wait-" he stops walking all of a sudden, and I almost fall out of my chair at the sudden stop. "This wasn't there last time we were here!" I turn to see where he's looking, and turn back to look at him confused. "<u>An Exhibit Full of Models of Famous Buildings and Architecture</u>?" I ask confused.

"We *need* to go in," he insists.

"I mean, you are driving..."

"Let's go!" He starts pushing me again, faster this time, and I fall back in my chair at the impact. I guess Kaid doesn't think when he's excited. It's cute.

The exhibit is one big room, with dividers making it into a maze of different countries.

I roll through the exhibit slowly, leaving Kaid gawking at the first model of the Colosseum. He'll catch up to me eventually, I'm sure. If not, I can meet him at the end and rest a bit before the next exhibit.

"Oh cool, it's Buckingham Palace," I muse, rolling myself closer to the display setup to my right. There's a miniature replica of the palace, about the size of a kitchen table.

"Would you look at that?" Kaid comes up from behind me, and leans closer to the replica. Unfortunately for him, he's forced to stop by a glass covering.

"Ah, damn," he mutters under his breath.

"Did you really expect to be able to get super close to these?" I ask, chuckling.

"I don't know, I didn't know this existed until five seconds ago."

I nod, he has a point there. I notice a card next to the display and skim through it.

"Oh cool, it's to scale," I tell him, ignoring the rest because it's general information and history about the attractions.

"IT'S TO SCALE?" Kaid yells in excitement. A group of people looking at another attraction turns around and shushes him aggressively. He blushes profusely and looks down at his feet, "I thought that was cool."

"It is cool," I reassure him, putting my hand on his arm. He turns to look at me, and smiles gently.

"Thanks," he says softly. He keeps eye contact with me for a few seconds too long and my heart beats erratically in my chest as he starts to lean towards me— am I reading this situation right?

"A CASTLE!" A kid yells all of a sudden, knocking us out of our stupor. Kaid immediately backs up, almost knocking into the kids that yelled, who ran up to look at the 'castle' closer.

"I, umm... will meet you at the end," I say quickly, before rolling myself around the next corner. I don't process the rest of the exhibit, my brain too concentrated on mine and Kaid's almost kiss.

7

I send a text to Adria and Caitlyn once Kaid and I get back from the science museum. After going through the architecture exhibit, I tried not to let myself think about the almost kiss for the rest of the day. Since I got home, I've been laying on my bed stuck in my thoughts.

There's no way that this is happening. I was supposed to stay here for a night, and probably never see him again after that night. That's not what happened, I'm going to be staying here for at least three more months and we've been getting super close.

How many horror stories are there of people dating their roommates? How bad could it be if we date and then break up? We'd be stuck with each other for months. I mean, I'm sure we would try to go back to being friends still, but I feel like it would be horribly awkward for both of us.

CAITLYN:

For the love, Clover, you know this is a bad
idea.

ME:

I didn't say that I was going to do anything
about it.

ADRIA:

Xe has a point

CAITLYN:

Yeah, but still. How likely is it that something
will happen between them?

ME:

I don't want to answer that…

ADRIA:

I don't know about you, but I want to see him

CAITLYN:

You're in a happy relationship!

ADRIA:

Doesn't mean I don't want to look at a hot
man every now and then

ME:

image

ADRIA:

Hot damn

CAITLYN:

I think you need to tell me more about him
before I decide if I think you'd be good for
each other

You've barely said anything about him- heck,
you've barely talked to us in general since you
moved.

ME:

I'm sorry, timezones suck and I'm scared of waking you up

ADRIA:

You know I don't sleep anyways, we might as well text

ME:

I hope you don't regret saying that, because I can and will text you at all hours of the day

ADRIA:

You know I won't

"HEY MISS CLOVER," Kaid walks into my room the next day. "I saw that there's a new record store by that bookstore we went to, do you want to go with me?"

"Oh that's cool," I turn to look at him. I've been working on my computer at my desk. "Sure, I could use a break, let's go."

"Yes!" He punches his fist in the air. "Let's go! There's been a few records I've been looking for."

"I didn't know you had a record player," I muse.

"I don't... yet."

"In theory, you should buy a record player before buying records."

"What if they have record players for sale there?"

"Then you better buy one, because if you're getting records I will be too."

"Do you have a record player?" He throws my question back at me.

"Yes, actually," I tell him, "I had to leave it at home, though."

"That sucks."

"If you buy a record player, I'm going to be buying records to round out my collection and use your player whenever I feel like it."

"Who's saying that I'll let you use it whenever?" He asks, jokingly.

"I don't know, but I feel like it'd be cheaper than shipping mine here."

"There's no guarantee that I'm actually going to buy a record player."

"Well then why are we going to the record store?"

"To buy records."

"To use in what? A CD player?"

He glares at me jokingly and I chuckle to myself. He takes the handles of my chair and pushes me down the hallway and out the door.

Kaid opens the door to the record store and props it open. There's a singular stair to get into the store, and Kaid doesn't even think before he comes up behind me and says, "Hold on tight," before pressing on the anti tip wheels on the back of the chair. The front wheels go shooting up. Before I know it, my wheelchair is on top of the step.

"Wow, that was impressive," I tell him.

He laughs, "It really wasn't that hard. I googled how to do it before we got here, it was easier than the article said it would be."

"You didn't have to do that," I blush, "and this wheelchair is old and used, I really need to get a better one. I just don't have the money."

"I can help you," Kaid immediately offers.

"No, you don't have to do that. Wheelchairs are expensive, and I don't have the extra to get a good one."

"Well here, they're probably cheaper and easier to get. I also have enough money to help you, my parents have given me way too much in allowance over the years, they're nasty rich."

"What do they do?"

"They're the CEOs of some big company. They were never at home when I was little, so they probably felt bad about that. They're better now, now that it's too late for them to raise me."

"That's- I'm so sorry, Kaid."

"Don't apologize."

"Okay... I revoke my apology."

He nods, "good."

"Seriously, though, I would love to help you get a new wheelchair," he changes the topic back to what we were talking about before.

"I'll think about it."

"That's good enough for me."

We drop the topic and I roll into the record store the rest of the way. Kaid walks in behind me. He immediately starts scouring the records on display. I roll my eyes, he really needs to find a record player before he starts buying a ton of records.

The store is small, but still full of records. The store has a small display at the front for new releases and the rest of the store has bookshelves. There are baskets on each shelf holding records.

I start looking through the records, looking for something to possibly add to my collection. I probably won't buy anything unless Kaid buys a record player today, or if I really want something and can't get it at home I will.

"Nightly Dreams!?" I hear Kaid exclaim from behind me. "I love them- and they have the new special edition vinyl? I need!" He reaches over my head to grab it, but can't quite reach. I reach my hand up and grab it, reaching my hand back to hand it to him.

"You like Nightly Dreams?" I ask, genuinely curious. Most Nightly Dreams fans are in the States, and I know there are overseas fans but not that many.

"I love them, their music is just so good."

"I agree."

"Really? Well I think they might need to be our music of choice now when we're driving or cooking together."

"For sure," I nod.

"I wasn't able to get tickets to their concert here," he tells me, flipping the record in his hand back and forth, "I'm still pissed about that."

"I would be too, Ticket Master really is a bitch."

"I had tickets, and then I didn't!"

"That's terrible."

"I just wish there was another way for me to get them."

"There might be, you just have to dig a bit deeper," I tell him, knowing there's literally no more tickets available, even the resell tickets are fully sold out. But I think I might be able to get some anyways. I have friends in high places.

"You're right," he tells me, "I'll have to look again when we get back home."

"Oh look," I change the subject, "They do sell record players here."

Kaid turns around immediately looking in the direction I was pointing. "Ooh, and they have different color options too!" He says excitedly, "Which one do you think I should get? The blue one or the green one?"

"I don't know, it's your record player."

"But you're going to be using it too."

"I have my own at home."

"You're not at home right now, which means that you're borrowing mine for the time being."

"Fine, I like the green one."

"Great, we're getting the green one," he announces before putting his records on top of it and picking it up.

"Am I ruling our household?"

"At the moment, I trust your opinion more than my own."

"In theory, you should trust your own opinion instead of someone else's."

"Yeah, but still, you have a better opinion most of the time."

"I'm not saying I don't trust my opinion over yours, just saying."

"WHICH RECORD SHOULD I PLAY FIRST?" Kaid asks me, holding up five different records.

"Why do you have so many records?" I ask confused, "you only just now got a record player."

"You're evading the question!" he exclaims. "Just help me!"

"I didn't realize that the first record you play in your first record player was so important."

"Just answer the damn question! I'm stressing out here!"

"Umm... I don't know, play the Queen record."

"... I don't know."

"You're the one who asked me! Are you not going to take my opinion?"

"I don't know, maybe?"

"I give up," I turn around in my chair and start wheeling back to my room.

"Wait, please? I need your help!" Kaid hollers as I roll

down the hallway back to my room. He can figure it out by himself, or he can't. Either way, not my problem.

I close the door to my room behind me and transfer to my bed. I pull my phone out of my pocket and look at the black screen, debating. Eventually I turn it on, and open up my messages. I open up my individual chat with Adria.

ME:

> Hey Adria, do you think you could get two tickets to the Newcastle Nightly Dreams concert for me?

ADRIA:

> I didn't know that you're interested in going, I would have gotten you tickets sooner— I don't know if it'll be possible to get tickets for this show

ME:

> I didn't know I was interested in going to the concert either, but Kaid told me that he loves the band today and wasn't able to get tickets

ADRIA:

> Ooh, giving concert tickets to your crush— that's a pretty big present

ME:

> I was hoping that we could go together... maybe for a first date

ADRIA:

> Don't worry, I'm on it. That's a pretty big date, a really big first date.

ME:

> We're really close friends, this is something that friends do for each other.

ADRIA:

Yeah… keep telling yourself that. You really
need to figure your feelings out.

ME:

When's the concert?

ADRIA:

Quit evading my question.

You told me that you think you have a crush
on him— you really need just admit to yourself
that you do have a crush on him

ME:

Fine. I have a crush on him

ADRIA:

Wow, that was easier than I thought. Shit, now
I owe Caitlyn five bucks.

ME:

You bet on me? Seriously?

Actually, I probably would bet on myself too.

ADRIA:

Sophie got back to me pretty fast— she owed
me one. Again. The show's in a month. You've
got backstage passes, everything you need is
in your email.

ME:

Thank you, thank you!! I owe you, big time.

ADRIA:

It's fine, our years and years of friendship
make up for it.

ME:

You're getting one hell of an amazing birthday
and Christmas present.

ADRIA:

You just need to worry about getting some

ME:

Okay. Eww. Gross. Don't say that.

ADRIA:

Yeah, I agree. I'm never doing that again.

ME:

Good.

8

———

"You found it on YouTube?" Zahra asks skeptically, sitting down on Kaid and mine's couch. "Are you sure that's a reliable source?"

"Yes it is. It was the only free one I could find. Do you want to pay for it yourself?"

"Nevermind, it's the most reliable source there is."

"That's what I thought," I roll back to the couch now that the tv is set up. I turn and ram my footrest into the couch, "Ow fu-"

"Clover, you really need a new wheelchair," Zahra says gently, concerned, "This one really doesn't fit your body well, and the footrests are so far out."

"I know," I lament, "but you know I don't have the money or resources to make that happen."

"It's so much better here, I promise, you should try."

"Maybe I will," I tell her just to make her shut up about the topic. As much as I want a new wheelchair, I just don't have a good way to do it right now.

"Are you two starting the *Sense and Sensibility* watch?" Kaid asks, walking into the room.

"No, we're watching *Pride and Prejudice*" I deadpan, transferring to the couch, "Of course we're watching *Sense and Sensibility*, it's only plastered across the tv a million times,"

"Ha ha," he rolls his eyes, "I'll get out of your way in a second, I promise, I just want to get a snack."

"Ooh we need movie snacks!" Zahra says, standing up, "you want popcorn? I'm making popcorn."

"We're watching a tv show, but sure I'll have popcorn if you're making it."

She makes her way into the kitchen, and I scroll on my phone as she makes the popcorn. After a few minutes, I prop myself up on my hands and turn around to see the kitchen. Zahra hasn't said anything since she left the couch. Kaid and Zahra are whispering to each other, the popcorn finished almost a minute ago.

"Umm.. Zahra? Are you going to get the popcorn, or am I expected to walk over there and do it myself?"

"Don't!" She exclaims louder than I expected.

"You know I was joking, right?"

"Oh, right."

"MORNING CLOVER," Zahra says as she sits down next to me in the lecture hall.

"Morning," I smile at her.

"You've read *Sense and Sensibility*, right?" She asks, confused.

"Yeah, are you trying to get out of reading it?"

"Umm.. not really?"

"Please explain," I tell her, narrowing my eyes at her. I feel like there's something she's holding back or not telling me.

"Well you know that Mom's favorite book was *Sense and*

Sensibility, and I want to read it I *really* do. I'm just worried that I won't have the same love of it after I read it. I'll read it eventually, maybe, but I'm scared," she says softly, looking down at her hands.

"I understand," I say, matching her quietness. "Don't worry about reading *Sense and Sensibility,* I'll compare it to the book. All you need to do is worry about comparing the movies."

"Thanks, Clover."

"Good morning class, it's time to talk about Austen," Professor Kingston announces, directing our attention away from our conversation. "As you all know, I'm starting a segment on Austen's most known novels to get everyone acquainted with them before your projects. Today's focus is *Sense and Sensibility.*"

She clicks her remote and pictures from one of the movie adaptations appears on the screen.

Zahra and I make eye contact and smile widely. This is the perfect way for Zahra to get to know the story basically without having the worry her connection with her mom.

"*Sense and Sensibility* is Austen's first novel. Most of her novels have themes mainly of romance, but this one also concentrates on sisterly love as well as coming of age..."

"That sounds boring," someone interjects.

"What was that?" Professor Kingston asks, putting her hands on her hips.

"This sounds boring," they repeat. A bunch of kids near them nod in agreement.

"Then why did you take this class?" She retorts, making intense eye-contact with the kid.

"Because I needed it for my degree?"

"Tell me the truth."

"...because I heard that we would be going on a trip to Hampshire at the end of the semester."

"You know," she tells him, "I have the ability to take you off the roster list for the trip. If you interrupt my class like this again, I won't hesitate."

"Yes ma'am," he says quietly.

"That goes for all of you," she looks around the classroom intimidatingly.

"What a badass," I mutter under my breath. I see Zahra nod aggressively from next to me. "She's probably the best professor I've ever had."

"You know," Professor Kingston says, coming up to mine and Zahra's seats. She just finished her lecture for the day, and is starting her rounds. As per usual, she starts with us. "*Sense and Sensibility* is probably my favorite Austen."

"It's my favorite book of all time," I tell her, shifting my chair so that I'm facing her.

"It really is a great all time favorite. So how's your presentation going? What are your plans?"

"We're currently watching all of the movie and tv adaptations, in time order of course," Zahra tells her. She pulls up our spreadsheet on her computer and tilts it towards Professor Kingston.

"From there, we're going to pick a scene from the book, and present clips from the different adaptations, and compare them," I add. Professor Kingston leans forward and looks at Zahra's computer. She nods, "That is probably one of the most aesthetic spreadsheets I've seen in awhile," she tells us happily, "Good job girl— I mean you two."

"Thanks Professor," we parrot as she goes down the stairs to talk to the next group. That group has been grumbling about having to do this project for the last week, eventually deciding on *Pride and Prejudice*, thinking it would be the easiest. Since it's one of the most well known Austen's, it probably is the most difficult because of all of the different adaptations out there.

"Alright, so we're onto the first movie, finally," I mutter to myself, looking at the spreadsheet; we've already watched two T.V. shows. "You want to meet tonight for dinner and watch it?"

"Oh, I have an obligatory roommate dinner tonight," she groans, leaning back in her chair. "We all hate each other, I really don't know why we bother with these dinners."

"Is that why I haven't been to your dorm?" I ask, curiosity seeping through my tone.

"Yeah, that and it's the opposite of wheelchair accessible."

"Ah, that makes sense."

"Yours and Kaid's apartment is just so much more comfortable and homey," she shrugs, "I wish I could live there with you two."

"If there were a spare room, it would be all yours."

"It's alright, you need that room more than I do," she says.

"Yeah, but still. Maybe we could have a sleepover some time," I offer, shrugging.

"How many *Sense and Sensibility* adaptations can we watch in one night?" She jokes. I laugh with her and nod. That probably would make this whole process a lot easier and faster since we have a limited time to get everything done.

"I'll have to text Kaid, but I don't see him minding," I tell her, pulling my phone out of my pocket and quickly texting him."He did say he wanted to watch the Bollywood version with us," The two of us laugh.

My phone buzzes and I pull my phone out again.

KAID:

Yeah sure, I don't mind. I can even stay at a friend's place if that makes you feel better.

ME:

That's not a problem, and you know it. You can even hang out with us if you want, we're going to watch the Bollywood adaptation of Sense and Sensibility

KAID:

I'm sold.

"Kaid's fine with it," I tell Zahra a few seconds later.

"Yes!" She pumps a fist in the air, "I'm so ready for a good night of sleep!"

"Do you really sleep that badly at your place?"

"Oh, you have no idea."

9
———

"You know, I've been thinking," Kaid says, sprawling on the couch next to me. It's dinner time, which we usually have on the couch. "I know you said that you just woke up one day and couldn't move, but that's just so wild. I can't imagine— that's not supposed to sound bad, I mean..."

"Stop rambling," I laugh, tossing my hand out and hitting his chest gently. I immediately freeze, a blush forming on my face. I slowly pull my hand away and avoid eye contact with him. "I-I'll explain." I tell him. I'm sure he thinks that my stuttering was my hesitation to talk about this, but it really is quite the opposite.

"It's nothing like you'd expect, really," I start, "I mean, to get in a wheelchair there's always that something beforehand. A car accident, an injury, birth complications, etcetera. But for me, there was never that type of reasoning," I look up at him, but he only looks at me with the most caring look in his eye. He doesn't say anything, only gestures for me to continue.

"The doctors still haven't figured out the reason this is going on, I mean I was completely normal, going to school, living life like everyone else. I never really had any existing health problems either, that is until July 6th of this year." A hand gently takes mine. Kaid. A small smile forms on my face as he squeezes my hand gently. "I don't know what happened, I mean the 5th was a normal day, and the 6th just... wasn't. I mean..." I feel tears start to form in my eyes and I sniffle, trying to hold them back. Kaid squeezes my hand again and I look at him. He smiles at me gently, "You don't have to continue if you don't want to,"

"No, it's fine," I tell him, squeezing his hand in return, "I don't have much else to say, there really isn't that much detail to give. Like I said, not even the doctors know what caused this and why it happened."

"I woke up on the 6th, and well, everything was different. I could immediately tell; my legs were numb; like they were asleep, I was nauseous, and dizzy. When I tried to move my legs they just wouldn't budge. I mean, it sounds crazy but mentally it felt like I had gotten my legs amputated overnight. I couldn't tell if they were even there until I could see them. From there I went to the hospital, had a lot of testing done, and since then I've been in a chair."

I look at him once I finish, and he's looking at me with wide eyes. Wide calculating eyes, like he's trying to figure out what happened too.

"Oh honey," he rubs the back of my hand gently. A blush immediately forms on my face, he's never called me honey before. "That must've been so traumatic, I'm so sorry that happened to you."

"There's nothing you could do to fix it, you don't need to apologize," I tell him, shaking my head. He sits up straighter, and lets go of my hand. He turns towards me and wraps me up in a hug.

I let out a shaky breath as I wrap my arms around him. I

rest my head on his shoulder and he rests his head on top of mine. I haven't had a hug this warm and comforting in so long, and I didn't realize how much I missed this. Missed having someone I'm close to hug me so warmly.

A tear falls down my face. I close my eyes, trying to prevent more from falling, but it doesn't work.

"It's okay Clover," Kaid whispers into my ear, tightening his grip on the hug. His efforts to make me feel better only make me want to cry more. "Let it out," he says softly. I shake my head, if I cry now I'm never going to stop.

He nods. "That's alright, I understand. I don't want you holding in your emotions, so make sure to let it out at some point okay?" He looks at me dead in my eyes and waits until I nod. "That's my good girl," he whispers, leaning in and kissing my cheek gently.

Unintentionally I cringe at his words, even though I have a blush forming on my face.

"What?" A look of panic washes across his face. "Did I say something wrong? What can I do to help? You can tell me every-thing, anything that's on your mind, I promise I won't be mad."

"O-oh, umm... I know you've been calling me 'Miss Clover' but..." I look down at my hands, avoiding his gaze, "I'm actu-ally nonbinary."

"What?" His tone is so shocked, I can't resist looking up at him, "Are you telling me that I've been using the wrong pronouns with you this entire time? Clover, we've been living together for almost two months!"

"Yeah..." I say shyly.

"Why? Why didn't you tell me?"

"I was scared," I shrug, "You were my only hope for a place to stay, and by the time I got to know you better it was just too awkward."

"Clover," he says softly, looking at me with sad eyes, "You never have to be worried to tell me something, I lo-like you so much you're my best friend."

My eyes widen at his slip up. Could it really be that he loves me? I know I've struggled to not say those words too... could it really be that we have similar feelings?

"You're my best friend too," I whisper to him, trying my best to not confuse my words like he did. "Can you use xe/xem pronouns with me?"

"Of course," he says immediately. He starts patting his pockets looking for his phone. Once he finds it, he pulls it out and starts typing on it. He mutters something under his breath, but I only catch 'pronouns'.

"What are you doing?" I ask, trying not to laugh at his confused expression.

"I'm learning about neopronouns, I never want to use the wrong pronouns with you again," he tells me, not looking up at me. He's so concerned about this, way more than I am for sure.

"Stop that," I laugh, pulling on his hand, trying to get him to let go of his phone, "It's not that big of a deal."

"It's a very big deal," he finally puts his phone down and looks at me seriously. He grabs the back of my neck and brings his head to mine. My mouth drops open at the movement, and I stutter a few times.

"Shh," he puts his pointer finger over my lips gently, "I'm talking right now," he tells me mock-sternly, "I never want to hear you say that your preferred pronouns aren't important or a big deal. They are a big deal, and I *never* want to undermine you again."

He moves his finger off my lips and leans forward, putting his forehead against mine. I stop breathing as I look into his eyes. Is he going to kiss me? I mean, I know we both have similar feelings.

He leans closer and leans his forehead against mine gently. My eyes shutter close as our breath ghosts across the others' lips.

"Not yet," he whispers, sounding pained, a few seconds. "I'm sorry, Clover, I can't do this yet."

He leans back and stands up from the couch. He turns to go to his room, and then turns back to look at me, before turning back and heading towards the hallway.

I DON'T KNOW how to feel. First he says all those sweet things about how much he cares about me and how he doesn't want me to think I'm not important. Then he gets super close and almost kisses me. AND I WANTED IT.

I've never been attracted to someone romantically like this before, and until he slipped up his words, I didn't realize how much I loved him. I love him so much, it's crazy. I've loved him since I first met him and he offered me his guest room, it only took me this long to figure it out.

He said, "not yet". Does that mean he wants to kiss me, but he didn't want to at that moment? But why? When is going to want to kiss me?

I sigh, shaking my head. I can't keep thinking about this, it'll drive me mad. If I keep thinking about it, I'll never stop. I scoot forward and transfer from the couch back into my wheelchair. Shaking my head, I wheel back to my room, not looking back at the couch where it all went down.

ME:

> Guys, something just happened with Kaid just now

ADRIA:

The hottie?

CAITLYN:

There isn't anyone else called Kaid, hon

What happened?

I text Adria and Caitlyn the second I close the door to my room. As I wheel over to my bed, and transfer, my phone won't stop buzzing. I know I said that I need to stop thinking about it, but I can't do it on my own. Maybe texting my friends will help.

I lay back against the head board and relay everything that just occurred.

ADRIA:

So he almost kissed you, and then left?

CAITLYN:

He said 'not yet' so obviously that means something

ME:

> Yeah, but still... something's been tickling my brain since it happened

ADRIA:

Wow, I've never heard anyone use that phrase.

CAITLYN:

You're in love with him, aren't you?

ME:

> ...

ADRIA:

YOU ARE!

YES I KNEW IT

CAITLYN:

Alright, lets not overwhelm xem, hon

Let's give xem the chance to talk

ME:

I think I am, yeah…

ADRIA:

OH MY GOD

ME:

He's literally the sweetest, like he gave me this
whole speech about how I'm important and
how my pronouns are important and how he
doesn't want to hear me say that they aren't

ADRIA:

THAT'S SO CUTE OMFG

CAITLYN:

She's right, that is adorable

ME:

I know, right? I'm just worried about what this
almost-kiss will mean for our relationship

CAITLYN:

It really could go either way. But I feel like if he
cares about you that much, he'll come back
to you and you'll have the same dynamic.

ME:

But he decided he didn't want to kiss me

ADRIA:

He said 'not yet', so obviously he wants to
kiss you. He just might not have been ready

ME:

Explain

ADRIA:

Maybe he hasn't been kissed before and mentally isn't ready to take that step

CAITLYN:

Or he cared so much about you that he didn't want to overwhelm you

ME:

That makes sense, yeah. Knowing him, it could be either one of those.

10

____

When I wheel out of my room the next morning for breakfast, Kaid's back is to me. He's not in his usual seat at the table, which immediately raises my suspicions. Usually, we sit next to each other facing the television. And now he's sitting facing me, instead of next to me. Does that mean he doesn't want to be near me? Or that he wants to have a serious conversation? I don't know which is worse.

I exhale, and wheel to my spot at the table. Kaid made breakfast this morning, as he usually does, and already made a plate for me. That's a good sign, right? I lock my chair and pick up my utensils and start eating breakfast, being careful to not look at Kaid too closely. I don't want to randomly burst into tears if I look at him for too long.

"Clover," he says softly, reaching one of his hands out and bumping mine gently. "Please look at me."

I look up at him slowly, my eyes stopping at his chin. He sighs, "You know what, I deserve that," A small smile forms on my face before I can stop it. Obviously, I'm terrible at holding a grudge against him.

"Mi- no that's not right... fuck I'm really not starting this right," he groans, putting his head in his hands. He takes a deep breath before looking up at me again. "Clover."

"Don't be so hard on yourself, I know you're trying your best."

"I really am trying. I googled last night what the gender neutral way of saying miss or mister is, but I just ended up confused."

"Its Mx."

"Mix?" He mimes mixing something with his hands.

"Yeah that's how it's pronounced, it's spelled M-X."

He nods, "Alright, Mx Clover, I would say I hoped you slept well last night, but if you slept anything like I did it wasn't good."

I nod again, he's exactly right. I was up all night, trying to sleep, but instead thinking about our almost-kiss.

"Look, Clover," he says my name with such emotion, I can't resist looking into his eyes, "I really wanted to kiss you last night, I really did, but I wasn't ready."

"You weren't ready?" I ask, relieved it wasn't something different.

"Yeah, I haven't kissed in a long time, and I've been wanting to kiss you for a long time but when I actually went to do it, I realized I wasn't ready."

"I've never been kissed," I admit quietly, picking at my breakfast. "I don't know, maybe I wasn't ready either."

He smiles at me, "I'm glad we're on the same page then."

"Yeah."

The two of us eat our breakfast in silence after that, and it feels like a normal morning again. Except for one thing... "Why are you sitting in that seat?"

"What?"

"You're sitting in a different seat than usual... why?"

"Oh." A blush appears on his cheeks, and he looks down at his hands, "I thought you wouldn't want to sit next to me after last night."

"What? Why wouldn't I want to sit next to you like normal?"

"Because I almost kissed you, and ran away, leaving you stranded on the couch."

"I wasn't stranded, you just always insist on helping me off the couch."

"So when are we going to have that sleepover?" Zahra asks me as I roll into class later on that morning.

"What sleepover?"

"What's going on Clover? You were so excited about this earlier," she questions, shifting in her seat to get a better glance at me.

"Oh right, the *Sense and Sensibility* sleepover... I can't believe that I forgot, I'm sorry. When're you free?"

"That's not important right now," she waves me off, "What happened? And why do I have a feeling it has something to do with Kaid?"

"You barely know him, how do you know?"

"You get this lovey-dovey look on your face whenever you talk about him."

"What? I do not," I argue, my mouth agape.

"You do. But I'm not going to get into this argument right now. Tell me what happened before class starts."

I sigh, "What if I'm trying to procrastinate until then?"

"Don't, I can tell you want to tell me."

"How do you know me so well?" I raise an eyebrow, she's really gotten a good grasp on me. Maybe too good of a grasp...

"Just tell me already!"

"Okay, okay, fine!" I exclaim exasperatedly, chuckling slightly, "Fine... Kaid almost kissed me last night."

"He... WHAT?!" Zahra's exclamation is like an explosion. A few of our classmates turn around to look at us, but Zahra doesn't blink. "I was waiting for this to happen! Wait-almost?"

"Yeah, almost," I blush, and fiddle with my hands, "I was a bit mad at first, but after he explained it was all good, and we're almost back to normal too."

"Oh no... don't tell me he backed away and left before saying anything..."

"Umm..."

"HE DIDN'T!" She yells, making me jump in my chair. Half the class turns around, staring at her. One of the boys in the row in front of us flips Zahra off, she responds by flipping him off without a second thought.

"Everything alright over here, ladies?" Professor Kingston asks as she walks into the classroom, "Usually I'd frown upon students flipping each other off, but I trust you had a good reason."

Zahra and I burst into giggles at her words, and she shrugs, "What? I know I'm right."

"You're right," I tell her in-between giggles.

"Everything all good, though?" Professor Kingston asks again.

"Oh yeah," Zahra says, "Well kinda, but we got it covered."

I roll my eyes, "Wow, cryptic much?"

"We're just going over some boy drama," she waves it off.

"Oh damn, I'd love to stick around, but I have a class to teach," she pauses for a second, "and to be honest, it's probably frowned upon to gossip with students... try and pay attention if you can, please. Or just be quiet," she looks pointedly at Zahra as she says the last sentence. I have to hold back my laugh.

"Will do," I smile at the professor.

"I'll try," Zahra grumbles. Professor Kingston nods, and makes her way down the stairs to her podium.

The second she's out of earshot, Zahra turns towards me again, "Now he better have a damn good reason for doing that."

"Well, that's none of your business, but I do know and I'm not mad at him for it."

"That's good enough for me, although that's literally the worst in books."

"Yeah, but usually they avoid each other after it happens. Not Kaid. No, the minute I wheeled into the kitchen this morning for breakfast, he was at the table with breakfast made ready to talk over everything."

"Why is he literally so adorable?" Zahra swoons.

11

———————

"Want to go back to that bookstore?" Kaid asks as I wheel into his apartment after my classes.

"Which bookstore?" I raise an eyebrow at him.

"The one I brought you to when you first moved in," he walks over and motions to my bag, "Want some help with that?"

Once I nod, he takes my book bag off the back of my wheelchair and puts it on the floor for me.

"I'd love to go back to that store, but I have a bunch of work to get done."

"How much classic literature do you have to read today?" I roll my eyes at his words. He really judges me for mainly reading classics, mostly jokingly, but I know he wants a gauge of how much work I need to do.

"Not much reading, I just have some writing to do," I shrug, rolling into the living room. "I figured I'd settle in here and get shit done."

"You could do that," he says walking up behind me, "or you could come with me to a coffee shop."

"I thought you were going to that bookstore?" I turn to look at him confused.

"I was thinking about it, but I'd much rather hang out with you," My heart melts as his confession, and I have to pay close attention to my words so I don't say something I'm not ready for him to know.

"Alright, fine, I'll go with you to the coffee shop."

I turn around and make my way back towards the door. Kaid pumps his fist in excitement, probably thinking I can't see him. I can, though, and I smile to myself.

He grabs my bag off the floor and hangs it off the back of my chair like it was second nature.

"One second," he tells me, rushing back towards his room. He comes back a minute later with his bag slinging off his shoulder. "Ready? Let's go!"

He pushes me down the Newcastle streets, giving me the chance to look closer at our neighborhood. We have to go the other way to go to school, so I'm not used to going this direction. I'm not sure which cafe he's going to bring us to, not like I really know where any cafes in this area are.

A few minutes later, he turns and we make our way down a side road. "Almost there," Kaid tells me. I can hear the smile in his voice, I guess he's excited to hang out with me. I'm hoping that I can get some work done, or at least talk to Kaid some more.

We make our way towards the door of the cafe. Kaid opens the door for me without me needing to say anything. I wheel in, and make my way to the counter to order my drink.

"You wanting a chai latte again?" He asks, making his way back behind me. I can feel him resting his arms on the back of my chair. Usually, it would annoy me but surprisingly it doesn't bother me when Kaid does it.

I shrug, "I don't know, I was kinda thinking a coffee of some sort."

"It's way too late for a coffee," I can hear the hesitation in his voice.

"I can tell it's going to be a late night."

"Have you had coffee before?"

"No," I shrug, "It sounds like something I'd need, though."

"Okay then you're not getting your own coffee," he tells me, "I'm getting my vanilla latte, and you can have a little bit. I'm a bit scared to see you with caffeine."

"Fine," I roll my eyes, but otherwise don't fight him.

I end up getting a chai latte. But I'm planning on stealing as much of Kaid's vanilla latte as I can get away with. We get a table towards the back of the cafe, and Kaid makes a spot for me instinctively. I can't believe how amazing he is, I've never had someone notice the small things so instinctively. Adria and Caitlyn tried their best, of course, but it was harder for them since they knew me for years before I was in the chair.

I grab my computer out of my bag and set it up on the table in front of me. I try to hold myself back from drinking my tea immediately, I tend to drink it when it's way too hot.

Kaid sets up his computer in front of him as well, and we start getting some work done.

"Can we talk?" Kaid asks a few hours later.

"Hmm?" I look up from my computer and blink at him. I was really in the zone just then, and I got a lot of work done.

"We need to talk about yesterday," he says gently.

"Yeah, we do. I'm so glad you aren't avoiding me."

"I would never," he looks and sounds offended.

"Well, I know that now," I tell him, not bothering to

suppress the smile on my face, "I've just heard of so many stories of things like this happening and it ends with the couple ignoring or avoiding each other for weeks to months on end."

"That sounds awful," he exclaims, eyes wide. I nod in agreement. "Either way, I just wanted to make sure that there wasn't anything you wanted to get out. I'm so thankful that nothing's really changed between us and that we're still friends."

"Me too," I say immediately, "It's not really relevant but if we're talking about what we're thankful for I wanted to say that I'm so thankful that you are always so caring when it comes to my chair. You don't treat me differently, you don't make me or my wheelchair feel like a problem, you always make sure everything is accessible for me. And if it's not accessible, you fix it without me needing to speak up and advocate for myself." I sniffle, trying not to get teary eyed at the admission. As a disabled person, I always get overlooked by the majority of society. Having someone who's always there for me and makes sure that places are accessible to me, means more to me than I ever knew.

"Clover," Kaid says, emotion swarming in his tone, "I-I... Clover... do people not make an effort to make life accessible for you?"

I shrug, "No, not really,"

His eyes go wide, "Please tell me you're joking,"

"I wish I could say I was. I mean, ask any disabled person. There are literally no places that are 100% accessible for wheelchair users among other disabled people. Most people don't think about it cause they don't experience it."

"Well... what about your friends you told me about? Kate and Amy?"

"Close," I laugh, "Caitlyn and Adria,"

"What about them? Don't they help you like I do?"

"Yeah, they do. But I knew them for years before I got into my chair, so it's not as much of an instinct for them. They try their best, though."

I look up at him again. My eyes go wide as I realize that he has tears in his eyes. "Kaid," I say quietly.

"Clover," he says quietly. He reaches out and grabs my hand, putting his other hand on top of it. He massages it gently as he says his next words. "I promise to help you as much as I possibly can, make you feel loved and accepted in society. I promise to be there for you as long as you'll have me by your side."

The tears that had been in my eyes previously fall as more tears appear in my eyes. Kaid's eyes go wide, but before he can say anything I unlock my chair and wheel back.

I brace myself on my armrests as I stand up. Kaid stands up in a panic, not sure what I'm doing. I waddle towards him as best I can and wrap him up in a hug.

"Thank you," I whisper into his shoulder. He wraps his arms around me tightly, both hugging me and keeping me upright.

"You don't need to thank me," he whispers. "This should be how it is for you."

"Never leave me," I whisper before it goes through my head, "Please, be my friend forever and never leave me."

"Never," he tells me immediately, "I'll never leave you."

12

KAID:

When's the sleepover with Zahra?

ME:

Tonight

KAID:

Shit, I totally forgot

ME:

We can always reschedule

KAID:

No, it's fine

I just need to get my homework done quickly,
and then we can watch the Bollywood movie

ME:

I didn't realize you were going to join us

KAID:

Yeah, you said I can- that still work for you?

ME:

Oh yeah, of course

"I'm so ready for today!" Zahra singsongs as she bounds into the lecture hall. She has a duffel bag slung over her shoulder along with her backpack. She puts the duffel bag on the floor and her backpack on the desk before sitting in her chair.

"I'm so excited!" I tell her, "I haven't had a sleepover in so long."

"Ooh, neither have I! This is my first college sleepover," She tells me.

"You have roommates," I say slowly, "Every night is a sleepover for you."

"I hate my roommates, you know that," she rolls her eyes, "It's the worst sleepover ever."

"WE SHOULD MAKE A FORT!" Kaid exclaims excitedly as I roll into the living room.

"Ooh! Gotta make it the whole sleepover vibe," I tell him, laughing. "Although, we probably should wait for Zahra."

"Shit, you're right,- wait I mean shoot."

I raise an eyebrow.

"There's going to be a girl present, I probably should restrain from cursing."

"Nice to know you don't care about cursing around me."

"Wait- that's not what I was trying to say," he says quickly in a panic.

"I was joking, Kaid, god. I'm just happy that you're not holding yourself back around me."

He smiles at me, and wraps an arm around my shoulders, squeezing gently. Now that we hugged at the cafe, he's been much more touchy with me. I can tell that physical touch is his love language, and he's opening up to me so much more than before.

"You're the best, you know that?" He says softly.

He releases me from the side-hug and goes back to setting up the living room for our sleepover. I'm probably going to sleep on the couch, Kaid has an air mattress blown up for him to sleep on in the middle of the living room, and Zahra can sleep on the armchair. I've never seen Kaid sit in that chair, he prefers to sit on the couch. I guess he has the chair to simply fill up space. Knowing Kaid, he got a super comfortable chair, so I'm not worried about Zahra being uncomfortable.

Kaid grabs a bunch of blankets and starts throwing them all over the living room dramatically. "You get a blanket! And you get a blanket!" He exclaims, imitating Oprah. I crack up, not able to hold back my laughter. He laughs with me, and we smile warmly at each other.

A knock sounds at the door and Kaid and I break our eye contact.

"Zahra's here," I say stupidly. I wheel to the door and open it, letting Zahra into Kaid's apartment. She had a few more classes than I did this morning, and she came straight here from her last class. I offered to let her stop at her dorm first, but she didn't want to. She said that she'll take any reason to not go to her dorm and deal with her roommates. With the way she talks about them, I hope I never have to meet them.

"Hi!" Zahra says excitedly as she walks into the apartment, "I'm so ready for this, I've been looking forward for this all day."

"Me too!" I exclaim, "Wanna order a pizza or something?"

"I wanna make a fort!" Kaid yells from the living room.

"Ooh, I wanna make a fort too!" Zahra agrees, rushing to the living room.

"But I'm hungry," I mutter to myself as I turn around to make my way back to the living room.

"Here," Kaid shows up out of nowhere, scaring me half to death. I have to stop suddenly, so I don't run over his toes and he cringes, "Sorry, I shouldn't have gotten that close. I won't do it again, promise."

"It's fine, it happens all the time."

"It's not fine, so I won't do it again."

"Thanks, Kaid," I say softly. His eyes sparkle as he looks at me for a few seconds before remembering what he was going to say.

"Take my credit card, order some takeout for us."

"Pizza?"

"Pizza sounds perfect," he passes me his card before turning back around to help Zahra build the fort.

AN HOUR OR SO LATER, the fort is complete and we're eating pizza while starting the first *Sense and Sensibility* movie. I wasn't really in the mood to build a fort, I wasn't sure how I would be able to do it in my chair, but Kaid and Zahra weren't letting me sit it out. They didn't make a big deal and had things for me to help that I was able to do without me needing to say anything. I really have the best friends in the entire world, I don't know how I got so lucky.

"We're starting with the Bollywood movie, right?" Kaid asks, stretching his legs out in front of him.

"Umm..." Zahra turns towards her computer and scrolls down the spreadsheet we made for this project, "No."

"Aw man."

"It's third."

"Wait- how many of these movies do we have to watch?" He asks, a grasp of panic in his voice.

"Well we've done two tv shows already, so we have seven adaptations to go," I tell him.

He blinks at me before his expression shifts to one of panic. "Wait, does this mean that I have to sit through seven *Sense and Sensibility* movies?"

"I mean..." Zahra drags the word out, not sure what to tell him.

"They aren't all movies, the first few are TV shows or old dramas." I tell him, referring to the spreadsheet I meticulously built with all the adaptations and where to find them.

He groans, "You two really are overachievers." He lays down on the air mattress fully, and I take that as confirmation that he's staying.

I set up the 1981 *Sense and Sensibility* TV show on the TV. Zahra and I have our computers open on our laps, our spread-sheets ready to go for note taking.

"Do you want to transfer out of your chair?" Zahra asks before I hit 'play' on the TV.

"I don't know," I shrug, "I'm fine."

"I can help you," Kaid offers, standing up and shifting parts of the fort around before I have the chance to say anything.

"Kaid," I shake my head. He ignores me, still adjusting the fort. He pushes an ottoman back in front of my spot on the couch.

"Nope, you're going to be as comfortable as possible," he insists, "Can I move you over a little bit?" I nod, and he moves me two feet closer to Zahra.

I'm sitting next to the armchair that Zahra's sitting in now. I smile at her, and she smirks at me with an odd look in her eye.

I raise an eyebrow at her. She leans forward so we can talk without Kaid listening.

"He's so lovesick, what the hell happened after you two almost kissed?"

"We've talked so much, it seems like we have similar love languages—"

"LOVE?" She yells before I finish my sentence. Kaid looks up at that, raising an eyebrow for a second before going back to resetting the fort. I put my head in my hands as I shake my head in embarrassment.

"Will you let me finish?" I hiss.

"Right... sorry,"

"We talked about how we both like physical touch with people we trust, so we decided that we'd hug more often. And now that we've talked about the deep things like that, we've gotten more comfortable with each other. And he realized how shitty wheelchair life can be, so he's been insistent that he needs to help me at any occurrence."

"That's adorable," she awes, "He's definitely a lovesick fool, though."

"He is not," I hiss.

"He tried to kiss you. You admitted you like him."

"Right... I'm not used to actually having that knowledge out in the open and not suppressed in my mind."

Zahra laughs, "Why is that the most relatable thing I've ever heard?"

"I don't know man, this is just my life."

"Alright Mx Clover," Kaid exclaims, smiling at getting my pronouns right, "Let's get you situated on the couch."

I roll to the side of the couch and lock my chair into place. I shuffle forward on the chair, and Kaid's hand in front of me stops me.

"Let me help," he insists.

"What? I can do it by myself."

"Yeah, but I know you're tired," he shrugs, "I can help you, no problem."

"Okay," I say shyly, not making eye contact with him as he gets closer to me.

He smiles at me gently, before wrapping his arm around my back, gently helping me stand up. Once I get up, he smiles at me before helping me turn around and sit down on the couch. He goes down onto his knees in front of me, and my heart stops. What is he doing? He grabs my legs and guides them onto the ottoman in front of me, making sure I'm the most comfortable I can be.

Zahra plops down on the couch next to me with her laptop. Kaid sits in the chair that Zahra was in before, and his eyes go wide.

"Damn," he exclaims, "How have I not sat in this chair before, it's seriously comfortable."

Zahra and I burst into giggles, "Just start the movie already," Kaid rolls his eyes.

I start the movie and snuggle up in the blankets and pillows always scattered across the couch.

Zahra and I make notes on the spreadsheet as the movie plays in the background. I watch as Zahra's long and nimble fingers fly across the keyboard faster than I can process. A small smile forms on my face as I watch her from the corner of my eye instead of watching the movie.

I WAKE up to the sounds of Kaid's snoring. My eyes fly open as I realize that I was supposed to be watching *Sense and Sensibility* with Zahra and taking notes.

"Have a nice sleep?" Zahra asks nonchalantly as I look around the living room in a panic.

"Wh-what?" I mutter, "I didn't realize I fell asleep, I'm so sorry I was supposed to be helping you."

"It's not that big of a deal," she tells me, typing something on her computer.

I look around, finding myself and Zahra still on the couch. In the night, I must've shifted onto my side. My blanket was adjusted, and I had a pillow under my head. *That definitely wasn't there before.* I feel a blush forming as I realize that it must've been Zahra.

Zahra, who's still sitting on the couch next to me. Who I fell asleep next to, and who made sure I was comfortable as she worked on our project. The project I was supposed to be helping her with, and wasn't.

"How much do we need to rewatch?" I ask her, trying not to make eye contact as I push myself into a sitting position slowly.

"Nothing."

"Nothing?" I repeat, adjusting my posture so I can see the TV, and Zahra, better. "Did you not sleep?"

"No I didn't, but I have insomnia so it's not that big of a deal."

"So you just can't sleep? That's terrible."

"It's not that bad," she shrugs, "I'm used to it, and I've needed an excuse to stay up all night."

"Sounds like you were productive," I grab my computer from next to me and start scrolling through the notes that Zahra wrote. "I still feel bad, I'll just have to put more work in later."

"Stop that," she scolds gently, "It's obvious you needed the sleep."

"How many adaptations are left? I'll watch them on my own time and write notes for us."

"If you insist," she rolls her eyes, "There are three left, and I watched three while you were sleeping."

"That's perfect," I yawn, "Wait, does that mean that I missed the Bollywood one?"

Zahra nods grimly, "I considered skipping it so you guys could watch it, but that kind of ruins the point of this entire project," I nod, she's right. Comparing each adaptation in order of publication to the original book, if you change the order you watch then the project doesn't make sense anymore.

"We missed the Bollywood?" Kaid mumbles sleepily from his chair, "Damn."

"It was amazing," she says, "Sorry, Kaid."

"Nah, it's fine. I don't want to ruin your project."

"We can watch it together once I finish the last three adaptations," I offer, "I want to watch it too."

"Yes!" He pumps his fist in the air dramatically, and then yawns. "I need some coffee."

He stands up from the chair and stretches before making his way to the kitchen to start his coffee maker.

"Can I have some of that?" Zahra turns to holler at him before turning back to whisper at me. "So are you two going to watch the Bollywood *Sense and Sensibility* as a date?"

A blush immediately forms on my face at her words. "I didn't even think of that," I whisper to her, not making eye contact.

"Well maybe you should start thinking about it, that'd be the perfect first date for you two."

"We're not dating yet," I tell her, my blush getting darker, "I don't know if either of us are ready to date yet."

"Well maybe you two need to talk about that."

"We're taking it slow," I tell her, "We need to figure out our feelings for each other, before we talk. Hopefully we can figure things out soon."

She nods, "With anyone else, I would be suspicious of that, but I can tell that you two are confused about your feelings."

"You've read too many romance books."

"So have you," she retorts, jokingly punching my arm.

"Do you want a chai latte, Clover?" Kaid hollers towards us, the coffee machine grinding beans behind him.

"Nah," I say after a few seconds of thinking, "I don't need the caffeine."

"I need the caffeine," Zahra hollers at him. I didn't realize she's so grumpy in the mornings, it's kind of adorable.

"I know!" Kaid exclaims exasperatedly, "I'm working on it!"

13

––––––––

I wake up to a text from Anders, Adria's brother. He's one of the members of Kaid's favorite band, Nightly Dreams. All the band members are so kind and down to earth.

I text Anders back quickly, asking him about the accessibility of the venue and thanking him a million times, before pocketing my phone and transferring into my chair. I wheel into the kitchen where I find Kaid sitting at the table, head in his hands.

"Isn't today your day to make breakfast?" I ask, glancing at the schedule I made for us. We switch off who makes meals, who does chores each day, among other things.

"Is it?"

"Yeah."

"Shit, I thought I asked you to switch with me."

"You didn't, but I don't mind making breakfast this morning," I tell him, rolling into the kitchen the rest of the way. I start pulling ingredients out of the cabinets, and start mixing together my omelette mix.

"No. No! No no no no no no..." Kaid exclaims. I hear a bang, and I quickly turn around to look at him. He's shaking his head, nursing his fist with one hand.

"What's going on?" I ask, worry seeping through my tone, "What's wrong?"

"I've been fighting TicketMaster all day, and I just got kicked out. I WAS NEXT IN LINE YOU BITCH!" He yells, throwing his hands in the air. His hands move towards his computer, and I quickly intervene, "Don't!"

His hands move back, and I wheel up next to him and grab them. Hoping to calm him down, and to give me an excuse to hold his hands. He turns to look at me, and his eyes soften as they meet mine.

"What were you trying to get tickets for?" I ask him.

"They added more tickets to the Nightly Dreams Newcastle concert, and I've been waiting in line for hours. But obviously TicketMaster hates me," I squeeze his hand in sympathy, and my mind reels.

Should I tell him about the tickets I have? By now they're definitely in my email, and I have the VIP passes coming in the mail soon. I study Kaid. He looks so disappointed in TicketMaster kicking him out, and I would do anything to make him feel better. So I'm going to tell him, but I think I'm going to leave out the backstage part for now.

"Well..." I say slyly, "I pulled some strings, and got us two VIP tickets to the concert."

"WHAT?" He exclaims, pulling back from my grip to look at me with wide eyes. "Did you just say..."

"That we have two VIP tickets? Yup," I smile at him and his jaw drops.

"You- wha- how did you-?" He stutters, barely able to say anything out loud, but I really want to surprise him at the concert later.

"I have friends in high places," I say, not giving him too much information. I have to hold myself back from telling him everything right now.

He stands up and throws himself into my arms. I get pushed back, and we run into some of the kitchen cabinets.

"Thank you, thank you so much," he mutters, his face in the crevice between my neck and shoulder. His breath on my neck makes me shudder, and I grip him tighter.

He leans out from the hug slightly, and our eyes meet. He puts his forehead against mine gently, and his eyes flutter closed softly.

My eyes widen, are we finally going to kiss? My eyes flutter shut as Kaid's hand comes up to cup my cheek. Our noses brush against each other's gently as we move closer together.

Kaid's lips brush against mine gently, and my breath hitches before his lips fully attach to mine. He kisses me gently, and I kiss him back. He leans back after a few seconds, avoiding eye contact.

"What's wrong?" I ask confused, trying to catch my breath. I'm sure I have a similar look on my face, but I try my best to mask it.

"I-I'm sorry," he says softly, still not looking me in the eye. He's still holding my hands which is a good sign... I think. "I thought I could do it, but I can't I'm sorry."

"W-what?" I stutter, trying to understand, but not quite being able to.

He lets out a deep exhale, "When I was younger, there was this girl. And I haven't seen her in years, but obviously she's still in my mind," he chuckles to himself, like he's in disbelief, "I haven't done anything with anyone since her."

"Oh Kaid," I sigh, "Are you worried I'm going to be mad or something?"

He nods silently, making my heart break.

"Of course I'm not mad at you," I tell him, "How were you supposed to know without trying?"

"I'm sorry Clover," he whispers, his voice breaking slightly.

"It's okay, it's not that big of a deal," I tell him, bringing him into a hug and try to joke. "Now I don't have to worry about my first kiss anymore."

His eyes widen, "I just took your first kiss?"

"Yeah," I shrug, "It's not really that big a deal."

"It is a big deal, it's your first kiss!"

"People'll make a big deal out of anything, obviously this isn't as chalked up as people make it out to be."

"Alright, now you just sound like a motivational book," he laughs, pulling up one of the kitchen chairs and sitting down in front of me.

I shrug, "I need to if you're talking nonsense."

"I wasn't talking nonsense!" He laughs. "Although there was something else I wanted to talk about."

"What?"

"I don't want this to change us... I don't want this to change our relationship in anyway. You're important to me, and I don't want this to change."

"Yeah," I tell him, feeling the same way. "Let's not change us."

"We're not going to change," he leans closer to me, putting his hands on my shoulders, "Promise."

"We better not," I threaten jokingly as I pull him into a hug.

ADRIA:

Do I have to push you to talk to Kaid?

ME:

No... We already talked, and we're set

ADRIA:

Seriously? I was expecting to have to push you in his direction

ME:

You're saying that like he wasn't going to push himself at me in the first place

ME:

He hates being in any sort of conflict with people, especially with us living together

ADRIA:

You two are really living a romance book, like seriously, forced proximity, roommates, and you two avoided miscommunication

ME:

Does everything have to do with books with you?

ADRIA:

Of course, books are my life

I heard you got tickets for Nightly Dreams' concert

ME:

Yeah, they're Kaid's favorite, so I wanted to surprise him

ADRIA:

So you're going to take him out on a date and surprise him with the concert?

ME:

Yes and no. I'll explain in a second. I told him this morning about the tickets, since he was trying to get tickets this morning. And we're not going to date.

ADRIA:

Wait, why not?

ME:

One sec, I need to switch to the group chat

CLOVER'S THIRD Wheeling

ME:

Kaid and I kissed this morning

ADRIA:

WHAT

CAITLYN:

Niceeee

ME:

Let me finish

Kaid realized he was still strung up over an ex of his, and so we decided we weren't going to date.

And after all that, I think I realized that I don't actually like him in a romantic way? Cause I didn't care about us, I was more worried about him and the girl he was strung up on.

ADRIA:

And that all happened this morning?

CAITLYN:

Damn, you weren't kidding when you said he doesn't like conflict

ME:

Yeah, we talked a bit yesterday, and then we kissed after I surprised him with Nightly Dreams tickets, and then we talked again

Now I'm kinda hiding from him, he doesn't need to know that though

CAITLYN:

You're hiding from him?

That sounds kinda counterproductive

ME:

I wouldn't say hiding, per say, I just need some alone time so I'm in my room

ADRIA:

And you needed time with your girls, of course

ME:

Of course

CAITLYN:

Wait I need to back up a bit, you're going to see Nightly Dreams?

ADRIA:

Bring earplugs, trust me

ME:

Yeah, I had Anders hook me up with some tickets for us

I was planning on that, but thank you

CAITLYN:

Oh, that's such a good gift, I'm sure you'll love it

ME:

Oh yeah, we're so excited about it

ADRIA:

Did Anders get you a wheelchair spot?

ME:

Yeah, he put us in a semi-private box too.

CAITLYN:

Niceeeee

"WANT TO WATCH A MOVIE?" Kaid asks as I roll into the living room.

"It's noon," I deadpan

"And?"

"We usually watch movies with dinner,"

He shrugs, "I don't know, I'm just in the mood to watch something."

"Well I have a few *Sense and Sensibility* adaptations I need to watch," I offer.

"How long till you need to have those finished?" he asks, raising an eyebrow at me.

"You're tired of watching *Sense and Sensibility*, aren't you?"

"How'd you guess?" He asks, a twinge of sarcasm in his voice.

I wheel into the kitchen and dig through the cabinets, hunting to find something edible to make for lunch. I hear Kaid shift on the couch, probably looking to see what I'm doing.

"I can make you a sandwich, if you want," he offers.

"I can make my own lunch, you know," I tell him instinctively. I cringe at my words, I didn't mean to be so standoffish. Kaid is good about letting me have my independence, he's probably one of the only people who does. "Shit, sorry,"

"It's fine, I understand," he shrugs me off. I shake my head, I'm being much too dramatic about the smallest things right now. Kaid and I have already had a long morning, with us redefining our relationship, I can't be here being a little bitch to him.

"I'm sorry," I repeat.

"Clover, it's fine, don't worry about it."

"Too late," I mutter under my breath. He sighs, and I hear the couch creak as he stands up. I turn around to face him as he crosses the combined living room and kitchen space.

He comes up to me and rests his arm on the top of my head. I blink, I don't know what I expected him to do, but that wasn't it.

"Whatcha making?" He asks leaning forward a bit to see what I'm doing.

"Nothing as of right now," I tell him, "You're kind of constricting my movement."

"Shit sorry," he immediately backs away from me, giving me my space, "I didn't think about that."

"It's fine," I say immediately chuckling softly, "Once I grab my ingredients and set up I won't need to move anymore."

Usually it would annoy me to have someone put their hand on my head like Kaid just did, but it doesn't bother me as much to have him do it. I guess he's just getting close enough to me where I don't care anymore.

"Ooh, okay!" He says excitedly, his tone becoming more excited within the second.

I pile the ingredients for my lunch quickly, before locking my chair in front of the kitchen island. Kaid bought it right after I moved in, claiming he needed more counter space. He won't admit it, but I know he bought it so I would have somewhere I could cook easily. I start building my sandwich and Kaid rests his arms on the top of my head again.

"You've seen *Friends*, right?" He asks randomly. I pause and look up at him confused. "Well, have you?"

"Yeah, I mean who hasn't?" I respond slowly, not sure where he's going with this.

"I've always wanted to try a Thanksgiving leftover sandwich."

"Random, but okay."

"I mean, what sandwich is so good that you get laid off your job from yelling at your boss eating your sandwich?"

I pause, "I never thought of it that way."

"It's kind of ridiculous to think about, I mean who gets so angry about a sandwich?"

"I guess it's the moist-maker's fault," I joke, referencing the gravy-soaked piece of bread that Monica adds to the middle of the leftovers sandwich.

Kaid shivers, "Please never say that again."

"What? Moist-maker?" I tease, trying to hold back my smirk.

"Stop, that's terrible," he groans, "I hate that word."

I laugh, "I didn't realize how easy it was to bother you. All I have to say is one measly phrase..."

"If you say it again, I'll flip your chair," he threatens, his tone immediately changing, "Actually I wouldn't, I'd probably tickle you but imagine I would flip your chair."

I laugh even harder, "You're terrible at threatening people."

"I'm not usually that bad at it, but I didn't want you to

think that I would actually flip your chair. I want you to feel safe here."

"I knew you were joking," I tell him, "You'd have to do a lot more to make me feel unsafe here."

14

___

"Kaid was being stubborn, but I finished watching all of the movies," I tell Zahra as she settles into the seat next to me. Today is one of the days Professor Kingston has set aside for questions and project work, and it seems Zahra and I are the only group in attendance. I'm not surprised, though, this class seems to be full of people who think this class is an easy A.

"Nice," she exclaims, "You wrote the notes and everything, right?"

I nod, "It's all in the spreadsheet, I figured we could go through and organize everything further and start seeing where we can compare and contrast for the main project."

"We also need to figure out the main project," she reminds me.

"Right..."

"Also I want updates, have you and Kaid kissed yet?"

I freeze, realizing that I've talked to basically everyone about this except for Zahra. "O-oh, umm, actually we decided we'd be better off as friends."

"Really? But your chemistry is off the charts, explosive, how do you think you'd be better off as friends?"

"Well, we kissed yesterday and realized that it felt wrong," I shrug, "We talked it through, and realized that our relationship wasn't meant to be romantic."

"Wow, that's very- uh- mature of you two," she stutters.

"It really was, wasn't it?" I chuckle, "Seriously, though, we're not going to be romantic, solely platonic," Zahra has a look of sheer excitement on her face for a split second before masking her expression- *I wonder what that was about?*

"Well I'm glad you two figured that out," she says before quickly changing the subject, "Man I can't believe how nobody showed up to class today."

"I know right," I say after a second of hesitation, agreeing to the conversation change. Professor Kingston looks up from her computer, noticing us sitting here and waves at us. We wave back before bringing our focus back to the project.

"I was thinking we could do a slideshow or a video for the presentation portion of the project," I tell Zahra, tapping my fingers on the desk in front of me, "but I feel like everyone's going to do that, and I want to be different."

"We could do a video," she muses, tapping her fingers on the desk like I am, "but to make it different, maybe I could animate everything."

"Animate everything?" I turn to look at her, eyebrow raised, "That sounds like a lot of work."

"Yeah, it probably would be, but I feel like I need to do it. For Mom."

"Well, you're more than welcome to, if you're insisting."

"I'm insisting," she nods, "Besides, I'm an animation major and none of my classes are letting me actually animate, I'm itching to do something artistic instead of boring and computery."

"Computery isn't a word, but I guess I'll let it slide," I tease, "But seriously, if you want to animate, I'm not going to stop you. Although I would like to help you with writing the dialogue."

"Oh of course, I wasn't going do it all by myself. I was probably going to have you help me with deciding details and probably voiceovers."

"I'm sure I could convince Kaid to be our narrator so we can be Elinor and Marianne."

"Oh good idea," she says excitedly, grabbing her computer and typing onto the spreadsheet, "I'll make a new document for us to write on, and we can get the first scene or two figured out today, hopefully, and I'll start thumbnails."

"Before I start writing," I say as I start a new document, "Do we want to go serious Austen English or more modern for the script?"

"Modern."

"Great that's what I was thinking too."

We start working on the script on our own computers, jumping between the new document and the already finished spreadsheet, making sure to make everything as simple as possible in the script while still being detailed so the video doesn't end up super long. I'm doing my best to make it so Zahra doesn't have a ton of things to animate, but she keeps adding more— so I guess it's her grave she's digging. She can't go blaming me in the end, because I have proof.

"Hey you two," Professor Kingston says happily a few minutes later as she stands up from her desk and makes her way up the stairs towards us, "Sorry this took so long, it's been bothering me for weeks."

"Oh I understand that," I mutter under my breath, knowing that I've had the same thing happen to me so many times in the past.

"Hi Professor!" Zahra says excitedly from next to me, I can tell she's getting and more excited about being able to animate for this project.

"Call me Melody," she corrects.

"Wh-huh?" I pause, rewinding my thoughts to make sure I heard her right. Yup, I did.

"Call me Melody," she repeats, "Don't tell anyone, but you two are my favorite students and I know for a fact that we're going to stay friends once this class is over."

"Ok Prof-I mean Melody," I correct myself mid-word, smiling at her, "I was hoping we would stay in touch."

"We will! I'll make sure of it," she smiles at me and then smiles at Zahra, "Either way, how's your project going?"

"We've got the big things planned out," Zahra explains to Melody, "Now we just need to finish our script, and get the thing done,"

"You've already watched all of the adaptations?" Melody asks surprised. When we nod, she continues, "Dang, I'm impressed with you two, there are *a lot* of *Sense and Sensibility* adaptations."

"There are," I chuckle, "We had fun with it, though. We had a sleepover and binged them all night."

"We were, until you and Kaid fell asleep," Zahra exclaims with mock-annoyance, crossing her arms over her chest,"It's a good thing I have insomnia."

"Hey, I finished the ones we couldn't," I protest instinctively.

"Oh, I know, I was just messing with you. I'm not mad, promise." She reaches out to me, like she wants to grab my hand, but pulls back at the last second.

Melody chuckles under her breath and sits down in the row in front of us, "So, what are you guys planning on doing for the second part of the project? If you don't know, it's not a problem, I'd be happy to talk through ideas with you."

"We just figured that out, actually," Zahra tells her, an excited hint in her voice. She goes through the entire project idea for Melody, who doesn't waver once.

"So what you're saying is that you're going to make a video together," she pauses as we nod, "and you're going to animate everything?" When Zahra nods, Melody's eyes go wide, "Wow, that's crazy. Don't tell anyone, but automatic A. I'm kidding... Or am I?"

The three of us laugh, Zahra and I sneaking a quick smile at each other. We definitely deserve that A, we're putting the work in that's for sure.

"Oh, speaking of, let me text Kaid before I forget about it," I tell Zahra, pulling my phone out. I freeze, pausing to look at Profes—Melody, "I hope you don't mind I'm using my phone in class."

"I don't mind," she waves me off, "We're the only ones in here, besides you are my favorite students. I wouldn't care if you were on your phones in regular class, cause I know you'd still be paying attention. You guys sit in the back, so nobody would see you and bitch about it to me anyways."

I laugh, "Good to know. I wouldn't pull my phone out unless it was important anyways."

She nods, "Exactly."

ME:

Hey Kaid, could you do me and Zahra a favor for our project?

KAID:

You mean more than watching Sense and Sensibility with you two all night.

ME:

First of all, you did that on your own free will. Secondly, it won't be that difficult.

KAID:

Hit me.

ME:

Zahra and I are making a video for our project, and we need a narrator

KAID:

And I'm assuming you want me to be that narrator?

ME:

I was going to say that, but yup

KAID:

Just send me the script and when you need the recording by and I'll get it to you

"Kaid's in," I tell Zahra and Melody, looking up from my phone.

"Now all we need to do is write the script..." Zahra grumbles. The two of us simultaneously look at our computer screens, still open with the blank document.

"I guess we better get started on this..."

"Do you want me to help you procrastinate, or just let you work?" Melody interjects, chuckling.

"Usually I wouldn't say this, but please help me procrastinate."

"This class is technically over as of three minutes ago," she tells us, "I don't have another class for another half hour, so you could stay if you want to."

"I have another class," Zahra says sadly. "I'll get started on designing characters tonight, if you can start on the script."

"I was about to suggest the same thing," I tell her, quickly packing my bag up so Zahra can hang it off the back of my chair on her way out of the classroom.

> ZAHRA:
>
> What do you think of me changing the animation style slightly for each movie?
>
> ZAHRA:
>
> Since you're probably sleeping, I made the executive decision to do it.
>
> ZAHRA:
>
> We need to have a coffee date or something- let me know your thoughts when you wake up.

I wake up to multiple texts from Zahra from throughout the night and I can't resist chuckling at her late night ramblings.

> ME:
>
> If you want to add more work for yourself, you're more than welcome to do whatever you want.
>
> ZAHRA:
>
> I've already got all the main people in each movie sketched out
>
> ME:
>
> Dang, you really got a lot done while I was sleeping
>
> ZAHRA:
>
> Insomnia's a bitch

After I get dressed for the day, I roll out of my room and into the kitchen. As per usual, Kaid's in the kitchen with breakfast almost ready.

"I made omelettes," he says in lieu of greetings, "I hope

you don't mind, I woke up a bit late this morning and wasn't able to make the breakfast bake I planned."

"I didn't realize you actually planned out what you're going to make everyday," I tell him, locking my chair into place when I get to my usual spot at the table.

"Of course I do, what do you think of me? That I'm crazy?"

"What? I didn't say anything about being crazy!"

"I have lists for everything, everything is always planned to the T. I mean, what else do you expect from me?"

"At this point, I don't know," I exhale, "I didn't know you were such an organization freak."

"It had to come up at some point," he says, "There's no way it didn't."

"Well way, since it didn't."

"I don't believe it," he mutters under his breath. He tosses the finished omelette from the pan onto a plate and slides it over, doing the same with his own omelette. "Cheese and spinach, your favorite, right?"

I nod, immediately grabbing the silverware he laid out for me, and dig in. "Ow," I recoil as I burn my mouth on the omelette.

"I was about to say 'be careful, it's hot,' like I always do, but it seems you beat me to it," he chuckles, blowing on his fork.

"At this point, you need to wait a few minutes to give me things so I don't burn my mouth immediately."

He laughs, "I really should start doing that, it would probably help your taste buds."

"I'd probably be grumpy about it, though."

"I don't know if I should do it then, keep burning your tongue."

I stick my tongue out at him, and he rolls his eyes. "I thought you loved me," I pout, scooping more eggs into my mouth.

"Come on," he exclaims, "You know I love you, Clover, don't doubt that. I know I joke a lot, but caring about you is one thing I will never, never, joke about. I hope you believe that."

His tone switched from joking to caring so fast, it almost gave me whiplash. "Of course I believe that," I say softly, "I was just trying to make a joke... obviously it didn't land."

"Oh, I thought you were serious for a second there," he chuckles awkwardly, "Can we agree not to make jokes about that anymore?"

"Deal."

15

———

I wake up having to use the bathroom. I yawn, and roll over. It's times like this that I forget that my legs don't work how they used to. I try to swing my legs over the edge of my mattress, going off instinct from years of my life. It doesn't work, but I do get into my chair eventually.

I roll to the bathroom, forcing myself to wake up a little bit. I do my business without any problems before I roll back into my room. I usually leave my door open, so I don't have to worry about having to open the door in the middle of the night.

I yawn, and my hand goes up to my mouth on instinct. My chair shifts to the left, and I have to quickly adjust my chair so I don't run into the doorframe. I close my eyes for a second, and hold my groan back. I need to get back into bed before I fall asleep in my chair.

I wheel up to my bed and lock my chair. I shift forward to get into my bed, but my chair goes flying backwards. I try my best to catch myself, but it doesn't work. I fall onto the floor, hitting my legs against the bed frame along the way.

My hands go flying towards my head, trying my best to protect it as a yelp comes out of my mouth.

All of this happens within a second, but it feels like it took forever. Now, I'm laying on the floor, in the dark. My phone's across the room, so I don't have any way to call anyone for help.

I lay on the floor, deep breathing, for a few seconds before trying to push myself closer to the bed or my chair. I mean, once I get there, I'm not sure if I'll be able to get up by myself, but that's the best I can do right now.

I get to my chair first, and I reach towards it. Immediately it moves, and at that moment I realize what happened. I swear I locked my chair when I went to transfer... I grab the chair and yank it towards me again. I grab the break closest to me and lock it. It immediately unlocks. Great. This is exactly what I need right now.

I lay down on the floor again, taking deep breaths, before doing my best to shuffle towards the bed. I shove the chair out of the way, and it goes flying across the room. I cringe, but go back to pulling my limp legs across my bedroom floor.

"What are you doing?" I hear someone say sleepily from the hallway. I yelp, and my hands shift making me fall flat on my face again. My head turns immediately towards the door, and I find Kaid standing there. "Is everything alright?" He asks, a worried tone seeping into his voice, "Did you fall?"

"I'm dancing," I deadpan, answering his question, "No, everything is not okay. Yes, I fell." My voice breaks then, and tears form in my eyes. I force them back, not wanting Kaid to see my tears.

"Here, let me help you," he comes over and helps me sit up. He holds my back up as he sits next to me, and lets me lean against him for extra support. I love how I didn't need to ask him for help before he did. I love how he immediately knew what to do to help, without needing to ask me.

I sniff, and blink frantically. I stare at my chair, that's sitting across the room, intensely and Kaid follows my gaze.

"Is your chair broken?" He asks softly, knowing it's my only way of getting around.

"Yeah," my voice cracks. It's going to be a lot harder than I thought to hide my emotions from Kaid.

"Everything's going to be okay, I promise," he whispers in my ear. He bumps his head gently against mine, and I can't hold back the small smile that appears on my face.

I sniffle again, and the first tear falls. I have to let it fall, my hands and arms are too tired from pulling myself across the room to wipe it. I stare at the chair again as the tears keep falling, wishing for them to stop.

Kaid's hand comes up to my face and gently wipes the tears from my cheeks. "Here's what we're going to do, okay? I'm going to stand up and lift you onto your bed. Then I'll look at your chair and see what needs to be done with it, and fix it as best I can."

I nod, still too emotional to get any words out. I still can't believe this is happening right now, I can't believe I didn't think to double check the breaks before I transferred. I can't believe I haven't been keeping an eye on the brakes, I could've prevented this.

"Stop playing the 'what if?' game," he chides, "We're going to figure this out together, I promise."

I smile at him again. Somehow he always manages to make me smile, even if I'm not in a good mood.

He stands up, keeping his hand on my back as promised, and bends down to pick me up. He puts one of his hands behind my back, while the other goes to my upper thighs before lifting me up.

I yelp, not knowing what to expect from this situation. Kaid chuckles and bends down to put a kiss on my temple as we get to my bed and he puts me down gently under the covers.

"I'm going to take this with me," he tells me, gesturing towards the chair, "and work on it in the living room so you can get your sleep. I should have it back to you by the time your alarm goes off in the morning, or I'll be in here to help you," He walks over to the chair, gently pushing it in front of him before turning the light off on his way out.

My ALARM the next morning shocks me out of my sleep. My eyes fly open, as I remember the events of last night. As I remember, my head snaps to the right, praying that my chair would be back and next to my bed. It's not.

I lose my breath for a second, as I look at where my chair should be. I know Kaid said he was going to fix it, but what if it was much more of a problem than he thought? What if he wasn't able to fix it, and can't fix it? What if I have to go without a chair today? All week?

"Clover, are you awake?" I hear Kaid holler from the hallway, before he rushes into my room. "I'm so so sorry, I know I promised that I'd have the chair, or me, in here before your alarm went off but I totally lost track of time, and..."

"It's fine, I'm fine," I tell him, mainly saying it to reassure myself instead of him.

"Your chair is fine," he tells me, probably noticing my panic, "I wanted to talk to you before I gave the chair back to you."

"Oh god, what's wrong with it? I don't have the money for a new chair, I barely had the money to get here."

"Nothing that much, you just have to be uber careful with the brakes. The breaks are broken, enough that they can't be fully fixed, but I fixed them enough that they'll work for the time being."

"Fuck, I don't have the money for this," I groan, my head falling into my hands.

"It's fine," he coos, putting a hand on my shoulder, "Your chair is working, I'll bring it in, I just wanted to help you the first time."

"Oh good, I have to pee."

He laughs as he rushes into the living room.

He comes back into my room, wheelchair in tow, a few seconds later. "Ta-da!" He exclaims, laughing and giving me jazz hands. I can't hold back my laugh.

"Alrighty, let's get you into this chair," he says excitedly. I toss the blankets off of my legs, and grip my pants lifting my legs and tossing them over the bed. Kaid puts the chair in place as I transfer into it.

"Take a look at this," he tells me, pointing to the brakes on the chair. My hands fly to them and immediately notice the difference, they're super loose. "As I'm sure you noticed yesterday, your brakes are loose and aren't staying in place very well. I did my best to fix that, it's doing much better now, but just be careful with it. The brakes are about at loose as they are before, but they'll stay locked longer, though I suggest keeping an extra hand on them when transferring in and out of the chair."

"Noted," I say, "Can we talk over this at breakfast? I wasn't lying when I said I have to pee."

"Go ahead," he holds his hands up, "I'll be in the kitchen setting the table. Keep an eye on those brakes, Clove."

"You don't need to worry about me, Kaid."

"Fuck," I grumble under my breath. I've been trying my best to concentrate on Professor Kingston (Melody??)'s lecture for the last 45 minutes, but my chair keeps unlocking and my concentration wavers. I hold back my groan as I lock my chair for what feels like the hundredth time this class.

I go back to my notes, and halfway through my next bullet point, my chair unlocks again. I never thought that my chair could bother me, especially since it's been a lifeline for me for months at this point, but at this point I just want to drag my body around instead of using the chair.

"Alright," Professor Kingston says, as she clicks her remote and the next slide of her slideshow shows up on the wall. "That's all I have for today's lesson, and it looks like I ended right on time," she glances at the clock and nods, "Don't forget to work on your projects, our next project workday is Wednesday at 11am, I'd love to see you there. Have a great day!" She dismisses the class, and like usual, the class empties out within a minute. I've given up trying to get out of the class right as class ends, if I tried I'd probably get run over.

"What the hell is going on?" Zahra turns in her chair. At first I thought she was going to leave, but I guess not.

"What?" I look at her confused. I put down the pencil I was about to put away.

"You kept grumbling under your breath and groaning, the entire class, I couldn't concentrate."

"I'm sorry," I tell her immediately, "I couldn't concentrate either. My wheelchair broke last night, and the brakes don't stay in place anymore."

"I was going to be mad at you, but now I can't. Ignore all of my annoyed-ness."

"Annoyed-ness isn't a word."

"Stop being the grammar police, just be happy I'm not mad at you," she laughs and goes back to packing her backpack up.

"I'm exhausted, and apparently I turn into the grammar police when I'm tired," I shrug, "It's weird, but it is what it is I guess."

We finish putting our things away, and Zahra and I make our way out of the classroom. Once we get outside, Zahra starts pushing me towards the cafe we agreed to hang out at afterwards.

"So you're saying that your wheelchair just broke on you last night?" It's the first thing she's said our whole walk, I guess it's been bothering her.

"Yeah," I sigh, "I don't really know what happened, but Kaid stayed up a lot of the night fixing it as best he could."

"That's so sweet, he's going to be an amazing boyfriend to someone one day."

"Yeah, for sure."

"I still can't get over the fact your wheelchair just... broke."

"I guess it makes some sense," I shrug, "It's a cheap, used wheelchair, and I've been using it nonstop for months. It makes sense."

"So when are you getting a new chair? Please tell me you're getting a new chair," she asks, partially begging at the end.

"I don't have the extra money right now, even if I wanted to get a new wheelchair."

"That's terrible," she says softly.

"I know Kaid's planning on looking at it more when I get home, so it should work better tomorrow."

"Yeah... that's good."

____

16

"**S**eriously, how many copies of _Sense and Sensibility_ do you have?" Kaid asks, making me look up from my computer. I'm working on some homework, and Kaid's supposed to be fixing my chair.

"Aren't you supposed to be fixing my chair?" I raise an eyebrow at Kaid, who's standing in front my bookshelves instead of on the floor fixing my chair.

"I finished," he says, not turning around to look at me.

"Mhm," I say skeptically, looking down at the floor and finding my chair with one wheel popped off.

"What?" He turns around and looks down at the floor. "Oh shit, how did that happen?" He bends down and starts trying to put the wheel back on the chair. I roll my eyes, even though he can be chaotic he's one of the few people I would trust to fix it.

I return my attention back to my homework, in particular the script for the _Sense and Sensibility_ project. I do have a lot of copies of the book, it's my favorite of all time. What I'm not going to tell Kaid, though, is that I only brought my favorites of my editions of the book. I have tons more at home in the US, and I'm not leaving here without buying a few more.

"Okay," Kaid announces a few seconds later, "Your chair is fixed now, for real this time."

I look up at him, and the chair and he has the biggest smile on his face. I don't know how much he knows about fixing wheelchairs, and probably not much considering how proud he is of his accomplishment.

"Good job!" I exclaim, happy that my chair's fixed and I don't have to worry about the brakes malfunctioning anymore.

"I'm not sure how well I did, but the breaks should be working for now... you really should look into getting a new chair though."

"Why?" I ask confused, "It works fine."

"Yeah, it works fine for what you need, but I can see parts starting to break down."

"Great," I mumble to myself under my breath, "That's exactly what I need right now."

"I'll look into it," I say louder, for Kaid to hear.

"I could always help you with payments, if you need," he says softly.

"No," I say immediately, my parent's mantra repeating in my head: "Never borrow money from friends."

"Hell, I'll buy it for you, I have the money for it."

"No, I don't want to have to owe you back."

"You wouldn't have to owe me back, consider it a present."

"That's too big for a present."

"Just think about it... please?" He asks, practically begging.

I can't resist the pleading look on his face, "Fine, I'll think about it."

"Thank you," he lets out a breath, "Thank you so much."

"No promises."

"It's not a problem, just look into it and think about accepting it as a present."

"I mean, it's just too big of a present from one person, that's the problem I have with it."

He nods slowly, "I understand what you're saying."

MOM:

> I hope you're doing well. Your Dad and I have been wanting to give you your space as you adjust into your new place. I'd love to hear all of the updates.

I reread Mom's text multiple times. It's been a few months since I moved to Newcastle. I know Mom's been busy, just like I have, so I don't blame her for not reaching out. I just haven't realized how long it's been since I saw her and Dad. I didn't realize how much I've missed them.

ME:

> Hi Mom! I've missed you and Dad so much! I've been doing good here in Newcastle. Once I got past the little dorm dilemma, and made a new best friend or two, it's been amazing. I've been working on a project based on Sense and Sensibility with one of my best friends and I've loved working on my classics degree.

MOM:

> That's great hon! I've talked to Adria a bit when I've run into her, and she's been keeping me updated. What was the situation with housing, though? I'm glad you got it fixed either way.

ME:

You didn't have to talk to Adria, you could've texted me easily. I've been easily reachable this whole time. Either way, the dorm I was assigned to wasn't anywhere close to wheelchair accessible. The room was, I guess, but the only entrance to the building is six big stairs. Either way, I met my friend Kaid, and I moved in with him and it's great.

MOM:

I don't know how I feel about you living with a boy.

I sigh to myself. I want her to be in the loop of things, but also I know she's judgmental as heck when it comes to things like this. Like there's no way that Kaid and I would be together romantically. She knows I'm not interested in dating anyone right now.

ME:

Mom, how many times have I told you that I'm not interested in dating? Either way, Kaid and I are friends and only friends, and we've talked about it. Besides, his apartment was the only option I had if I wanted to have a place to stay anyways. I've decided to stay here.

MOM:

You're an adult now, living in another country, so I'm not going to lecture you about this. I'm too tired, and I trust your judgement.

That's her way of ending the conversation, I guess. I toss my phone onto the bed and drop my head onto the mattress. Mom's always been this way, kind of just letting me do my own thing and following my dreams. I guess that's a good thing, but she doesn't really care much. We moved a lot when I was little and I never really made close friends until Adria and Caitlyn.

She'll probably reach out in another month, when she remembers I exist again. I groan into the blanket, that being the only way I can express my frustration right now.

At least I have my chair fixed... that's all I have for now.

$4,844.70.

$4,844.70.

$4,844.70

I knew getting a custom wheelchair would be incredibly expensive... but damn. I went online, just trying to get an estimate of how much it would cost. I definitely didn't expect it to be that expensive. I groan, and close my laptop, there's no way that I'm going to be able to afford that.

I'm struggling to afford my tuition payments right now, there's absolutely no way I'm going to be able to afford a new, nice wheelchair, on top of all of that.

Kaid hasn't been letting me pay for rent, so I've been trying to pay him back any way that I can. I've been sending groceries to the apartment when he's not here, and filling the fridge and pantry when I can. I need to go to the actual store at some point, cause the online ordering doesn't always work in the way I need to.

He's probably noticed me doing this, since he does the majority of the cooking, but he hasn't said anything about it. So I'm going to keep grocery shopping for us until he says something— the only thing is I can't save for the chair as much as I'd like.

From what I know, I have a 'medical grade' chair- at least that's what people call it back home. I could get another one of these, but obviously they aren't the best quality if mines breaking down on me.

I've seen other wheelchair users with custom chairs, and I guess that's the next jump up. And that's too damn expensive for me right now. I guess I'm just going to have to deal with this for now.

I move to unlock my chair and hold back my groan as I find it already unlocked. This is going to drive me nuts, but I'm going to have to deal with it until I can get the extra to get this.

In the living room, I find Kaid sitting on the couch writing in a little orange notebook. When he hears me wheel in, he quickly closes it. He puts it in his pocket and turns to look at me wide-eyed.

"What?" I ask, holding back a shocked chuckle, "Don't worry, I'm not going to ask or look."

"R-right," he laughs awkwardly, pulling it back out of his pocket slowly to fiddle with it. "I know you wouldn't, I'm just so used to people invading my privacy."

"I'm sorry."

"Don't apologize. I've long since learned that family is found not forced."

"That's a good lesson."

"It is," he says quietly under his breath, looking at the notebook with a sense of longing.

"I'll make some lunch," I say quietly, wanting to give him some space.

I go to the fridge and try to open it, but with my chair's locks not working, every time I try I end up flying back.

I grip the counter next to me for stability, and am able to get the door open after a few hard yanks. I grab the leftovers that Kaid packed in individual serving sizes the other day and toss them in the microwave.

I look over at Kaid, and he's still sitting on the couch

looking at his notebook. He's obviously having a moment, and I'm pretty sure I see a tear fall down his face.

I look down, and try not to cry myself. Kaid's my best friend, and he's done so much for me over these past few months. I don't want him to be sad, or suffering.

I grab one of the bowls and start wheeling slowly towards him. He looks up at me and gives me a small smile. Once I get closer I pass him the bowl and he puts the notebook down.

"Thanks Clove."

"I'm always here if you want to talk," I tell him as I wheel back into the kitchen to grab my food.

"Can we talk now?" He asks softly. I barely hear him.

"Of course," I tell him, quickly putting my bowl down on the table before starting to transfer.

Kaid puts his bowl on the table and puts his hands up towards my chair, silently asking if he could stabilize the chair while I transfer. I nod, and he puts his hands on the front of the chair above the front wheels making sure they don't move.

I transfer to the couch easily, finally getting the hang of doing it by myself. Kaid smiles at me as I pull my pants to move my legs onto a cushion before leaning back into the couch.

"Alright, I'm ready." I tell him, "You can start wherever and whenever you're ready."

17

———

He takes a deep breath and lets it out slowly. "I know I told you that my parents were rich and left me with a nanny for most of my childhood, throwing money at me as they traveled the world doing whatever the fuck they wanted. My nanny, Nonna Helen, basically raised me. I honestly think of her more as a Mom than my real Mom."

"I lived with her in Manchester, going between her cottage and my parent's mansion. I spent my days playing outside in the woods, learning Italian, playing with my friends, and so much more. My parents only ever reached out around the holidays, and excessively sent me money for any occasion they could think of. Eventually they gave up on parenting, and let Nonna raise me fully."

"I-I mean they haven't reached out in years," he sniffs, rubbing his eyes and nose, "I kinda forgot they existed in a sense. I went to therapy and don't resent them anymore, I'm just neutral about them. B-but now that I'm older and in college and an 'adult' they insist on seeing me, and trying to bring me into the family business."

"Well that's total bullshit," I interject before I can stop myself. He laughs sadly.

"I really don't know what they want from me, but they're basically trying to make me join in the family business, and threatening a bunch of shit I don't want to get into. It's just really hard right now..."

"Yeah, I'm sure it's so hard for you." I say quietly, looking down at the couch, trying to take in what he said. I don't really know what else to say so I lean over and hug him as best I can. He sighs and wraps his arms around me as well, tucking his head in the crook of my neck and crying.

A few hours later, we're still laying on the couch together, but we've put on a show in the background as we each stew in our thoughts.

"I wanna go visit Nonna Helen," he says, "I think I need to go and talk over this with her, and I have the money for flights."

"I think that's a good idea," I tell him, squeezing his thigh gently in encouragement. It's a better idea than any I could come up with.

"I don't think I'm going to be able to go until the end of term, I know that I'd want to go for a month, maybe more, at a time and I can't do that during term."

"I was going to suggest at least a week, but I think staying for a month is a much better idea. Spend some time with Nonna, go over everything that's happened and maybe even talk to your parents together."

"Yeah, that's a good plan." He nods. "Although, I've been thinking about this for too long, so I want to change the topic."

"...to what?" I ask skeptically.

He looks over at my ratty wheelchair and it's shitty brakes and doesn't say anything.

"Your chair." He says finally.

I look over at the chair as well.

"I've looked into getting a new one," I tell him, "But I just don't have the money for it. Frankly I don't think I have the energy to go to all of the appointments just to be told I'm faking."

"Has someone told you you're faking?" He sits up so fast a pillow goes flying across the room.

I shrug, but he immediately sees through me. "That's bullshit. What the fuck? Who would say that to someone? You're obviously not faking, you're one of the strongest people I know."

"Thank you, but the healthcare system sucks."

"You're not in America anymore," he says softly, putting a hand on my shoulder, "It's not as expensive for appointments, doctors actually care here, and me and Zahra are here for you. Always."

I take a deep breath, looking up at the ceiling for a split second. As much as I love the idea of getting a new chair, or even getting this one fixed, I just don't have the money right now— and I probably never will.

"I really want to," I tell him, trying to hold back my tears, "I really do. I just don't have the money."

"Well that's what me and Zahra are here for,"

"No." I say immediately, "Fuck no."

"Hear me out, though," he says quickly, just as passionately as I am. "I have too much fucking money, and even though I donate a lot of it, I still have a lot. It's all from my parents, so I hate using it on myself unless I have to, but I'll gladly take money out for you. It'll barely be a dent, and if you're really worried about it, I'll call it a Christmas gift."

"A Christmas gift? I wouldn't let you buy me anything for ten years if you bought my chair, it's just too much."

"Well ten years is a bit excessive," he chuckles, "but I don't care, as long as you're taken care of. Zahra and I talked about it, she'd help you to appointments and be there to support you — if you're comfortable with that, of course, we can always find her something else to do..."

He starts rambling and I stop him, "I'll consider it— that is if we even get to that point."

"Oh we will." He gives me a look that begs me to fight him on this. "And I'll pay, obviously help you around the apartment if you need it."

"You're not paying."

"Yes, I will."

"No."

"Stop fighting me on this Mx Clover, you're not going to win."

I stop for a minute and consider the options. He's right, I'm not going to win, cause he's one of the most fiercely stubborn people I know. He'd do anything for the people he loves, and I guess I've made my way onto that list within the four months we've known each other.

"How about we split it?" I offer, knowing that's the only option I have where we're both happy enough.

"Fine, 90/10."

"You're fucking with me." I narrow my eyes at him. "50/50 sounds better to me."

He scoffs, "No way, that's not happening. How's 30/70?"

"40/60?"

"20/80."

"No."

"40/60 is the lowest I'll go." I barter.

"Fine, it's a deal." He glowers at me jokingly— I think—

and reaches out his hand. "It's a pleasure doing business with you. I'll reach out once we get closer to the first appointment."

I reach out and shake his hand, trying to act serious but holding back a laugh.

We shake hands and he pulls me into a hug. I immediately hug him back, and the laughter I was holding back turns into tears. I start shaking as the tears fall down my face and onto Kaid's shirt, but I can't get myself to stop them.

"Oh Clove..." he says in my ear softly, scooting closer to me on the couch so he can tighten the hug, "Let it all out, I know it's a lot. Me and Zahra are here for you, always."

"T-thank you," I hiccup.

I feel odd all of a sudden, and grip onto Kaid's shirt as dizziness takes over my entire body.

"Clover?" He asks, worry seeped into his tone, "Clover, are you okay?"

I try to answer, but nothing comes out. I don't know what I'd say anyways, my brain is so messed up.

The world starts to go dark around me and I panic even more. *What'll happen if the room goes dark?*

I can't stay awake enough to figure out the answer.

18

———

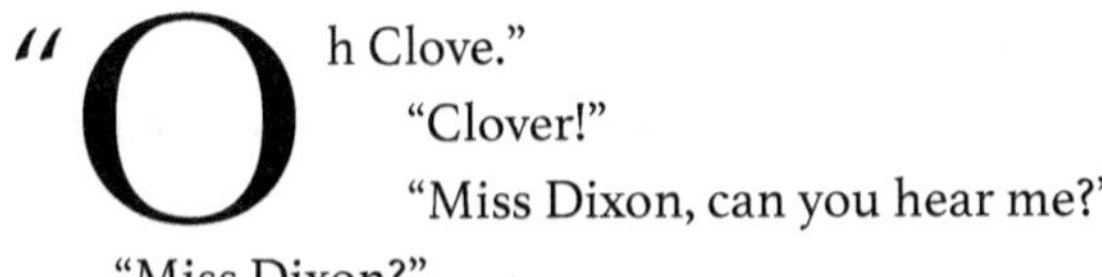

"Oh Clove."

"Clover!"

"Miss Dixon, can you hear me?"

"Miss Dixon?"

I hear voices faintly, but I can't open my eyes. I can't move either, but I'd rather stay here. It's peaceful here, the most peaceful I've been in awhile. I know that when I open my eyes, it'll be stressful— possibly even more than before.

The voices grow louder, but they aren't as frantic as before. Kind of like they're chattering amongst themselves instead of talking directly at me. I relax a bit more, falling back into my deep sleep.

MY EYES slowly open and blink multiple times. I can't move any of my limbs, and there is an incredibly bright light in my eyes. I don't recognize the ceiling above me and my brain immediately starts racing.

"Clover!" Someone exclaims, and I hear them rushing

towards me. "Clover, it's alright, I promise." Zahra, I realize as she comes into view.

I calm down a bit, but still don't understand what's going on. "W-what?" It's the best I can get out, my mouth is so dry.

"Shh, you don't need to talk." Zahra says softly, moving her hand up to brush the hair off my forehead. "I'll explain every-thing," Her hand lingers afterwards, and her hand slowly brushes across my forehead back and forth like she's doing it without realizing.

"You passed out in your apartment earlier, and since you weren't responding, Kaid called an ambulance for you. He went with you, and called me. Since then we've been waiting for you to wake up to get more information, and Kaid literally just went to the bathroom."

There's a knock on the door, before it creaks open. Zahra turns around and smiles gently.

"Ah, you're awake," she says, and a cart rolls into the room with her. She's an older nurse, with curly white-ish grey hair and a bounce in her step. "I'm going to go ahead and get your vitals, and then I'll go ahead and call the Doctor in for you."

I try my best to smile, but it doesn't work very well. She smiles at me anyways, and she starts mindlessly chattering while she takes my vitals.

I have to resist rolling my eyes, I always forget how hard it is going to the hospital. Kaid said it was easier to get health-care here, and that staff are much nicer, but I've still had too many bad experiences to feel comfortable here immediately. Especially since I can't talk and stand up for myself at the moment.

"Alright, dearie, your doctor will be in here soon and I really hope we can help make you feel better." She gives me a massive smile before making her way out of the small room with her cart.

"So Kaid should be back any second now," Zahra says after a few seconds, "he's been out a few minutes, but maybe he stopped for something."

"I got snacks!" I hear Kaid exclaim excitedly as he comes through the door. I immediately feel happier, like another piece of my heart has come back.

"Anything good?" Zahra asks, standing up and rushing towards Kaid and the pile of snacks he has in his arms.

He scoffs, "Of course I got good snacks, who do you think I am?"

"Right, I forgot I was talking to a snack connoisseur," I can't see her face, but I'm sure Zahra rolls her eyes at him. She looks a bit closer before nicking a bag of cheese and onion off the top of the pile. She opens it up and falls back into the chair next to my bed.

Kaid goes through the remaining snack bags, picking one and putting the rest on a small table against the wall.

"So how's our favorite Clover?" He asks, opening the bag and sitting in a chair.

"Xeir awake," she says slowly. A small smile comes onto my face as Kaid processes Zahra's words.

He stands up and rushes over to my bed, "Oh my god, Clove!" He exclaims relieved. "I was so worried, are you okay?" He reaches his arm out like he wants to give me a hug, but hesitates and squeezes my arm gently instead.

"Xe aren't able to talk or move right now, but xeir vitals have been taken and the Doctor has been called."

"Oh good, hopefully we'll get some answers soon."

I must make a face or something, cause Kaid adjusts his tone. "I promise, Clover, it's going to be okay. I don't know much about your health situation, but based on how you talk about them you don't like hospitals. I promise the staff in these hospitals are much nicer, and will do anything to help you get the care you need. I had the ambulance bring you to Nonna Helen's hospital of choice, so I promise that this will be a good experience compared to your other ones."

"I haven't had many hospital experiences," Zahra comes to my other side and says, "But I promise to make this as good as possible for you."

I smile at them, and I think I'm able to get it a bit wider than before. That's a good sign, I think I'm slowly improving. Although it really doesn't feel like it.

A knock sounds on the door and the door creaks open.

"Hello," a soft, kind voice says. She's a younger doctor, and I feel better having her as my doctor immediately. "I'm Doctor Councit, the neurologist assigned to your case. Before I start talking to you about you and your symptoms, I want you to know that if you ever feel that you need a second opinion or wish to change doctors, you have the right to do so and we will never judge."

If I could raise my eyebrows, I would. That was one of the last things I expected her to say.

She goes over basic information about me and my medical history quickly before moving onto why I'm here today.

"So, you passed out." She states, looking at me waiting for a reaction. I try to talk, but nothing comes out other than a few grunts.

"Uh, xe-"

"You can't talk right now, or move any part of your body? I can tell by your body language, sorry I don't know why I expected you to answer. I'll ask you yes or no questions and I'll have you blink once for yes and twice for no." Dr Councit says kindly.

"Wow, that's a good idea," Kaid mutters.

"Alright, I want to start from the beginning here." She says.

Kaid nods, and explains our conversation in the living

room. He explains how we were talking and then I passed out pretty much out of nowhere.

The doctor taps her pen against her clipboard as she thinks.

"This is the first time this has happened, then?" She looks at me and I blink once. Yes.

"But from your medical history, you've had a lot of other doctors look at you. Your legs went numb this past July, and your PT doesn't really have many notes here..." I blink once at her words, even though she's not looking at me. That PT really sucked... maybe I could have been able to walk now but he didn't really work with me.

"Okay," she stops tapping her pen, and she looks up at me, Kaid, and Zahra. "The first thing I want to do is get an MRI scheduled, to see if there's anything going on inside. Then I want to set you up to an EKG, monitor you for maybe 36 hours. Get you started with PT in the meantime, see how we can make your life outside the hospital easier for you."

Kaid nods, "Thank you Doctor." Zahra thanks her as well before she leaves. I try to smile, but still can barely move.

"This Doctor seems really nice," Zahra says softly, looking down at the hospital bed.

"From what Clove's told me, I think this is going to be a good match compared to past doctors." Kaid puts a hand on Zahra's shoulder, doing his best to comfort her.

"Y-ya-" I try to say 'yes' but it doesn't come out right. I want to cry, because of how unfulfilled I feel about not being able to move or talk anymore.

"Hey, you're able to talk a bit now!" Zahra exclaims, excitement and relief flying through her tone. "I'm so proud of you, Clove, you're doing amazing!"

A blush forms on my face, but there's nothing I could do about it.

"Oh, and you're getting less pale," Kaid notices, relief etched in his tone as well. *I guess they won't notice the blush either way.*

They continue talking amongst themselves, as I fall in and out of consciousness.

THE MRI and the EEG aren't the worst things in the world. I mean, yeah, they're uncomfortable, but every medical test is on the uncomfortable side.

"Are you alright now?" Kaid asks, hovering over my hospital bed. *Again.*

"Kaid, I swear, you don't need to ask me every five seconds. I'm alright, just a little bit uncomfortable," I tell him, for what feels like the millionth time.

"You only have," he looks at his phone and hesitates, "...32 hours left."

"I'm counting down the seconds," I deadpan, making a small smile form on Kaid's face.

A knock on the door sounds and it creaks open. Doctor Council comes into the room, and into my sight.

"From what I can tell, your MRI doesn't have anything unusual on it, and we won't have anyone bother looking at the EEG until after your 36 hours are up. But as of right now, the best I can tell you is that there isn't anything extremely pressing or dangerous right now, and all we can do right now is get you into PT and wait on the EEG to finish." She looks up and smiles at each of us gently.

I nod, "Thank you Dr."

"So, what do we want to do in the meantime?" Kaid asks, sitting back on the couch and twiddling his thumbs.

"Kaid, you need to relax." Zahra tells him gently, "We're

going to be here for the next 32 hours, and in the meantime we talk to anyone who comes in and do our best to get caught up with our schoolwork."

"Wait, what do you mean 'caught up'?" I interject.

"Well it's been three days since you got here, you were 'out' for maybe three hours and then you were in and out of consciousness until you woke up." Kaid explains. "It's Thursday now."

"Oh my god, I can't believe I've missed so much class— I'm never going to be able to catch up!" My brain starts spiraling out of control as I try to figure out how long it'll take me to catch up on a full class load.

"Don't worry about it," Zahra puts her hand on top of mine and squeezes gently. "I've already emailed your profs on your behalf, and reached out to disability services to see if they can help as well."

I exhale, feeling better already. I mentally scan through the rest of this week's schedule and remember— "I missed my call with my friends back home! God, they must be so worried."

"Don't worry about that. I called the first three people on your call log, your Mom and two people called Adria and Caitlyn. They were worried, but I promised to help you call them once you're feeling up to it. I've been using your phone to text them updates, I hope you don't mind."

"Usually I'd be pissed, but I think this is the only time where I'm not."

"That's what I told him too," Zahra nods.

"Sounds like you two have everything settled." I say under my breath.

"All you need to worry about now is resting."

19

"I'm so glad you're alright!" Adria exclaims through the phone, eyes scanning me as best she can through the blurry screen. Caitlyn wraps her arm around her girlfriend, bringing her closer. "I know that Kaid said you were alright, but I wanted to see with my own eyes."

"Xe looks really good," Caitlyn nods, "How are you doing Clover? We miss you here."

"I'm doing better," I nod, "I'm pretty much just waiting on tests and stuff— both for tests to be finished and for results." I motion to the EEG wires surrounding my head. "I think PT is going to come in eventually, and once tests are done I should be out of here."

"Out of here on Thursday," Kaid says, walking in. It's currently Tuesday. "That's the estimate the nurse just gave me."

"Home on Thursday," I smile to myself, "I can do two more days of nothingness."

"Not 'nothingness'," Adria tells me, an infectious smile on her face that I can't resist from reciprocating, "We each ordered you a book from a local store and had them shipped to your apartment."

"And they reached out to me, to bring them to the hospital with me today. Along with a few snacks, since I figured you were tired of eating hospital food and overpaying for the good snacks."

I laugh, "Yeah, I was getting a bit annoyed with that, but it's nothing compared to US prices. Besides, I'd pay anything if I was craving it enough."

"But now, you don't have to," Caitlyn says.

"Here," Kaid hands me a cutely wrapped present that he had hiding behind his tote bag.

"This wrapping is so cute!" I exclaim, flipping the bag around and looking at the design closely.

"It is!" Adria exclaims, "I don't remember hitting 'giftwrap' online but it looks so good!"

"You didn't hit 'giftwrap'," Caitlyn clarifies, "I remember that, because it was insanely expensive."

"Then how did...?"

"Zahra did it," Kaid sits in the chair next to me, and I tilt the computer towards him so he can see better. "She had class today and felt bad that she didn't have a gift for you, so she wrote you a card and wrapped everyone else's gifts. Also, it's nice to officially meet you two."

They repeat the sentiment.

"Open the present!" Adria exclaims excitedly, sitting on her hands.

"Okay, okay," I laugh, and start pulling the first piece of tissue paper out of the bag.

I start pulling the second piece out and Kaid exclaims, "Don't tell me that you're one of those people who unwraps super slowly to keep the pretty paper?"

"Not fully," I say, pulling another sheet out, "I just don't like ripping things." I toss the paper at him jokingly, and he swats it on the floor.

I reach my hand into the bag and grab a few of my favorite snacks that Kaid got for me. I immediately open the pretzels and eat a few before moving on to the two wrapped packages I felt.

I grab the first one out of the bag and laugh as I move to unwrap it. "It's so big," I pull the tape off the back, and before I can open it the rest of the way, Kaid snorts, "That's what she said."

Adria and Caitlyn hold back their giggles and Kaid freezes. "That's not offensive to you, is it? I-I didn't mean to misgender you, it was a joke. A-a reference."

"No, no, you're good." I have to hold back my laugh, "I know the reference, and I don't mind misgendering if it's a reference— and if it's someone I trust."

"Okay," he lets out a dramatic deep breath, and I can't hold back my laugh anymore.

"Stop laughing at me and open your damn present," he grumbles, crossing his arms to complete the effect.

Adria, Caitlyn, and I laugh even louder as he pouts at us. I haven't laughed like this in awhile, and I think he realizes that so he's just letting it happen. I see a small smile in the corner of his mouth, as he shakes his head dramatically.

I unwrap the paper the rest of the way, and I gasp excitedly as I flip the book to see the cover.

"*The Count of Monte Cristo!*" I exclaim, holding the book up to show Kaid, then Adria and Caitlyn, "You guys! You didn't have to get me this!"

"Well we know you've been wanting to read it, and you have plenty of time in the hospital, so we split the cost."

"It's still so expensive!" I exclaim, flipping the book in my hands and looking at it. I've been wanting a copy for so long, but it's always been too expensive for me to buy.

"You're worth it," Adria and Caitlyn say in sync. They laugh as they realize, and Caitlyn drops a kiss on Adria's temple.

"Thanks guys," I tell them sincerely, "I cannot wait to read this."

"Yeah, and on the off-chance you finish it, there's another book in there for you."

"You know, finding new classics for you that you haven't read yet is really hard." Caitlyn says, "We had fun finding one, though, and honestly I might read it once you're done if you like it."

"I'd prefer a movie, cause classics are hard for me, but I doubt they'll ever do that since it's not as popular," Adria sighs. As many times as I've tried to help her read a classic, it's never worked well. Although, she's never complained as she struggled through. If that doesn't tell you anything about my best friend, I don't know what will.

"*The Prisoner of Zenda...* by Anthony Hope." I read as I unwrap the second book. "I've never heard of this, but I love a good adventure especially in a classic novel."

"I was going between two but ultimately decided on this one," Caitlyn tells me, "The only reason I got this one is because I wanted to read it after you."

I laugh, "I'll definitely lend it to you when I come back to the states on break."

"I almost bought both of them, before we decided to get the Count."

"I don't need three books to read, this is perfect guys, even if it's a bit expensive, thank you guys." I turn to Kaid, "All of you, and I'll text Zahra once we're off the phone too."

A KNOCK SOUNDS on my door. I resist a groan— I just want to go home, but I can't. Not yet. The door creaks open, and a tall redhead walks in.

"Hello, my name's Esme, and I'm here to help you with PT. You'll have someone come in later for OT, usually we come in together but unfortunately she had to step out last minute."

"Is everything alright?" I ask her.

"Oh yeah, everything's fine, but she just needs an extended lunch for today."

I nod.

"So you still can't move your legs?" She asks, gently lifting my blanket off my legs.

I nod, and she makes a sound of acknowledgement.

"For today, I'm going to help you stand up so I can get a general idea of where we're starting, and then we'll talk about what we can get to help you out even more as you recover."

"Sounds good to me," I gulp, looking down at my legs. I don't know how this is going to work... but I guess we're about to find out.

"Umm..." Kaid interjects, as Esme lowers my hospital bed and puts the side down so I can get out easily. "Do you want me to leave?"

"No, Kaid, it's fine." I can't look at him, but I don't want him to leave. I see him sit down in the corner of my eye.

"Alright, let's get started."

I use my arms to push myself into a sitting position. I try to move my legs, but of course, nothing happens. I sigh and pick up my left leg and swing it over the side of the bed. I repeat with the other leg.

I feel the floor on the bottoms of my feet, and it feels weird. I don't know why, because I make an effort to stand up once a day when my body is able to. But it feels different this time.

"Here," Esme holds an arm out to me, I reach out and grab it to stabilize myself. I grab the hospital bed with my other hand.

I take a deep breath and hoist myself up as best I can. I try to stand up straight, but my legs won't hold me up and I fall back onto the bed.

Tears form in my eyes, and I look down at my legs. I close my eyes tightly, trying to hold the tears back, but more just form and I can't keep my eyes closed anymore. My eyes open and the tears fall down my face rapidly. I quickly wipe them.

"I know it's super frustrating that they aren't working, but I need you to try again."

"I understand," I tell her, my voice heavy.

I try again, and immediately fall back onto the bed.

"Hey," Kaid says softly from behind me. I hear him stand up from his chair, and he comes to stand next to me. "I'll help you. I'll hold your back, and make sure you don't fall. I mean, as long as that's alright with you," he looks at Esme.

She nods, "I was actually about to suggest that I do it. It's probably easier for all of us for you to do it."

I nod at both of them, "Okay. Let's do it."

I take another deep breath, and as I exhale I push myself up off the bed. I grip the hospital bed and Esme's arm as I push myself up off the bed. I feel myself about to fall—and I almost give in— but I feel Kaid's hand on my lower back. I inhale and concentrate even harder on standing, knowing that Kaid has my back. Literally.

"Good job, Clover!" Esme exclaims happily as I'm finally up on my feet somewhat balanced.

"I knew you could do it," Kaid says proudly, squeezing my shoulder.

"I can't do it anymore," I say quickly, sweat beading on my forehead.

"Alright, not a problem. You did amazing, that's all I needed to see," Esme says quickly, helping me back onto the bed with ease.

Kaid passes me my water bottle, and helps me hold it up to my mouth as I take small sips.

"I'm so proud of you," he whispers in my ear, before kissing my temple. He sits back down in his chair and puts my water bottle in reach.

"Like I said, I only really needed to see that. Now we can just talk, not as physically difficult, promise." Esme explains. "So, how's your living situation right now? Are you able to use your chair at your place?"

"Yeah, when I first got here there was a bit of a situation, but Kaid's apartment is completely wheelchair accessible." I explain.

"Ok, that's great," she nods and puts a note on her clipboard, "So you use a wheelchair full time?" I nod. "Is it this one over here?" I nod again. She moves to take a look at my chair in more detail.

"It's a shit chair," Kaid interjects.

"Kaid!"

"What? It is!"

"... yeah, you've got a point there actually."

"You need a custom chair."

"Actually I was about to ask that," Esme stands up from looking at the chair, writes something down, and looks at Kaid.

"I can see there's been some at-home repairs, is this your doing?" Kaid nods. "You did a good job, from what I can tell, eventually this chair's going to just break."

"Oh good, now you have an excuse to get a new chair." Kaid looks at me pointedly, and I roll my eyes.

"I still don't have money, Kaid."

"What did I tell you, Clove, Zahra and I are here to help you," he sing-songs.

"I have a new chair for you to use in the meantime, and I'll send you a site for you to order your custom chair. I'll get your measurements before I leave, so you shouldn't have a problem with anything." Esme explains, smiling at me.

"Oh good, that's what I was about to ask," Kaid nods.

She explains how she'll bring a new chair for me and get rid of the old one. She grabs a measuring tape from her pocket, and quickly takes my measurements, writing them down for me.

MY NEW CUSTOM chair is ordered, it's going to be light blue. My new chair to use in the meantime, is sitting in the corner of my hospital room. I can't stop looking at it, still processing my PT appointment from earlier today. My old chair was so raggedy and uncomfortable, and even though I haven't sat in the new one yet, I know it's going to be so much more comfortable.

The chair I have for now isn't much, but a million times better than the chair I had before. The size is more adept to my body size, so I'm not swimming in it anymore. The cushion looks thicker and more stabilizing than the sloppy piece of fabric that the old one had.

I honestly can't believe this is real, I think to myself, I have this amazing new chair and another chair that's being built specifically for me on the way. This wouldn't have been possible back home, and now thanks to my new friends and some amazing medical staff, it's possible for me.

"Not meaning to interrupt sexy time or anything," Kaid interjects, breaking me gazing at my wheelchair, "But when do you want to take it for a spin? I kinda wanted to get some food."

I throw a half-eaten roll from my lunch tray at him, "Oh fuck off."

The little shit catches it mid-air and takes a bite out of it, "Oh geez, this is a lot worse than I thought it'd be."

"Why do you think I didn't finish it? It's like a fucking rock."

"I should've known, you always finish your bread," he turns and throws the bread in the trash can, "There, now there's no evidence of us not finishing the bread."

"I don't think they care, but thanks," I roll my eyes jokingly, but a small smile still forms on my face. Even though I've been in the hospital for the last four days almost, Kaid's never failed to leave my side. Never. He's been sleeping here, taking his classes on Zoom instead of going in person, eating here, literally never leaving my side unless he has to.

"Yeah, you're right," I tell him after a few seconds of comfortable silence, "I haven't really been out of this room since I got here and I wanna try out this new chair. Let's go explore!"

THE CHAIR WAS BETTER than I ever could've imagined. Just by looking at it, I knew it'd be good, but actually sitting in it and it serving as an extension of my body, it's a completely different experience. In such a good way. This chair rolls so smoothly, the turns are crisp and short, and the brakes stay put well without me needing to put all my strength into unlocking.

We got Kaid some food, and he pushed me around for a few minutes too. He was also super impressed by the chair, and honestly he might even be more excited about it than me. He had been the one pushing me to get a new chair in the first place, but even he didn't realize how much my old one was a piece of shit compared to this one.

We're back in my hospital room now, our little adventure being much shorter than I would've liked. I'm getting tired of looking at these same four walls, but I know I'm going home soon. I just need to wait for the results that my doctors are looking over now.

I got my EEG taken off earlier this evening, and even though I have a migraine from all the stickers, I feel amazing. Not having wires attached to my head and upper body, moving with every move I make and getting tangled when I have to go to the bathroom. Now all I need to do is wait.

The doctors said that I'd have results in the morning at my neurology appointment. All I need to do is wait.

20

———

The door opening suddenly is what wakes me up the next morning. My migraine must've really made me sleep well, cause I'm pretty sure I slept through all the vitals throughout the night.

"Good morning," Dr. Councit says sweetly as she comes into the room the rest of the way. I have to stifle a yawn as I watch her sit down, her clipboard resting gently on her legs.

I look over at Kaid, and it looks like he just woke up as well. He doesn't bother stifling his yawn as he sits up and puts his attention on the Doctor.

"Sorry to have woken you," she says, looking down at her notes.

I shrug and deadpan, "It's the hospital, you don't come here to get a good night's sleep."

"She laughs, "That, is a very good point," she chuckles to herself and she fiddles with her fingers.

"Now I usually don't do this, but I'm going to cut to the chase here and tell you the results I know you're stressed about. The nerve tests can wait."

"Thank you," I say, trying not to let the relief stem from my voice. I fail completely.

"So, I looked over your results last night, and good news is that you don't have epilepsy."

"Then what *does* xe have?" Kaid asks.

"That's where it gets a bit more difficult," she explains, "So the passing out you've been experiencing is what we call 'non epileptic seizures' — which basically means that you have a seizure like someone with epilepsy would have but without all the crazy brain stuff. Think of it like your body turning off and back on again." I try not to chuckle at the mental image of someone running around inside my brain yelling for a reboot.

"With your symptoms, there are lots of different conditions that you may have, and in my opinion it doesn't matter what it's called as long as symptoms get better. So, with that being said, I've prescribed you some medicine to help with pain and with your nerves. I'll have the nurses give them to you when they come around next."

"So what do we do now?" Kaid pulls the words from my head before I can say them.

"Well, I'll be referring you to one of my colleagues who's more in tune with these types of conditions. She knows the difference between a lot of these diagnoses better than I do, and I hope she can help you on a higher level. For now, though, you're free to go once the nurses are finished with your discharge paperwork."

"Well, thank you so much," I tell her, trying to tie my words together. My brain feels like mush with the information overload, but I think she gets the point. She smiles at me and Kaid softly, and leaves the room.

IT FEELS LIKE FOREVER, but it's only been four days. I roll into Kaid's apartment, and immediately feel a sense of relief. I had no idea how quickly Newcastle would end up feeling like home, somehow I feel more at home here than I did back in the States.

I roll further into the apartment, and start smelling something good coming from the kitchen. I look behind me, confused, Kaid's standing behind me holding our bags. He just gives me a sly smile.

"What...?" As I turn the corner into the kitchen, I see Zahra. In the kitchen, making food.

"What are you doing here?" I'm able to finally get out my words and confusion. "Wait shouldn't you be in class?"

"I skipped," she shrugs, flipping something on the stove.

I gape at her. I don't think she's ever skipped class before.

"Oh don't look at me like that," she says, and Kaid laughs, "I do skip class from time to time, when it's important."

"Me coming home from the hospital isn't that important."

The room goes silent, and there's barely a sound except for something sizzling in a pan.

Kaid puts his bags down behind me and moves in front of my chair slowly, positioning himself directly in my eyesight. "Don't ever insinuate that you aren't important, ever again," he says, deadly serious. I blink a few times, and nod.

He smiles at me, back to his usual happy-go-lucky self. He quickly boops my nose before moving out of my way again.

Zahra nods in agreement, and turns back to work on the food. "I hope you're hungry, cause I've been cooking up a storm for you guys."

"Please tell me you listened when I said I wanted a full English breakfast," Kaid asks, sitting on his usual barstool.

"Not a *full* English, but I have a lot so you'll survive," she chides, and I laugh.

"You were in on this?" I raise my eyebrow at him.

He laughs, "How else was she supposed to get in?"

"Ah, so she has a key now."

"Yup, and I'm keeping it." Zahra says decisively, like we don't have a say. "I'm going to use it all the time when I need to sleep on your couch."

We all laugh, and I wheel closer to the island so I can see what Zahra's making. She has a stack of pancakes, bacon, sausages, toast, and multiple varieties of potatoes.

"I'm just finishing the last pancake now, and then we can sit and eat." Zahra tells us, flipping a pancake.

"As long as we don't have to watch a *Sense and Sensibility* retelling, I'm good." Kaid deadpans.

I laugh, "Now we're going to have to watch *Sense and Sensibility* just to annoy you. And because I haven't watched one in a few days."

"Ok but seriously, how many do you have left?"

"I'm done," Zahra shrugs, "I wanna watch something else for a change."

"I have one left," I tell them, "And don't worry about it, we don't need to watch it now, I'll worry about it later."

"Then I claim we watch *New Girl*," Zahra says.

I nod, and Kaid shrugs. Zahra grabs plates and silverware from the cabinet and passes them out to us. I immediately start piling food onto my plate, dodging Kaid and Zahra's hands as they do the same.

I pour syrup onto my pancakes and turn slightly to see the TV better.

Zahra grabs the remote and starts pulling the show up on the TV.

21

I scowl as I pound the delete button on my computer as I release that I misspelled *Marianne*. You know how it's spelled, Clover, this isn't the time for stupid mistakes. You need to get this project done before you get back to school. For Zahra. For Zahra's Mom. For your grade.

I pick up my pencil and twirl it between my fingers as I read what I've written. I'm not the most proud of it, but I'm prouder than I was before so it's a start. I haven't been feeling good about anything since I left the hospital, but I know this is good work nonetheless.

A knock sounds at my door, and I sigh. Kaid's probably wanting to check in with me *again*. He's been relentless, checking in on me every few hours, and making sure I eat all three meals.

"Come in," I say. The knob twists and I don't bother looking up, knowing that it's Kaid. I grab my handwritten notes on the 2011 adaption, as well as my paperback copy of the book.

"Woah, it looks like a battlefield in here," I hear a feminine voice say as the door closes. I look up confused, and see Zahra leaning against my door.

She raises an eyebrow, "You can't spend all of your time avoiding your thoughts. Especially not by doing homework."

"Since when can you tell me what to do?" I grumble without thinking as I type another line comparison on the graph I made.

"Since you moved to Newcastle by yourself, and your parents are in a completely different country. Kaid and I have put ourselves in charge of you and your care since you, obviously, are focused on other things at the moment."

"Well that's not fair," I grumble, not looking at Zahra.

"The only instance that this wouldn't be fair, is if you actually cared about your health on the level that me and Kaid do," she explains softly.

Zahra slowly makes her way closer to me.

"I'll care more once I finish this. I'm almost done!" I continue typing on my computer.

She sighs, "I didn't want it to come to this," and grabs my laptop off my lap mid word.

"Hey!" I holler, trying to grab the laptop back from Zahra, but not working well. Ignoring my protests, she puts my laptop on my desk out of my reach.

I sigh, and grab a notebook and pen. Before I can click the pen and start writing, Zahra's snatched that out of my grasp too.

"What the hell is going on right now?" I exclaim, extremely annoyed at Zahra for messing with my system and our almost finished project. She grabs everything else off my bed and stacks it neatly on my desk.

"Listen to me," she sits down next to me and gently grabs my face. I gasp as she moves my face towards her to initiate eye contact. Or as close to eye contact as we can get, since I can't get myself to look her in the eye.

I feel a blush form on my face, which makes it even harder for me to make eye contact.

Zahra continues, not caring about eye contact. "You need to get out of this room. You've been cooped up in here for days, Kaid and I are worried about you."

"What do you want me to do about that?" I say softly, fiddling with my hands.

"Go out on a date with me."

"Wh-what?" I stutter, trying to process Zahra's words. There's no way I heard her correctly, right?

Zahra smirks, "You heard me."

"Did I really though?"

"Yeah you did," she smiles softly at me, "I've had a crush on you for awhile, and I really hope you feel the same way. Otherwise, this'll be very, very, awkward for me."

I freeze, and blink multiple times in a row. A date. A *date*. With Zahra. The Zahra I've been friends with and working with for months now. When Kaid and I had this conversation, I didn't feel this way. I didn't feel like my heart was going to pound out of my chest, and I didn't feel like the world was going to end if this didn't end out.

"I-I like you too," I say softly, still not able to make full eye contact but doing a bit better than before. "I've never dated before, but I am interested in trying. But slowly."

Zahra nods and smiles super largely, "Slowly sounds perfect to me."

I nod, and Zahra grabs one of my hands gently smiling one of the most beautiful smiles I've ever seen.

22

"Are we there yet?" I ask again, my leg bouncing in excitement.

"You know, the more you ask, the more you sound like an insolent child," Zahra chuckles, seeming like she doesn't care how many times I ask.

"Well then, how bout you tell me where we're going?"

"Not happening," she singsongs.

"Fine then, I shall continue my questioning."

"Fineeeeee," she drags the syllable out, and tilts her head back in a laugh.

"The Highland Cattle Centre?" I squint as I read a sign as we drive past it. It takes me a second to process, but then a picture of a fluffy highland cow flashes through my head.

A smile forms on my face and grows as Zahra turns into the parking lot to the cattle center. I didn't realize that I wanted to see and pet highland cows, but now that I'm here I'm seriously excited.

"How did you know?"

"Know what?" Zahra asks, looking at me, "I just figured this was the best way to get you out of your slump."

I remember when everyone was talking about how adorable highland cows are, and the obsession the internet had with them. Especially baby highland cows. I don't remember exactly what the babies look like, but if the adults are that cute I'm sure the babies are absolutely adorable.

"Are there baby cows here?"

"Is it really a highland cow farm if there's no babies? That's what everyone wants to see, especially with everyone under the sun wanting one as a pet." *Damn, I didn't realize the obsession went that far. These things better be adorable.*

"That does make sense..." I nod as I think about it more.

Zahra parks the car and turns it off. Her words knock me from my highland cow filled thoughts, "Can you walk me through how to put together your chair?"

"What?"

"You really gotta stop doubting that I want to make things as easy as possible for you, and that I care," she says softly, grabbing my hand softly. She squeezes it once before bringing it up to her lips and kissing it gently.

"You're right," I say softly. "I'll show you this time, and you can try next time we go out."

"Are you saying you want another date?" Zahra asks slyly, a smirk forming on her face.

"I don't know," I shrug, and wink, feeling flirtier by the moment."Ask me again after."

"Now this is Nessie," our kind tour guide explains as we

make our way up to the first enclosure. Our guide is an older lady with a strong southern accent.

There are three cows in this enclosure, including Nessie, but Nessie is the only one standing near the fence. It seems like she desperately wants pets, she keeps butting her head in our direction. The guide laughs and pets her head gently.

"Nessie?" I can't resist asking, "Like the Loch Ness Monster, Nessie?"

The guide laughs, "I'm so glad you mentioned that. I seriously don't know how this happened since she's lived here pretty much her entire life, but she only responds to 'Nessie' instead of her full name 'Anastasia.'"

"That's absolutely hilarious," Zahra cackles.

"Nessie is one of our oldest cows, and she's always been one of the calmest cows I've ever met— and trust me I've met a lot of cows throughout my life. Who wants to pet her?"

"I want to pet her!" Zahra exclaims excitedly, rushing up to get closer. She holds back her excitement, to not spook Nessie, as she learns how Nessie likes being pet.

I stay where I am, watching the interaction from afar. I used to love being up in the action, but since I'm in my chair full time I've been getting used to watching things from farther back. I don't want to be in anyone's way, plus I can see lots of things at once from here.

I mean, yes, I do want to pet a fluffy highland cow. But it's not something I absolutely need to do, so I'm fine being on the sidelines.

"Hey, Clover," Zahra turns around and raises an eyebrow at me, "What do you think you're doing right now?"

"Umm... I don't know, sitting?"

"Yeah, sitting. Over there, away from me and Nessie. Don't you want to pet her?"

"I mean, yeah, she seems soft, but I don't need to."

"I'll help you."

"You don't need to..."

"I'll help you."

"You don't need to."

"Clover. The reason we're here is for you to be outside the apartment, on a date, and I want you to be a part of this experience with me. I specifically picked this farm because they do really well with accessibility, and I wanted to make this as easy as possible for you," she smiles at me, and I can't resist smiling back.

I look around and realize that she's right. All the paths are concrete, all the way up to the fences. There are benches placed strategically so people can sit and rest as they watch the cows. Right up by the fences, I think I see grab bars that double as a second layer of the fence.

"That's so sweet," I talk to my hands, a blush forming on my face as I think about how much thought and research Zahra put into this date. She wanted to make this as easy as possible for me, and is putting everything into making sure I'm comfortable and able to experience this like a 'normal' person.

Zahra slowly pushes my chair closer to the fence, and locks my chair. "Okay, do you want help with standing up?"

I think for a second, and nod almost without a second thought. I don't trust many people to help me with standing and readjusting myself, hell I barely trust people to push my chair, but Zahra has always been someone that I could trust with anything.

"Wrap my hands around my shoulders, and support me as I stand." I explain, and Zahra immediately nods, following my instructions. We easily get my standing in front of the fence without a hitch, leaning against and holding the grab bars. *I think I need to accept help more often.*

Zahra doesn't make a big deal of helping me, just stands behind me helping me stay balanced. She continues chattering to keep it as normal as possible even though my legs are throbbing and I'm dizzy. Her chatter actually helps me distract from the dizziness and helps me recover sooner.

"She's so soft, Clove, you won't believe it. Seriously, I don't understand how she's *this* soft."

Once I'm less dizzy, I reach my shaky hand towards Nessie, and she moves closer. She barely moves, twitches or even breathes for the second it takes my hand to land on her head.

Nessie looks super soft and fluffy, but like Zahra said she's insanely soft. She's even softer than I ever could've imagined. I can feel her muscles under her fur, but they aren't sharp. It's a smooth feeling, I can't really describe it. She's definitely a healthy weight, and is being treated well, which makes me feel good.

Nessie shifts her head like she's a cat begging for more pets as I scratch her under her neck. I chuckle and roll my eyes, continuing to spoil the cow with pets.

THE GUIDE LEADS us down a concrete path and towards a barn on the far side of the property.

"You guys came on a good day, the babies are in a good mood, and they haven't had many guests come today," the guide explains. She opens the barn door, and Zahra pushes me in.

The inside of the barn is a lot different than I thought it would be. Instead of stalls for animals, there's one big enclosure for all the baby cows to play in together. There are seven baby cows in the enclosure, all tumbling over each other adorably.

There are benches and hand sanitizer stations inside and outside of the enclosure as well.

"What do you mean?" Zahra asks.

"Sometimes the cows aren't in the mood for human interaction, or have just had too much. That's the only time they tend to bite, because they don't understand it's bad. They won't bite otherwise, cause they love humans," she explains as we make our way closer to the fence.

She's definitely not lying, I realize immediately. The cows are all by the edge of the fence, having run over the second they noticed us. They're jumping up and down in excitement.

The guide closes the barn door and opens the fence for us to make our way in. The cows get even more excited, but don't go past where the fence was.

"They're trained to not go past the fence, but we close the doors just in case."

"That's so cool," I mumble under my breath, looking at the cows. They'd put one hoof past the 'line' but that's the farthest they'd go.

"Do you want to stand and walk instead of using your chair? We can share that bench," Zahra asks, pointing at a bench not far from where my wheelchair's parked.

I nod, and Zahra immediately puts her hands up silently asking if I want help like last time. I nod, and have to hold back my blush. There's a feeling in my gut, full of love that showed up out of nowhere. I've never had this feeling before, definitely not this overwhelming. I have no idea what it means, but I can't let myself worry about it right now.

I'm standing within seconds, faster and smoother than last time, and she helps me to the bench slowly. Without saying anything, the guide corrals the cows out of our way.

Once we sit down, the cows come running over to us

awkwardly with their too-big hooves, tripping over each other in excitement wanting pets and snuggles from us.

Zahra holds her hands up excitedly, trying to hold back her squeals of excitement. One of the cows comes up to Zahra, and jumps up on her legs with two paws like a little puppy. Another cow comes up to me and nudges my hands with his nose.

I can't help but smile as I pet the cow in front of me. Zahra picks up her cow, and puts it in her lap. The cow moos softly and curls up in her lap, basically begging for chin scratches.

I keep petting my cow, and somehow he's even softer than the adult cow was. I didn't think that was even possible, but somehow it is. When the cow rolls over onto its back, I coo and lean over to rub its belly. Even though my back is killing me at this angle, and my body is not going to like me later, it's very worth it.

"I can't adopt one, can I?" I ask, definitely joking but I do consider it for half a second.

"You don't have the space," Zahra reminds me. I think she sounds a bit remorseful.

"Damn."

"Do they have names?" I ask instead.

"Most of them are up for adoption, actually. We might keep some of them, but we tend to sell all of them each year," the guide explains, "If you could name one, what would you name it?"

I study my cow, but can't come up with anything. Zahra cocks her head and says, "I'd name her Moos, but spelled M-O-O-S— like moo, but not."

"That's so stupid," I laugh, "But I love it."

Through my laughter, something clicks in my brain.

I think I'd love anything that Zahra says.

23

Kaid bursts into my room a few days later, hollering something, but I don't understand a word.

"What?" I repeat, confused, turning around to look at him.

"I'm taking you out," he repeats, leaning over me to see what I'm working on, "Oh, nice to see you're still busting ass on this paper."

"I need to make sure it's perfect," I grumble to myself, while I edit a typo I somehow missed before.

"Clover, you're obsessed," Kaid says, worried, "I'm pretty sure this is your fourth time going over this project in the last four days."

Actually, the sixth in four days... I probably shouldn't tell Kaid that though.

I shrug.

"Clover, seriously, you need to find another project. It isn't healthy for you to put this much energy into your homework."

"It isn't healthy to put this much energy into anything," I grumble, "If I'm going to do it, I might as well put my energy towards this."

"Well *this* isn't that important in the long run."

"I beg to differ," I type a note in the margins.

Kaid grabs my computer off my lap, and I try to grab it back, but he's too fast.

"How about this," he asks, "We go to Lights and Ledgers, and I'll buy you a book. Then we can hang out and read on the couch."

"I don't know if I'm in the mood for that," I shrug. Usually, I'd never say no to a bookstore visit and a free book, but I'm definitely not in the mood to go anywhere or do anything.

"How about we try anyway?" I raise an eyebrow at his words, "For me?"

I sigh, "Fine, if you insist."

"I definitely insist."

I groan.

"I'll meet you by the door in ten," he singsongs as he leaves my room, putting my laptop on my desk.

I close my eyes, and let out a deep breath as my door clicks closed. I can't believe that Kaid's making me leave the comfort of my bedroom, and making me stop my project. It needs to be perfect, it has to be perfect for me and Zahra.

I transfer out of my bed and into my chair to get ready. I don't feel like looking cute or anything right now, so I just toss on a new pair of sweats and a hoodie.

I wheel into the kitchen after freshening up. Surprisingly, I'm ready before Kaid is, so I put my shoes on and start digging through the cabinets.

"Anything you need me to grab for you?" Kaid asks as he comes into the room and puts his shoes on.

"I don't think so, thanks, though."

"Have you eaten anything today?"

"Umm... actually I don't think so."

He 'hmms' and goes into the kitchen the rest of the way,

opening one of the cabinets. He grabs a granola bar and tosses it in my directions.

"Eat." He says, pointing at me.

"Fine," I roll my eyes as I unwrap the bar.

"You ready to head out?" Kaid asks, tapping his hands on the handles of my chair twice.

I nod, my mouth full of granola bar, and Kaid opens the door and pushes me out.

"I'M NOT REALLY in the mood for caffeine, are you?" I shake my head, the idea of getting anything to eat or drink makes me feel physically sick. Kaid's been holding this conversation since we left the apartment. I'm not in the mood for anything, but Kaid insisted so here I am. It's a good thing he's chatting, cause I'm definitely not in the mood.

We turn the corner, and make our way towards the back door of Lights and Ledgers. The concrete wasn't bad last time, honestly it was better than most of Newcastle combined, but it seems like they updated it and made it even more accessible.

They changed the concrete to tile, added multiple more streetlights to light the alleyway, added art and signs on the walls. Made it seem like you're making your way to the front of the store, but better. Made it seem like it's anything but the alleyway it actually is.

There's no trashcans, no litter, no grime, nothing like an ordinary alleyway. I remember Kaid saying that the owners are disabled also, but this is beyond my wildest dreams. I never would've thought that a business— especially a small business— would put so much effort into making entrances accessible.

It brings a smile to my face, and I marginally feel better.

Kaid opens the door, and I wheel through to a wonderland full of fairy lights. Because it's a back entrance, the door opens to a hallway, but the staff have hung fairy lights from the ceiling and down the walls.

Every time I come here, they make the experience even better than the previous time. I don't understand how it's possible, I could never be that creative, but they are.

The hallway ends and Kaid and I are greeted by a seating area and aisles upon aisles of books. My head tilts as I study the shelves, trying to figure out where I want to start.

"I hope you're in the mood for books— cause I want you to pick one out. If you don't, I'll pick one out for you, and I can't guarantee you'll like it." Kaid says, smiling at me. He's trying to be mean about it, but he can't. After a few seconds of attempting intense eye contact, he breaks and starts laughing.

"You're terrible at threats," I laugh.

"I don't care, I still want you to pick out a book."

"I'll do my best," I promise.

He nods, and heads into the stacks to find a book for himself.

I stay where I am for a few more seconds, taking in my surroundings. The fairy lights strung everywhere, the faux hanging plants hung strategically from the ceiling, the faux plants sitting on tables and bookshelves.

I start slowly pushing my chair into the stacks, trying to figure out what I'm in the mood for. Cause the more I'm outside of the apartment, the more I'm realizing that I don't want to be sitting in my bedroom revising my stupid project over and over and over forever. I want to be doing the things I love, with my favorite people.

I wheel down the first aisle slowly, eyes skimming over book titles as my brain battles with decisions. I still don't feel up to doing anything other than sitting and revising my assignment— which is kind of a problem if I want to break this streak.

I sigh, and keep going over the spines of the books in this aisle. I'm sitting in the middle of the history aisle, which doesn't particularly fascinate me much. I mean, it does, but I'm definitely not in the mood for reading about history. I never really have been, but I figured I might as well glance.

I shake my head, going through the aisle and into the heart of the store. Lights and Ledgers is a beautiful store, full of beautiful special editions alongside all the books you can find at other bookstores. This is the most accessible bookstore for me, so I'll buy anything that interests me here instead of going elsewhere for it.

Most stores aren't anywhere near as accessible, set in historic areas where they can't fix the sidewalks or stairs to enter. No ramps over those stairs, or decent working elevators. Knowing this store exists, run by people just like me... it just isn't the same going to any other store. So I'll continue going to this store as long as I'm in Newcastle, and regret the day I have to leave it. That is, *if* I have to leave it.

Do I actually have to leave Newcastle? I think about it for a second. I'm an adult, both here and back home, and I can make whatever decisions I want to. At this point, Newcastle feels more like home to me than the states ever have.

I lived in the States for eighteen years, and I've only been in Newcastle for a few months... and in these few months I've made more of a home here than anywhere else. Why would I leave?

I consider the possibility of leaving Newcastle. Considering it for less than a second leaves a massive gap in my chest, way more of a gap than leaving the States did.

I'd be leaving behind my friends and family if I stayed here. But as we've learned, over these last few months; these relationships work long distance. Adria and Caitlyn's books are very quickly gaining popularity, and they're starting to go on tours.

They have an amazing agent, they've told me. I'm sure if they tell her they have a friend here, she'd put a tour stop here and they can visit. They have each other, and we text all the time it's like we still live in the same country.

"Hey, what's the matter?" Kaid asks softly, coming out of seemingly nowhere. He puts his hand out and slowly wipes a tear from my cheek. *I didn't even know I was crying.*

"Shit, did I overwhelm you with making you pick out a book? I'm so sorry, I won't do it again, I'll help you find a book tonight," he keeps rambling on, but I can't process his words. I can barely process my feelings right now.

I swear I see a tear in his eyes, and that makes even more tears flow down my face. His hands shake as he wipes more of my tears, bends down, and pulls me into a hug.

"I'm so sorry," he keeps whispering in my ear. He didn't do anything wrong, but I still haven't been able to tell him that.

I open and close my mouth, trying to get the words out. It feels like forever, but after a few tries I'm able to stutter out "N-n-no, it's n-not you."

He unwraps his arms from my shoulders and looks at me, "It's not?"

"N-no," I tell him, "You actually helped me."

"Helped? How?"

"Helped me realize I don't want to live my life cooped up in my room, helped me realize it's time to change the narrative."

"I'm so proud of you, Clover."

24

———

I lay in bed, struggling more mentally than physically for once. It's been a few days since I decided to try and break through my depression, but it's a lot harder said than done. I don't know what I've done the last few days, but it probably didn't do much to break me out of my depression slump.

I sigh, and transfer into my chair. If I sit here thinking about what I could do, I'm never going to get up and do something. I'm going to try a new method, and go around to try and find something to do. Besides, I haven't really eaten so I should do that as well.

I roll into the kitchen and start going through the cabinets, looking for something, anything, that sounds good enough for me to eat right now. Nothing does.

The cabinets are pretty bare, actually. Kaid usually keeps the cabinets full with both of our favorites, but I guess he must have been extra busy these last few days because he hasn't refilled everything.

I look around, still nothing sounds good. Maybe I should go to the store, I mean it gives me a new experience *and* something to do right now. Also it'd give me a lot more options to find new things and something to eat now.

I shrug to myself, it's the best idea I can think of right now. I roll back to my room and slowly get dressed.

The roll to the store wasn't terribly long, my arms are yelling at me because they aren't used to being this used, but it's tolerable. By the time I get back to the apartment, though, that'll be a different story.

I roll through the automatic doors and grab a cart before making my way into the main store. I position the cart in front of my chair and use one hand to control the cart and the other to push the chair. Having the cart directly in front of my chair makes the cart go as well— making it incredibly easy to do both at once.

Most people think wheelchair users can't do anything, but that's because the world is built to accommodate able bodied people. The truth is, we're innovative as fuck. We figure out ways to accommodate ourselves because nobody else will.

As I make my way around the produce, I realize that I haven't been in a European grocery store before. Actually, I haven't really done any day to day errands or things in general. I'm going to have to change that. I'm going to change that because I need to make my life my own again.

I grab some fruits and vegetables that I like and put them in the cart. I go aimlessly down the aisles, grabbing things I think we need and some new snacks to try. There are so many things I've never seen or heard of before, right next to things I see all of the time, it's absolutely bizarre in the best way.

I turn into the bread aisle and stop in front of the white loaves. I look between a loaf that's sliced thinner and a loaf that's sliced thicker, mentally debating over which one to get, when an arm shows up next to me trying to grab a loaf.

I startle, not expecting anyone to get up in my personal

space, especially not that close. I've barely experienced people invading my personal space since I've been here.

"Sorry," I say instinctively. I don't know why, because they're the one in my space, but they don't say anything anyways.

The hand reaches and grabs a pack of bagels and tosses it in my cart. I blink, and turn to face them more. They nod, like they just accomplished their one act of kindness for the day, and walk away.

I look down at the bagels. They are everything flavored, and I look up at the shelf and find that they're too high for me to put away by myself.

I sigh, hoping that Kaid likes everything bagels, because there's nothing I can do about them now.

I grab a random loaf of bread, not caring anymore about the thickness of the cut. My thoughts are full of thoughts like 'why don't people understand that wheelchair users are people just like them?'.

I'm so annoyed by the random person in the bread aisle, that I quickly go through the rest of the aisles, barely grabbing anything. It's a good thing that I got most of my groceries before getting to the bread.

I GET BACK to the apartment, with most of the groceries in two large tote bags hanging off the back of my chair. I find Kaid sitting at the table, scrolling on his phone.

"Did you just go to the grocery?" He asks, raising an eyebrow at me.

"What? Did you think I wouldn't?"

"I don't know what I was expecting from you, honestly, but it's just more ironic than anything because I was just putting a pickup order in. I usually do pickup more than going in— the people there can really be pricks."

"Tell me about it," I grumble, twisting my upper body to grab one of the bags. I pass it to Kaid, who immediately starts picking through it, getting more and more excited by the second.

"Damn, Clover!" he exclaims, "I need to have you pick out the shopping more often! You pick out the best snack foods!" He pulls a bag of chips and opens it.

"I'm glad you approve, but if I always did the shopping, we'd probably never have healthy food again." I chuckle, grabbing another bag off the back of my chair.

"You bought some apples," he says, pulling some out of the bag and putting them in the fruit bowl. "Those are healthy."

"That's true," I grab a bag and peek in it, "Actually this bag is mostly healthy things, so maybe I should take over the shopping."

"Ooh!" Kaid exclaims, pulling something out of the bag, "I love everything bagels! How did you know?"

"Well, I'm glad someone does."

"I'D LOVE to hear about your project progress, now that we're in the home stretch," Professor Kingston says, coming up the stairs to where Zahra and I are sitting after her lecture the next day.

"Well I've finished my part, and I've finally corralled Kaid enough to get him to record his lines, so I think that means I'm finally done." I tell her, letting out a loud sigh of relief as I tap my book.

"Wow... are we sure the work is even?" Professor Kingston asks, raising an eyebrow at me.

"Oh for sure," Zahra exclaims, nodding her head enthusiastically as she continues drawing on her iPad. "Xe wrote the script, revised it multiple times, rewatched the adaptations multiple times each to make sure everything is as accurate as possible, and xe corralled everyone who volunteered to speak for us and got everything filmed and organized. Kinda undermines my work a bit..."

"Don't say that!" I exclaim, "You designed and made everything look amazing for the animation, and you're animating everything by hand. You helped me make the notes, watch the adaptations, *and* knocked me out of my depression when I couldn't stop editing."

"What do you mean when you say 'depression'...?" Professor Kingston raises an eyebrow at me again.

I sigh, "Well I hyper-fixated on making the script absolutely perfect, and Zahra broke me out of it." I explain, shrugging. I understate it a bit, knowing that Melody would get worried about me.

Zahra looks at me and raises an eyebrow. I gently shake my head, silently telling her not to say anything. I know she would if I didn't.

"I'm glad you're doing better," Melody says softly, probably noting our small interaction but not saying anything, "Don't forget that campus has mental health resources you can use without any additional cost— believe me when I say they're amazing and have helped me through so much, especially with my gender identity."

I smile at her and nod. "I'll definitely look into that."

I usually wouldn't consider therapy, as it's never felt like something that could help me, but because Melody recommended it... it might be different.

I've always looked up to Melody, in a different way than I've ever looked up to anyone before. Maybe it's because I'm in a new time of my life, or maybe it's because Melody has gone through a similar experience with her gender identity, but it still surprises me that I'm actually considering therapy.

"I'm incredibly excited to see your finished project," Professor Kingston smiles at the two of us before making her way down to the next group. I'm not certain, but for a second it seems like Professor Kingston didn't want to stop talking to us, but she had to move onto the other groups.

I'm about to pick up my book again, but I pause as Professor Kingston makes her way to the next group. I see the panic arise in the other students' eyes, and the two of them quickly start closing all of the tabs on their computers. Obviously, they weren't paying attention during the lecture, and are most likely severely slacking on their project. I chuckle at the look in Melody's eye; it's obvious she can tell as well, but can't say anything about it.

___

25

"**I** cannot believe this is happening!" Kaid exclaims excitedly from behind me as we wait in line to get into Utilia Arena to see Nightly Dreams' concert a few days later. It's been a long time coming, but the day is finally here.

Anders had given me the highest ticket possible, with early entry to get merch and into a lounge area with snacks and drinks. We have amazing seats— although not the best because of my chair. After the concert, we're going to go to the meet and greet, and then we'll go to the dressing room. Not that Kaid knows any of this; I'm going to surprise him as the night progresses.

Once we get to the front of the line, I flash my phone with the tickets, and she lets us in. We enter the venue and stand in the lobby, taking in our surroundings.

"So, do we want to get merch first, and then go to the lounge?" I ask, turning to face Kaid.

"Wait— what do you mean, lounge?" He asks, raising an eyebrow at me, "How much did you spend on these tickets?"

"Nothing, really?" I tell him, not lying.

"What ticket tier is this? I feel like you already went above and beyond with this."

"Well, you deserve it, after all you've done for me."

"Oh, Cloverrrrrr," he hugs me from behind, and squeezes me before letting go.

"How about this?" I ask, "Let's get merch first, then we can explore the lounge and then the actual arena."

"Oh yes, let's get merch first! I want my pick of everything."

"There's not any risk of it selling out, and the line will be short since general admission hasn't been let in yet."

"Seriously, Clover, you thought of everything and went above and fucking beyond," he sighs happily, and we start making our way towards the merch booth.

The merch booth is massive, and there is absolutely no line. We immediately go up and start looking at all of the options.

"Wow," Kaid says, awe evident in his tone, "There are so many options."

"Take your time," the clerk says, a smile on his face, "If you want to see anything closer, feel the fabric, or try it on, just let one of us know and we'll pull one for you."

"Oh, before you start picking things out," I turn and tap Kaid on the shoulder multiple times so he turns to look at me. "I'm paying for the merch too."

"What the fuck?" He exclaims, "Absolutely not, I'll pay for my merch, and yours too. You've done way too much for me."

I raise an eyebrow at him, and he does the same for me. I do my best to not blink, feeling like this is an unspoken staring contest. My eyes water, and I hold them wider than ever, as long as I possibly can... until I blink and lose.

"Hah." Kaid says smugly, smirking at me.

"How about I pay for my merch and you pay for yours," I grumble, not making eye contact with him.

"Deal," he nods and continues looking at the merch.

"Aww, you two are such a cute couple," the clerk coos, smiling at the two of us.

Kaid and I look at each other. I awkwardly chuckle as Kaid stutters that we aren't a couple.

"O-oh... umm, sorry about that," he says, scratching the back of his head with a hand, "I'll leave you to it."

He walks to the side, giving Kaid and I the chance to look at the merch clearer. There are four different shirt options, two sweatshirts options, a few hats and so many small things.

I spot a cream shirt that has the tour logo on the front, while the back has a notebook design with three lines like their latest album cover 'From the Depths of the Songbook'— but it's blank, like it was made for the band to sign. I might have Adria embroider the signatures on the shirt after we get them signed, she's so talented at embroidery and clothing design— she actually made most, if not all of Nightly Dreams' outfits for their music videos before they were picked up by their management company.

I skim the rest of the options quickly, noticing the line growing behind us but not feeling incredibly bad knowing there are three more clerks ready to check people out.

"Can I have two of shirt C, both larges please—" I start, asking the clerk to grab my shirts when Kaid interrupts.

"What did I say about getting me merch?" He says, a slight growl in his tone meaning he's mad, but I can't take him seriously like this.

"It's for Zahra, chill out," I say immediately, lying to him but knowing he'll be appreciative once he realizes he's going to the meet and greet. "Those two, as well as a pin and a tote bag."

The clerk nods, quickly bagging my items and telling me

the total. I swipe my card and finish the transaction while Kaid asks the clerk for his merch.

THE LOUNGE IS A SIMPLE, yet aesthetic room. The furniture is black, while the walls have black and cream posters of the band. There are couches and tables filled to the brim with snacks and sodas. There's even a minibar with a bartender in the corner I didn't notice at first.

"I hope you're hungry," I joke, seeing the look of pure shock on Kaid's face.

"It's a good thing I didn't have lunch today," he declares before bee-lining towards the food line.

"I've been ready for this," I mutter to myself excitedly as I wheel towards the food. I didn't eat much today in preparation for this snack buffet, remembering the pictures that Adria and Caitlyn sent last time Nightly Dreams were in their hometown.

I grab a plate and start filling it up with all the best snacks from America and Britain. Sweet and salty, hard and soft, any popular snack you've seen on the internet is probably sitting on these tables.

Kaid is already sitting down on a couch, an end table next to him by the time I'm finished going through the line. He waves at me excitedly, and motions for me to park my chair next to the end table.

"Holy shit, I've never had these before, but I think I need to get some," he tells me, his mouth full of a cookie.

"Which ones are they?" I ask, having not recognized a lot of the cookies on the table. He holds up a sandwich cookie with an elf embedded in it and chocolate filling.

I laugh, "I actually know that one! It's called an E.L. Fudge."

"Why's it called E.L.?" he asks, after taking another bite.

I pause, "I don't know, actually. Google it." I haven't actually thought about it before, and now that he mentions it, I want to know why as well.

"I need to buy a pack of these for the apartment, or maybe not... there is a chance I'll eat the entire thing in one sitting," he jokes, pulling his phone out of his pocket and putting his plate on the end table.

I grab an E.L. Fudge off my plate, take a bite, and moan in happiness. E.L. Fudge has always been one of my favorite cookies, and I haven't seen them since I moved here. I didn't realize how much I've missed the taste of home until now... looking at my snack plate and seeing E.L. Fudges, Cheez It's, Chip's Ahoy!, Goldfish, and so many other snacks are making me kind of emotional. Yes, some of these are available here in Newcastle, but they just don't taste the same. What's allowed in food here is so much stricter than back home. They try to make it the same, but it just doesn't taste the same. Although, I have felt so much healthier since I moved.

"Oh! It stands for 'Everyone Loves'! And the entire name spells elf! Hah, that's so punny, I love it." Kaid tells me, reading from his phone.

"Hah, especially since the Keebler elves are the ones who supposedly manufacture and make the cookies," I chuckle, thinking of the packaging covered in little elves.

"They aren't wrong, though, I'm sure everyone does love these cookies." Kaid devours another EL Fudge.

"Do they even have these here? I think I'm going to be craving these again soon," I ponder.

"They were on the American table I think," Kaid says

disappointedly, "I wonder how much it'll cost to get some shipped here..."

"I'll just have Adria and Caitlyn ship some with my birthday present, it'll be cheaper in the long run." I tell him, getting my phone out of my pocket to text them before I forget.

"Wait, when's your birthday?" Kaid looks up at me, eyes wide.

"October 17th."

"Clover, why didn't you tell me?"

"I-I don't know," I stutter, "I didn't really think about it?"

He rolls his eyes lovingly, before making a note on his phone to go back to later.

26

"Holy shit," Kaid hasn't stopped saying that since we've gotten to our seats, "How the fuck did you get these seats?"

"I told you, I have my sources," I repeat for what feels like the millionth time, doing my best to not reveal my connection to the band. At least not just yet.

"You're going to drive me crazy one day," he grumbles, grabbing his phone and taking even more pictures of the stage.

"It'll all be revealed in due time, don't you worry," I tell him. When I look over at him, he isn't paying attention to me anymore, and probably didn't hear me.

I pull a portable charger from my bag, passing it to Kaid and saying, "I think you'll need this more than me... maybe save some storage for the actual concert, yeah?"

"Fuck, you're right," he mutters, quickly plugging his phone into the charger and putting it on his lap.

For the next twenty minutes leading up to the show, he moves between twiddling his thumbs, looking around him in awe, or scrolling each member's social media page plus the band's shared account. *You gotta appreciate the man's commitment.*

The second the countdown starts, Kaid's on his feet screaming in excitement along with the other 15,800 people in the arena— *yes I looked it up before we got here, I had to know what we were getting into.*

I've been a Dreamer since I moved to Lockwoods Lake and met Caitlyn and Adria. From seeing Caitlyn's intense love for the boy band, to eventually meeting them in their basement on a random day after school. I've seen my fair share of Nightly Dreams performances, between practices and rehearsals and actual concerts, but seeing Kaid watch his first concert... It was a whole new experience for me, and it might be my favorite.

We're seated up high, in a semi-private box, but still close enough to the stage to be able to see what's happening. While I do feel kind of bad that we can't be on the floor super close to the stage, I think Kaid's truly loving his experience from up here regardless.

It's not super crowded, but he's still around some people. He has plenty of space to sing and dance without getting in anyone's way, which would not be the case closer to the stage. The only thing is that any freebies that might be chucked off the stage don't have any chance of reaching us... here's hoping that Kaid can forgive me for that one. I'm sure being able to see backstage and meet the band one on one should make up for that.

We enjoy the concert, Kaid having the time of his life, singing and dancing while I record fancams for him when he asks. There are also tears, for Kaid... Kaid pretty much cries every time one of his favorite songs gets performed, which happens a lot. Now, I've heard a lot of their ballads live before, but when they perform Little Mix's *Between Us*? It throws me off guard so bad I start bawling my eyes out thinking about my friends back in the States.

Kaid notices my tears, and grabs my hand. His other arm, held up towards the stage recording a video, twitches as his attention veers towards me.

"Kaid—" I insist, watching his phone shake and stutter.

"You're more important, period." He tells me, putting his phone down. He squeezes my hand before letting go and reaching up to wipe my tears.

"Thanks," I whisper, wiping my tears fully.

"Anytime, Clover, anytime."

A MAJOR PERK of being in a private box that I didn't take into consideration until now: it's a hell of a lot easier to get out of the arena once the concert ends. Everyone below us is stampeding to get out, and Kaid and I are mindlessly strolling towards the elevator. Yes, it is a bit crowded up here, but it's lightyears less crowded than below.

We make our way to the elevator, hitting the down button before the doors open. Kaid pushes my chair in, and hits the button for Street Level before anyone can get on after us.

I lean forward and hit the button for the Main Floor, saying "Actually..."

"You're shitting me," Kaid says, stuttering over his words in shock, "You already got early entry, and the lounge, *and* the amazing seats. What else is there to do? Meet the band?"

I say nothing and smirk. I know Kaid can't see me, but he gets what I'm putting down within seconds.

"You're shitting me," he says, "There's no way... there's no fucking way."

"Way. Start thinking of what to say, and something for them to sign."

"Fuck I didn't think of that! I don't have something for them to sign! What do I even say?"

I turn and pull the shirt I bought him earlier out of my new totebag and pass it to him wordlessly.

He blinks in shock. "Damn, you really do think of everything."

"Beep beep!" Kaid yells as we rush through the almost empty hallway to get into the meet and greet on the other side of the venue. I definitely didn't take this into consideration when I was planning out the day... who knew the venue was so fucking massive?

Kaid yells again and I can't control my laughter. As he cuts a corner, almost loses control of the chair, and yells "Ah, fuck, shit, motherfucker!" within a span of three seconds, I laugh even harder making it nearly impossible for me to breathe.

We cut another corner— more carefully this time— and the door to the meet and greet comes into view. There's a security guard standing in front of the door, his eyes on his watch. As we get closer, he notices us and lets us in. He closes the door right as we pass through the threshold. Kaid lets out a sigh of relief as he stands on his tiptoes, trying to see what's going on in front of us.

There's probably fifty people in the large room with us, all squished up to the barrier trying to talk to the band while a group of security officers tries to make a line.

"I think I'm going to stay back here for a bit..." Kaid says softly. I turn my chair to look at him, and he looks both over-stimulated, excited, and super pale. I grab his hand and help guide him towards a chair set against the back wall. It's probably for a security guard, but they're all busy, so it's Kaid's now.

"Here," I pass him a set of headphones and a bottle of water. "Drink, and put some of your favorite music on, and just take some deep breaths for a few minutes." He nods, grabbing the water first, taking a few sips and putting the bottle on the back of his neck.

Once he's settled with his headphones on and taking deep breaths, I park my chair next to him. I pull my phone out of my pocket and start aimlessly scrolling on it. I want to be here for him, but not overwhelmingly so. I'll let him do his thing while I do mine. Once he's ready, then we'll continue.

After a few minutes, he taps my arm and I look up at him. He has my headphones on still, and he looks much better.

"Ready?" I ask, and he nods excitedly.

He stands to get in the line, that's shrunk considerably since I looked at it last. We're the last ones in line, which is best for what's coming next.

Kaid chats with the people in the line in front of us about the concert, their favorite moments, and songs sung while I take the time to update Adria and Caitlyn.

ME:

We're the last ones in line for the meet and greet now, the concert was amazing

CAITLYN:

How have Kaid's reactions been?

ADRIA:

Yeah, how'd he react to you actually knowing the band?

ME:

I haven't told him that part yet, I was kinda just letting things unravel as they come along. I don't want to overwhelm him too much.

He's been mostly flabbergasted, although it's probably all going to click sooner or later.

ADRIA:

Probably once you guys actually talk to the band, Anders won't be able to keep his big mouth shut

CAITLYN:

Yeah, you've always been his favorite— he's probably going to want a hug

ME:

Third wheels always have to stick together— although I'm not a third wheel anymore

ADRIA:

WHAT

CAITLYN:

SINCE WHEN

ME:

Do you two finish each other's sentences often?

ADRIA:

Yes, it happens a lot actually— especially since we're writing books together full time now

ME:

Ah, makes sense

And yes, me and Zahra are dating. She took me out to a highland cow farm, once I got out of the hospital, after asking me out

CAITLYN:

Aww that's so cute, I'm so happy for you

ADRIA:

Your best friend? The one you're doing your Jane Austen project with?

ME:

Yes to both of those

ADRIA:

The only one I haven't talked to yet!

ME:

I only have two friends here…

ADRIA:

I want to talk to her next time you call

ME:

Fine. Whatever, I'm sure she'll want to meet you too.

ADRIA:

Yay

Shit, did one of us tell them that you're in a chair? Not that it's a bad thing, but I don't want them to be surprised

ME:

I figured you did when I had you ask for accessible seating

ADRIA:

Oh yeah, I did

Kaid and I finally get to the front of the line, and I let him talk first.

"H-hi," he says softly, and I blink surprised. I've never heard him stutter or stumble over his words before so I don't know how to respond.

"It's nice to meet you," Niro says nicely, smiling at him as he hands them his shirt to sign, "What's your name?"

"Kaid," he introduces himself, "Wow, I never stutter anymore," he chuckles at himself awkwardly.

"We don't mind," Anders says, "We stutter sometimes too,"

"Yeah, it happens to Kenji all the time," Niro says, throwing their boyfriend under the bus. I snort, unable to hold back my laugh.

Kenji looks up from signing the shirt and sees me. It takes him a second, but once recognition glistens in his gaze, his eyes go wide. Niro notices and jabs him in the side with their elbow before he can say anything.

Kaid looks at me and raises an eyebrow, probably thinking he's ableist, but it's actually the complete opposite. They're just waiting for the last fans who were in before us to leave before they move from behind the barricade.

"Do you want a picture?" Anders asks. Kaid nods excitedly, handing me his phone. I roll my eyes and prep the phone to get pictures for him.

"Okay, everyone smile!" I prompt, holding the phone up and taking a picture. I turn the phone to get another angle, knowing Kaid will want them all.

"Alright I took multiple pictures from multiple angles so you should have a few good ones." I pass Kaid's phone back to him, and he excitedly flips through the pictures to make sure they all look good.

Anders looks behind me and nods after a second. He looks back to me and gives me a huge smile as I hear the thunk of the doors closing behind the last of the fans.

"Why do I feel like the mood just considerably shifted?" Kaid whispers to me, still looking through the pictures.

"Can I go *now?*" Kenji asks his partner, impatiently.

"Yes, you can," Niro chuckles. At their words, Kenji stands up and rushes to the barrier from behind his signing table. He lifts the chainlink barrier and shimmies under it before rushing over to me.

He's about to drag me into a hug, but stops right before

making contact. Kaid looks up from his phone, sees Kenji, and his eyes go wide.

"I'm not going to hurt you, am I? I've been waiting to hug you since I heard from Adria about your chair, but I don't want to hurt you." Kenji exclaims. I hear Anders (probably) snort from behind him, having made his way to this side of the barrier with Niro.

"It'll be fine," I chuckle, holding my arms up to meet Kenji's in a hug.

He drags me into one of his massive bear hugs, and almost pulls me out of my chair. I don't care, though, cause I know he won't drop me and I feel safe in his arms. Adria's brother and friends are some of the first masculine people I've felt comfortable with and become close to.

I hug him back with the same enthusiasm.

"Wait a minute," Kaid asks confused, finally putting the clues together, "What the fuck is going on here? Do you guys know each other?"

Kenji lets go of the hug and starts cracking up at Kaid's words.

"You didn't tell him?" He cackles, and the more he laughs, the more he starts to sound evil.

"Kenji stop that, you sound deranged," *Not how I would've phrased it, but he's not wrong.*

"Shut up, Anders."

Anders rolls his eyes and comes over to Kaid. "We've known Clover here for years, xeir friends with my sister."

"Why didn't you tell me?" Kaid exclaims, looking between me and the band and back again.

"Because I wanted to see how long it would take you to figure out, and to see your reaction." I shrug.

Kaid flips me off and everyone laughs.

"You and Adria have grown up so much over these past

few years, I'm so proud of you guys," Anders comes over to me and wraps me up in a quick hug. I've known him for years, and he's still not a big fan of hugs. Although he's gotten better, since he sees his loved ones less often than before.

I hug him back before he's done with the hug. He holds on for longer than I expected him to and it makes me feel better. He's always been like an older brother to me, like Adria is like a sister.

"Adria's your sister?" Kaid looks at Niro and tilts his head, trying to see the resemblance.

"Not me," they say, "Anders."

Kaid turns his head to look at Anders, who waves. "I see the resemblance, actually."

"That's not public knowledge, though, so don't tell."

"Oh, I'm going to go to the forums and tell everyone," Kaid says, sarcasm dripping from his tone. It takes Anders a second to realize, but once he does, he cracks up.

"Happy birthday, man. It's a good thing I like you cause we set up a birthday surprise for you," Kenji says, putting an arm around Kaid's shoulders and walks him towards the back door.

"You have a birthday surprise for me? H-how did you?" Kaid stutters as Kenji excitedly drags him towards the dressing room.

"You forgot how detailed I am; I texted Anders months ago and we planned out everything to make today the best day ever for you." I explain as Niro comes up behind me and offers to push me towards the dressing room.

"I really need to stop underestimating you," I hear Kaid mutter.

"I'm shocked you haven't learned this by now," Kenji laughs.

27

———————

Once we get to the dressing room, the band starts showing Kaid around.

Their bathroom is covered in makeup and hair products that Kenji explains "are only used by our team cause none of us know what the fuck these are for."

On our way back to the main room, both Anders and Niro snag a makeup wipe to take off their stage makeup.

Niro sits down on the couch, already halfway through with their makeup removal. They gesture for Kaid to sit next to them, and he does.

"Ask me any questions you have," they tell him, "I'm sure you're brimming with them."

"You should've given me some warning," Kaid laughs, "I feel like I usually would have more questions, but there's so much going on right now."

"Give me one," they challenge.

"Do you three seriously get along so well all of the time?" Kaid blurts.

The entire band laughs, and I join them, as Anders leans across the back of the couch.

"We do get along well, and I won't give you an interview answer saying we don't fight, because we do; but we know each other well enough now that we know when someone needs alone time or a break, and we always have each other's backs for that." Anders tells Kaid, after a moment of hesitation.

Kenji and Niro nod solemnly, like this is a more serious matter than it is.

"I heard, though, that you aren't a third wheel anymore, Clover," Anders says, changing the subject, "Congrats, I can't wait to meet her!"

"What are you talking about?" Kaid looks at me confused.

"Well I've been third wheeling these two for years, " Anders explains before I get to, gesturing towards the happy couple, Kenji and Niro. "And Clover has been Adria and Caitlyn's third wheel since they became friends basically— so we've always joked about us both being third wheels."

Kaid laughs, "How do you deal with the third wheel constantly?"

"It's a good thing these two don't like PDA and act the same with me as they did before— I don't think I'd be able to cope otherwise."

"You're welcome," Kenji announces from behind us, holding his hands up, making everyone laugh.

EVERYONE'S SITTING on the couch now, chatting amongst themselves, but noticing that the conversations are starting to waver.

Out of nowhere, Kenji stands up and exclaims, "I know what we can do!"

Everyone looks at him confused.

"Oh shush, we promised Clover that we would make tonight a night to remember for Kaid. And we're going to do it — I just bought a new karaoke system, and have been meaning to try it out."

"You bought a karaoke kit?" I ask confused, "Don't you guys sing as a job? Why would you buy a karaoke kit?"

"I was wondering the same thing," Anders deadpans.

"I figured this could make warmups more fun," Kenji shrugs, "And it comes in clutch for times like this."

"Sounds fun," Kaid smiles, "Let's do it!"

"Great!" Kenji jumps off the couch excitedly and grabs everything he needs to set it up. "Kaid, you wanna go first, or should I?"

"You go first," Kaid says, "I don't know what song I want to sing."

"I heard you do a great 'I See the Light'" I joke, remembering when Adria told me that Kenji sang Rapunzel's part when they were watching *Tangled* once.

Kenji's head snaps in my direction so fast, as Anders and Niro burst into laughter. "Of course she told you that," Kenji sulks, "Of course she did."

I can't resist bursting into laughter with Anders and Niro.

"For your information, I will *not* be singing anything Disney. I thought I'd sing Queen or something." Kenji tells us, flipping through the song options on the TV.

"You aren't sophisticated enough to sing Queen," Anders deadpans, "You're more apt to sing One Direction or something."

"What if I wanted to sing Queen?" Kenji starts flipping through the options faster than before.

"Do you even know a Queen song?" Niro raises an eyebrow at their boyfriend.

"Out of anyone, I thought you'd be on my side," Kenji looks at his partner, feigning sadness.

"I'm just asking a question," they raise their hands up in an act of surrender.

Kenji sighs, turning back to the tv, and finally choosing a song. He picks up the mic and starts singing *Don't Stop Me Now*.

"Tonight... I'm gonna have myself, a real good time!"

"You've got to be shitting me," Anders mumbles, deliberately loud enough for Kenji to hear. Without missing a beat, he flips him off and sings the next lines of the song.

Niro snorts a laugh and holds their phone out to start filming.

Kaid holds a hand over his mouth to conceal his laughter as Kenji tries to hit a high note.

The song ends as Kenji dramatically puts his right hand up in the air like Freddy Mercury. He hands Kaid the microphone and collapses on the couch next to Niro without hesitation moments later.

"You did good, hon," Niro compliments their boyfriend, pushing the hair away from Kenji's face.

Kaid slowly scrolls through the list of karaoke songs, eventually deciding on the Beatles' *Eleanor Rigby*.

"A solid choice, a bit slow, but a classic nonetheless," Anders nods.

Kaid freezes up, like he forgot that he's doing karaoke in front of his favorite band. The music starts and he misses the first few lines. He freezes for a second before breaking himself out of his slump and performing the hell out of the song.

I'd never heard Kaid sing karaoke before, but knowing his personality I had a feeling that he'd be secretly amazing at it. And boy, was I right. By the time he got to the end of the song, every member of Nightly Dreams was slack jawed and in shock.

Kaid turns around and holds the mic out for someone to grab, oblivious to everyone's shock. Niro grabs the mic, breaking out of their slump and gives Kaid a nod before flipping through the options.

"Holy..." Anders says as Kaid sits back on the couch next to him.

"That was amazing!" Kenji exclaims loudly, eyes wide. He reaches over Anders to shake Kaid's shoulders, "You're such a good singer, you totally could join the band!"

"I will admit, I was a bit skeptical going into this, but you blew me away." Anders adds, making Kaid blush.

28

"Happy Birthday to youuuuuuuuuuuu," I jolt awake, not realizing what's going on for a split second. Kaid's singing to me, I realize, and it's my birthday.

In the two weeks after the Nightly Dreams concert, Kaid has been living on cloud nine. He was constantly having their music playing throughout the apartment, and going through the photos and videos he took from the night. Everyday he reminds me how grateful he is to have that experience, and it melts my heart in happiness every time.

I crack my eyes open and blink multiple times as I see Kaid holding a cake in front of me and continuing to sing.

"Wha-?"

"Happy birthday, Clover," Kaid says softly, putting the cake on my nightstand. He leans down and gives me a hug. I try to lift my arms to hug him back, but I can't. He stands back up, grabs my desk chair, and sits down.

"Let's have some cake for breakfast," he said excitedly, grabbing a cake cutter I haven't seen until now.

I laugh, and try to sit up. It doesn't work. I try to pull my arms up over my mattress to push myself up, but I can't move my arms.

I look over at Kaid, who's excitedly laying out plates and silverware for our breakfast of cake.

I sigh, "Kaid."

He looks up, sees the look on my face, and immediately stands up.

"What's wrong?"

"I can't move my arms, and my legs are extra sensitive. Something's wrong."

"Oh Clover..." he says softly, standing up. He stands directly next to me and asks, "Can I help you out? Then we can take a bit of a closer look at how your body is acting."

"Yeah," I tell him, already starting to feel defeated. I trust Kaid with my life, basically, I'm just pissed at my body. Of course my body decided to fuck with me today.

He gently takes my upper body into his hand and pulls my body into a seated position, the position I was trying to get in before. He picks my arm up, lifts it, and drops it. Unsurprisingly, my arm flops back onto the mattress like a limp noodle. He leans over me to pick up my other arm to do the same test. The same results occur.

Tears form in my eyes as I realize how badly my body feels and how badly I feel in general.

"Oh Clover," Kaid says quietly, grabbing one of my limp noodle hands in his. He grabs his phone and quickly types something.

He sighs again a few seconds later, "I think we're going to have to go to the hospital... I'm sorry Clover, I don't think I can help you by myself."

"I had a feeling this was going to happen," I whisper, defeat in my tone.

"I still think we should have some cake before we get you

ready to go," he says, not giving me any room to say 'no'. "It's your birthday, we already have a cake. We were already going to have cake in bed anyways."

"I can't move my hands, Kaid."

"Stop being such a worrywart," he says, waving me off, "I can feed you."

"That's embarrassing."

"And?"

"What about you? Don't you want some cake too?"

"Of course I do. But I have two hands, don't I?"

"... fine."

The biggest smile forms on his face before he turns back to the cake and utensils he'd already set up. He quickly cuts the cake, putting two generous slices on plates. He puts a bite on a fork, and holds it up to my mouth. I open my mouth, and he slides the fork in gently, letting me eat the cake piece.

The cake is frosted with a teal color, and has 'happy birthday clove' written in black with a cursive font. I groan happily when I taste it, an airy vanilla cake with strawberry frosting.

"Where did you get this?" I ask, mouth still half full of cake, "It's fucking incredible!"

"Zahra and I made it last night," he tells me sheepishly.

"You did?" I ask shocked, "Holy shit, you two are incredible."

A blush forms on his face, and he looks down at his plate, taking a bite of his own to avoid saying anything.

He changes the subject as we continue to eat our cake. I appreciate him so much for that, since I'm still freaking out mentally about my body not responding.

Once we're finished, Kaid helps me transfer into my chair, making sure my arms and hands are safely away from the wheels before pushing me towards the bathroom.

"I can do it by myself," I tell him, definitely lying as I look at the toilet. I definitely can't do it by myself easily, but I'm willing to find a way to do it alone.

"You can't move your arms or legs, Clover, let me help you. It won't be that big of a deal, and it's a bit of a drive to the hospital."

I sigh and close my eyes, knowing he's right. "You're right." I say quietly, "Please help."

He quickly transfers me from my wheelchair to the toilet, and pulls my pants and underwear down, making sure to not make it awkward.

He leaves the room quickly as I do my business, probably laying out clothes and packing a bag for the hospital.

All my birthday plans are off.

"NEUROLOGY?" The receptionist at the ER's main desk asks. When I nod, she types something into the computer and without hesitation tells me, "We're going to have to admit you. It'll be a bit of a wait before we can get you into a room." *Happy fucking birthday to me.* I sigh internally as Kaid turns my chair around and brings us to a spot in the corner to wait.

He settles us into the corner, the two of us facing each other. Kaid puts his bag in-between the two of us, and reaches into it to grab something.

"Here," he says softly, grabbing a pair of over the ear headphones and putting them on my head for me. He makes sure they're connected before grabbing my phone and putting in the password I tell him. "Do you want to listen to a podcast, audiobook, or music? Or nothing. I guess nothing is also an option."

"I need to keep an ear out to listen for my name." I tell him.

"I'm not going to have headphones or anything on, I have some homework to do. You need to calm down and have a bit of a mental reset while we're waiting. So I'll ask again, what do you want to listen to?"

I think for a second. I need to listen to something that'll keep my attention, but won't be too hard for me to focus on. Something that'll keep me away from my internal thoughts that are already out of control. I usually would read a classic, but my brain isn't in the right mindset for that, for once in my life.

"How about you go to my Libby app, it's an online library basically, and download whatever books by Adria Altherton or Caitlyn Blake you can find that are available." I tell Kaid, shrugging.

I've never really taken an interest in reading their books before, although I'm always a huge supporter of them. Newer fiction just isn't my thing most of the time, but at this point I'll listen to anything that I think will comfort me. And a story told by my best friends sounds like the perfect medicine.

"I found one," he tells me a few seconds later, and the audiobook starts playing in the headphones on cue.

"Thanks," I tell him and then realize, "Wait, what about them? Have you updated Caitlyn and Adria? And Zahra?"

"That was gonna be my next step, actually. I know that Zahra's in class, and Adria and Caitlyn aren't awake yet anyways."

"Has anyone reached out yet?"

"Yeah, Adria and Caitlyn reached out at 5am— which I think is midnight their time— and Zahra reached out around 7."

I sigh, "I don't know what to do about that..."

"For now, don't worry about it. I'm about to reach out to them, and then they'll understand why you haven't answered. Once we get a room, we can have Zahra come visit and call Adria and Caitlyn if we're going to be here awhile."

"I have a bad feeling we will be..." I tell him, the feeling sinking deeper and deeper in my gut.

AFTER MULTIPLE HOURS of listening to my audiobook waiting in the ER waiting room, we get a room in the back of the ER. Technically I'm admitted at this point, and I have a bed in the hospital... but it's still in the ER. It's a cramped room, with a shitty paper bed, but at least I'm laying down flat.

"Here's your remote," A kind nurse explains, "Hit these to put the bed up or down, and if you need something, hit the big red call button and someone will be here as soon as possible."

"Thank you," I tell her, trying my best to smile and be polite, but really struggling.

The nurse leaves the room, and I let out a rough exhale as my body adjusts to laying down flat. Usually this is the best position for me, but since I've been sitting up for most of the day, it's going to take a minute to adjust.

My audiobook is still going in my ears, and I'm enjoying it a lot more than I thought I would. It's the perfect comfort read for me right now, and if I close my eyes and listen, it feels like my best friends are here with me.

"Zahra said she's going to try and swing by after class," Kaid tells me.

"We're probably going to be in this room for awhile," I say, "I don't think she can visit if I'm in this room."

"Actually she can," Kaid says, shocking me, "and the nurse

I was talking to earlier said that there are a few people in Neurology who are being discharged today."

"So it should be a bit quicker than we originally thought?"

"Hopefully?"

"I'll take that," I tell him, closing my eyes and returning back to my book.

Uncomfortable paper and the lack of a pillow makes it so hard for me to feel comfortable.

Within the next few hours, multiple nurses come in and check on me. I go to the bathroom a few times, and I get an IV put in on the assumption I'm going to need it later.

"Hello!" A cheerful voice exclaims from outside my door, startling me to death.

An older Black lady with bright lipstick comes in with a massive smile on her face.

"Hi?" I say, trying to be polite again, but also being incredibly confused.

"Good news," she singsongs, "I'm here to bring you to a new, and better, and more private room."

It's been about seven hours since we arrived. That's a normal time to be waiting with how busy this hospital gets, however, I'm so done with this room, the uncomfortable bed, and the sounds of the ER.

Kaid stands up, quickly grabbing his things and standing next to my head so I can see him. He does all these things mindlessly, it feels like. I've never had to ask him for help or tell him my preferences. He just knows, and I love him so much for that.

The three of us make our way to the neurology wing of the hospital, go up to the fourth floor, and go into my new room.

It's a bit cramped, but it's much less cramped than my first room. There's lots of natural light, a larger TV, and even a couch for Kaid to sit and sleep on.

"Here's your new remote," the lady explains, pointing out all the buttons quickly. She tells me that my nurse will be in shortly, before leaving my room.

"WE'RE GOING to get you started with an MRI, and once we get the results back, I'll have your neurologist look over the results and we'll figure out where to go from there." My nurse explains after doing a quick physical.

I nod, I've had a feeling all day that this was what we were going to do. I'm already sensing a pattern through these hospital visits, and there's a good chance that this is going to be what happens every time I come in.

"I've put in the MRI request, but I'm not sure how long it's going to take for you to get in. But I'll pop in every hour or so to check in. Don't hesitate to hit the call button if you need me, though." The nurse explains before leaving the room.

Kaid sighs, and closes his laptop happily. "I'm finally done."

"I'm sorry you had to miss class, and you've been trying to catch up all day."

"Clover. Shut the fuck up." Kaid stands up from the couch and pulls a chair over to sit next to my bed. "I'm helping you, and I don't care what I have to do to catch up."

"Thanks, Kaid."

"I just feel terrible because we've been here for your birthday instead of celebrating."

"Yeah, it does kinda suck," I shrug to the best of my ability, "It's just more annoying spending my day waiting and not really able to do anything."

"How's your audiobook?" He asks, sitting in the chair he moved. He grabs my hand in his, and gently massages it.

"I think it's almost done, although I can't check."

Kaid taps on my phone screen and looks, "I think you have about an hour left."

I nod, "I'm enjoying the book, but I'm getting tired of just staring at the ceiling."

"Do you want to pause the audiobook? I'll help move the bed up and we can watch some tv while we eat."

At the mention of food, my stomach growls loudly, making me laugh. My stomach sinks a minute later as I realize I still can't move my arms.

"I didn't realize I was hungry, dammit it's going to take awhile for something to get delivered up here," I grumble under my breath. I don't really know what I want to eat, but it's going to take a long time for the hospital cafeteria to deliver it to my room.

"Hello!" A knock sounds on my door, and it creaks open. I can't see who's there, but the voice makes me feel warm inside.

"Oh Zahra, you have perfect timing!" Kaid exclaims happily, standing up to help her out.

Zahra. That explains the warm feeling inside my chest. She's the one I didn't realize I've needed here all day.

"I had Zahra stop by the apartment and grab comfort food for you," Kaid explains, unloading a bag of snacks onto the table.

"Happy Birthday Clover," Zahra tells me, coming over to the other side of my bed. She leans down and gives me a soft kiss.

"Thank you, babe," I say softly, tilting my head to look at her. She has her hair pulled back, like she hasn't bothered touching it since she pulled it back to study a few hours ago. She looks absolutely beautiful.

"What are you in the mood for?" She asks, putting her bag

down and going over to the table. She unloads her bag of snacks onto the table.

"I don't really know… I don't feel too good."

"Have you eaten much today?"

"Only some birthday cake before we left the apartment this morning," Kaid tells her. "I packed you a slice by the way Za-Za."

"Za-Za?" I ask, smiling at the nickname.

"We've become good friends, and I wanted to give her a fun nickname." Kaid explains.

"I don't like it." She says immediately, like she's said it a million times before.

"I do," Kaid singsongs, making Zahra groan.

"How about we start with crackers?" Zahra suggests, "I grabbed both Ritz crackers and saltines— do you have a preference?"

"I don't know… let's start with Ritz, I guess."

Kaid grabs my remote and slowly starts raising my bed up after asking my permission, while Zahra pulls out an iPad and scrolls through it to find something for us to watch.

Once Kaid finishes putting the bed up, my body falls onto itself. I groan, my head and chest falling down the mattress.

He quickly turns around when he hears me groan. He quickly adjusts the bed again, and helps me reposition my limp body so it doesn't fall again. He makes sure that I can see well and that I'm sitting up enough to eat and drink.

Zahra sits down next to me and open the sleeve of crackers. She wordlessly starts holding them up to my mouth, as we watch the show she picked out.

29

I had my MRI at two in the morning, and my neurologist came in with results at noon.

"So, I didn't see anything we haven't already seen on the MRI," my neurologist explains as he goes and checks my limbs in the standard test that anyone who's admitted into the neurology department gets done at least once per hour.

"So what does that mean?" I ask, trying to distract myself from the pain. It's not working.

"I'm going to put you on a three day steroid infusion track, and hopefully by the end you're going to be feeling better. We're going to keep you here to monitor, because these can be brutal to the body and we want to monitor and adjust as needed. We'll start in a few hours, make sure to order some food now and eat before you start, because you probably won't want to eat during or afterwards."

I nod, feeling like something's supposed to be happening in these next new days, but I can't place it. I shake my head, and think of the hospital's menu and what I might want to eat. The answer is nothing, but I definitely believe I won't want to eat afterwards.

The doctor leaves, and Zahra brings me the tablet the hospital provided for me to order food from. She starts going through the options with me, but nothing's popping out at me. I want to get something that sounds good, but also something that would be easy for Zahra to help me eat.

"Nothing sounds good," I lament, groaning and throwing my head against the pillow as best I can. It barely moves, but I still want to be a bit dramatic.

"Do you just want to eat some crackers?" Zahra offers, "I have more Ritz, and a few sleeves of saltines you haven't touched."

I sigh, "Yeah, I'll just have the saltines."

I redirect my attention to the tv mounted on the wall where cartoons have been playing on a low volume all day.

I let my mind wander as Zahra feeds me crackers, not letting myself think about it too much, knowing I'd be embarrassed.

Her and Kaid have been switching off who's staying with me, no matter how many times I tell them I can be here alone. As much as I insist I don't need them here, and for them to go home, I really am grateful they're staying with me. I don't think I'd be able to get through this experience otherwise.

After an episode of random cartoons, I finally realize what was supposed to be happening over the next few days while I'm stuck here. Mine and Zahra's <u>Jane Austen's Impact</u> project. We were supposed to present our video to the class and Melody in two days.

My head falls to my chest as I try not to cry. We've spent the whole semester making this project the best it could possibly be, and I know for a fact that Zahra was taking this class and going above and beyond because she felt like she had to for her mom.

"What's wrong?" Zahra asks, looking over at me worriedly.

"Our project," I blubber, "We're supposed to present our project the day after tomorrow."

"It's okay, honey, I know Melody's gonna understand. I'll email her now, don't worry about it."

"I don't care about Melody," I tell her, completely lying. "You took this class for your mom, and now I'm preventing you from presenting the project you've put your life and soul into basically."

"It's not that big of a deal," Zahra says softly, "I took this class to have the opportunity to read and watch *Sense and Sensibility* to get to know her better, and I did. And through that, I met you, and we've gotten to know each other so well and now I have the best partner ever. I've gotten everything I need from this class, and more."

My tears fall down my face even stronger at her words.

"How did I get such a great girlfriend?" I blubber, not sure if she can understand me through my tears.

Zahra grabs my hand, and brings it up to her mouth, kissing it gently. She kisses it again, and I feel something wet hit the back of my hand. *Tears. Zahra's crying too.*

"All you, hon," she whispers onto my hand, "All that matters is that we have each other."

She puts my hand back onto the mattress, and holds it in hers, softly squeezing three times every few seconds.

She wipes away her tears, and leans over to wipe mine for me. I sniffle, she knows me too well. She always knows exactly what I need, and I appreciate her so much for it.

"I think this is a good time to give you your birthday gift. I have some cake that Kaid left here for you, if you want it."

"The cake," I groan, remembering the soft, velvety, moist vanilla cake with the most beautiful frosting. "That's the only thing that sounds good to me right now."

Zahra laughs, leaning over the side of my bed to kiss my

temple. She grabs a Tupperware from a bag I didn't see before, grabs a fork out and opens the container.

She feeds me my cake as we talk about our project. We decide that Zahra can present it by herself, since it's a video anyways, all she'll have to do is say something quick at the beginning, if that.

Another part of the grade for this class is taking notes on other presentations and giving feedback. Zahra's going to do that as well— we figure I can just get the same grade as her if I'm not exempt from the assignment. We've emailed Melody, but it's after hours right now. I'm sure she'll be fine with it, we're pretty much the only ones who've done anything in the class, and she likes us.

As I finish my slice of cake, a nurse comes in with an infusion stand and starts to connect my IV to the bag.

"This infusion will be about three hours, and I'll come in and disconnect you from the drip once you're done. You're probably going to be super tired and feeling weird afterwards, so just a head's up." She gently adjusts my IV placement, and adds another piece of tape to my arm. "I'll come in and check on you in a little bit." I nod as she pats my arm gently before leaving.

Zahra and I talked through the first hour of my infusion, but once the first hour mark hit I was so tired and feeling like shit I ended up falling asleep mid-sentence. I can't even remember what we were talking about now, I barely remember them disconnecting me from the IV, or any of my vitals checks that happened overnight.

When I wake up the next morning for my now daily blood

draws, Zahra's gone to class and Kaid's replaced her on the couch.

"Good morning, sleepyhead," he says, smiling at me.

I roll my eyes in response, and when I instinctively stretch my body, my hands move slightly. My eyes go wide and I do it again, just like the first time my hand moves slightly.

It isn't much, but it's so much better than it was before. I'll take this slight movement over no movement or feeling any day of the week.

"Did I just see your hand move?" Kaid asks, raising an eyebrow at me. As I nod, a smile grows on his face and he jumps up off the couch excitedly. He rushes forward and wraps me up in a big hug. I can't move my arms to hug him back yet, so I nuzzle my face into his shoulder blade, smiling widely as I do. *I think he understands.*

"Well that's perfect timing," he tells me, "I was going to suggest that I help you open your birthday presents once Zahra gets here, she mentioned you fell asleep before you could yesterday. I guess in the meantime, we should turn your cartoons back on and have some cake for breakfast before your infusion."

"Sounds good to me," I say as Kaid turns on the TV, it automatically turns back onto the channel of cartoons we were watching before.

He grabs another Tupperware with a slice of cake— *seriously, how many of these does he have?* Not *complaining though.*— and opens it up. He grabs a fork and grabs a bite for for me. He goes to bring it up to my mouth, but pauses.

"How about you try?"

"What if I drop it?"

"I'll help you."

I nod. Kaid lifts my hand and puts the fork in it. I try to close my fingers around the fork, but it doesn't really work. My pointer finger twitches pathetically instead of listening to my command.

Kaid gently closes my hand around the fork wordlessly, and my hand miraculously stays in the position. Yes, it's twitchy, but it's not unraveling from its grasp around the fork. I'm taking it as a win.

I put all my energy into bringing my hand with the fork up to my mouth. Somehow, it works. It's very slow going, and my hand is trembling all the way, but it works. The trembling makes some of the cake fall off my fork, but Kaid's had his hand resting under mine in preparation for that.

I finally get the fork into my mouth after what feels like forever. Once my hand lets go of the fork, my hand flops back onto the mattress. I take deep breaths, feeling like I just ran a marathon.

How pathetic is this? I can barely lift a fork to my mouth, and my body's acting like I ran a fucking marathon instead. I used to be able to lift things easily, use my hands easily, and now I can barely move my hands in general.

Kaid quickly grabs the fork from my mouth, allowing me to breathe deeply through my mouth.

"You did good, Clover," Kaid tells me softly, grabbing my water bottle and holding it up to my mouth so I can take a sip.

"I BROUGHT THE PRESENTS!" Zahra exclaims as she comes into the hospital room. She's holding a box full of different presents, wrapped in numerous colors and packages.

"Woah, that's a lot of presents!" My eyes widen as I see the box.

"You deserve them!" Kaid and Zahra say at the same time, making me blush.

"Come on," Kaid exclaims excitedly, standing up from the couch. He's practically jumping in excitement, and rushes over to Zahra to help her unpack the box of presents. "Ooh, I need to call Adria and Caitlyn too!" He rushes back to the couch, grabbing his phone and dialing them.

"Hello?" A sleepy voice comes from Kaid's phone and yawns.

"Oh shit, I didn't think about the time difference, sorry Adria..."

"Why'd you wake me up then?"

"Oh, me and Zahra were going to help Clover open xeir birthday presents."

"Oh! Okay, that's a good reason to wake me up then. Gimme a sec, let me wake Caitlyn real quick, and we can switch to FaceTime. I'll call you back in a second." A dial tone rings before Kaid can even open his mouth to say anything.

I laugh at Kaid's befuddled expression, and Zahra looks up at me and smiles. She hasn't really talked to Adria and Caitlyn before, and I know both her and them are excited to meet each other. They're all such important people in my life, and I cannot wait for them to finally meet each other.

Zahra grabs the chair she usually sits in and pulls it towards the end of the bed. She starts going through the box again, stacking my presents on the end of my bed where my legs don't reach.

"Kaid?" She asks, "Can you hand me my present? It's in the bag I left here last night by accident."

"Wha-" Oh yeah, here it is," he grabs the wrapped present from where Zahra said it was. He goes to pass it to her, but his phone goes off. He jumps, startled, and almost drops the present onto my leg.

I cringe preemptively, expecting the fuck ton of pain that's about to come (yes, that is an official neurological term when it comes to pain). But it doesn't.

When I open my eyes, I see Zahra leaning over the bed, the package in her hands, mere inches from my leg. I sigh in relief, and my body relaxes.

"I am so sorry," Kaid says, one of his hands over his mouth with his eyes wide.

"It's fine," I say, just relieved it didn't actually hit my legs. "Just answer the phone before it goes to voicemail."

"O-oh right!" He exclaims, having forgotten about the ringing phone in his hands for a second. "Good morning, lovely ladies."

"Quit trying to charm us because you feel bad about waking us up." Caitlyn says bluntly, "Give the phone to my best friend, I haven't been able to talk to xem for days."

Kaid nods and diligently sets the phone up on my table for me. Yes, I can move my hands and arms a bit now, but I don't trust myself to not drop the phone a lot. I'm sure Kaid's also going to insist that I try and open my presents by myself anyways. I can't open presents and hold my phone at the same time.

"We sent you some goodies," Adria tells us, "Some gifts, and some American essentials I'm sure you're missing."

"Oh yeah, *some* goodies," Kaid grumbles, knowing Adria and Caitlyn well enough that they won't be offended. They know him well enough that he cares more about me than carrying a large package every now and then anyways.

"We've missed you so much," Caitlyn tells me, leaning forward to see me a bit closer. "You're looking a bit rough, there, are you sure you're doing all right?"

"Oh yeah, I'm on a steroid track to help me feel better but it's super rough going at the moment." I explain and shrug.

They both nod, "How long are you on? When should you start feeling better?"

"I'm on the track for three days, this is going to be day two. My body's starting to feel a bit better now, I'm able to move my hand a bit—" Kaid whoops as I say that and hold my hand up to demonstrate, interrupting my sentence and making me laugh. "And I'm hoping to be able to be back to normal by the time I leave— hands wise I mean. Apparently, these steroids are pretty strong, so I'll feel like shit for a while though. One of those switching one bad thing for another type of situations."

"That sucks, but I'm glad it's starting to help a bit." Adria says, a small frown forming on her face.

"And I'm glad you're going to be going home soon," Caitlyn adds, "Even though you're going to feel like shit once you're done with the steroids, at least you'll be back in your apartment."

"You're so right," I nod in agreement.

"Can we have xem open xeir presents now? Kaid asks impatiently. I don't blame him, he has been looking at them since they've come in the mail, slowly accumulating a pile in his room.

"Yes!" Adria exclaims, then backtracks, "Actually wait, I want to meet your girlfriend first."

I laugh, "Alright, alright, Zahra come over here so you can meet my best friends."

Zahra walks over to be in frame and holds my hand.

"Wait, I thought I was your best friend!" Kaid jokingly exclaims.

"You all know I love you so much," I tell them, blushing a bit at thinking that I just insinuated I loved Zahra. She doesn't respond in any way, so I relax marginally. Kaid smiles at me, and I do my best to smile back.

"Hi, I'm Zahra," she introduces herself, smiling cutely at the screen.

"Hi, I'm Adria! And this is my girlfriend, Caitlyn," she introduces quickly, gesturing to Caitlyn before waving at Zahra.

"I'm so glad to meet you two, Clover talks about you all of the time. I'm so glad to put faces to your names."

"You too!" Caitlyn tells her. "Although since we aren't in Newcastle, make sure you guys take care of xem, okay?"

"I will," Zahra says softly, putting her hand on my shoulder and smiling gently at me.

Kaid comes up on my other side, nodding his head at Caitlyn and Adria, as he puts his hand on my shoulder as well.

I haven't seen Caitlyn this vulnerable in a long time, if ever. She tends to be like this only with Adria. Sometimes she'll be vulnerable around me, but only if I need to be in the know. And definitely never *about* me.

Caitlyn nods, smiling softly at both Kaid and Zahra individually before saying, "Thank you."

30

───────

"What present should I grab first?" Kaid asks, moving towards the end of the bed to grab me a present.

"The snack box?" Adria looks at Caitlyn for her opinion and she nods. "I put something in there for you as well, Kaid."

"You did?" he asks confused, "Do you want me to open this one, or do you want to?"

I think for a second before deciding, "How about you open this one, and I'll open the more personal ones. N-not like this isn't a personal gift," I quickly backtrack, eyes, "All of the gifts are special, and I appreciate them all immensely..."

"Calm down Clo," Caitlyn says, using a nickname she rarely uses but I love. "We understand what you mean, don't worry about it."

I sigh in relief, a small smile forming on my face. I hear Kaid ripping open the package excitedly, making sure I can see it. Zahra grabs my phone and flips the camera, holding it up so Adria and Caitlyn can see me and Kaid as well.

"Oh my fucking god," Kaid exclaims excitedly, grabbing something out of the box. He holds it up to me, a package of double stuffed E.L. Fudges with a post-it labeled 'Kaid' on top. "I didn't know they made double stuffed ones!"

"They're superior in my opinion, so I figured you'd appreciate them." Adria says excitedly, "If it wasn't so early here, I'd go and break into my package, but I'm not hungry yet."

Kaid smiles, thanking the girls before putting the cookies on the table behind him. He reaches into the box and grabs two wrapped gifts, putting them to the side as well. "I figured we'd go through the snacks first and then you can open the packages," he exclaims.

I nod, ready to have an amazing snack stash ready for me. I do love the snacks here, but American snacks are just so much better. It might be because I grew up with those snacks, and I have nostalgia for them, but I don't care.

Kaid goes through the box of snacks quickly, holding them up for me easily since they aren't wrapped. They packed Cheeze-Its, and Goldfish, and various types of cookies and chips. Last but not least, they included my favorite snack that isn't available here: Cheez It Snack Mix. They packed me three family sized boxes, more than enough to last me multiple months.

"Ooh, these look good," Kaid says, turning the box around for him to take a closer look at it.

"I'm not sharing," I say immediately, making Adria and Caitlyn burst into laughter.

"Shit, okay," he puts his hands up jokingly as he puts the box on the table with the rest of the snacks.

"Open mine next!" Adria exclaims excitedly. I can't see her, but I can imagine her bouncing in her seat.

Kaid grabs a small box, wrapped in red paper with bows. He puts it on the table in front of me, and grabs my hand.

"Want me to help you?"

"At least getting it on the table, I should be able to get it from there."

He nods, and does what I told him.

I take a deep breath and move my hand onto the package. I try my best to grab the edge of the paper to open it, but struggle a few times before I finally get it. I triumphantly grab the edge of the paper and rip it as best as I can.

It takes me a long time to open the gift, but nobody says anything as I struggle. I finally get the package open, and there's a cute gift box there.

"Can you...?" I ask Kaid to cut the tape for me. He grabs scissors and grabs the box before I can finish my sentence.

He quickly cuts the tape, and lifts the lid off. He gasps, accidentally seeing the gift before he tilts the box towards me.

There's a blue and green swirled fabric I can see, but I can't tell exactly what it is. I know this is Adria's gift, so there's a good chance this is handmade by her.

I bring my hands up slowly, shaking but not falling, and grab the fabric. It's so soft, and I gasp as I feel it. I yank on it, and it falls out the side of the box. It goes on forever, it feels like, as I bring my hands back to my lap.

"Adria, this fabric is stunning," I tell her in awe. "What is it? I can't wait to style this."

"It's a pair of pants!" she exclaims excitedly, "I found the fabric and *knew* I had to make you something with it. It took me a while to decide on pants, but I thought you'd look so good in that fabric as pants."

"You made those?" Zahra exclaims, shock evident in her tone. Kaid grabs the phone from her, as she goes to grab the pants from my lap. She holds them up and they flare out towards the floor, but not hitting.

"Yeah, I did," Adria says softly, probably blushing and shy

about it. She's so talented, but she doesn't like to flaunt her creations to people she doesn't know well.

"Holy shit, this is amazing. You're so talented."

"Yes, you are," Caitlyn says, and I can hear them kiss quickly.

I look at the pants closer now that Zahra's holding them up. They look like they're going to be my perfect fit. They have a nice waist seam, and no buttons to clasp. My eyes widen as I notice the pockets on the side, and the zippers on the hips instead of the front to make putting them on easier.

I didn't even have to say anything, and Adria did her research to make them easier for me— and executed it seamlessly.

Zahra gently folds the pants and puts them back in the gift box for me. She moves the box off my table, and puts it aside.

Kaid excitedly grabs his gift for me to open next, and puts it on the table for me. I do my best to get my hands up onto the table to open the present, and even though it burns like all hell, it's faster than before.

Kaid's present is wrapped in paper with oranges all over. I don't know what his obsession with the fruit and the color orange is, but it's very endearing. Orange is slowly growing on me.

I grasp the paper easier this time, but I still struggle pulling it open. I yank it aggressively, and the gifts inside go flying in different directions. I yelp, and laugh as I look down at my hands holding the paper.

"I caught them!" Zahra exclaims, laughing along with me. I look over and she's triumphantly holding two DVDs.

"Lies, you only caught one." Kaid says, ribbing at her like siblings would. "Adria and Caitlyn can back me up, I know they say as well."

"Dammit, Kaid, I could've gotten away with it. I know Clove didn't see me," she pouts.

I laugh, and can hear Adria and Caitlyn laugh through the phone as Zahra and Kaid glare at each other.

"I believe you hon," I tell her, definitely lying but wanting her to feel better.

"I know you don't, but thank you." Zahra immediately sees through me.

"Here you go," Kaid bends down and picks up the last present that flew towards him when I ripped the paper. He puts it on the table and I lean forward to see it better.

It's another clothing gift box, this time not taped so I can open it easier. I flick the top off the box, and see a light green pattern and... is that his face? And Zahra's? And Caitlyn and Adria's?

I blink, am I imagining this? No, no, I'm not, I realize as I'm able to grasp the fabric and pull them out of the box.

I look over at Kaid, who has the biggest shit-eating grin on his mouth. His grin goes wider at the bemused and confused expression on my face. I hear Zahra laugh for a split second before biting her tongue.

"What is this?" I ask, somehow managing to hold back my laughter but not my smile.

"Pajamas."

"Pajamas with your face on it? With her face and their faces?" I motion towards each person as I talk.

"Yes," he bites his lip to hide his amusement. "I bought them months ago, and honestly this is the perfect time for you to get them."

I can't hold back my laughter anymore, and it explodes out of me. I laugh so hard, tears fall down my cheeks, unable to stop when everyone joins me.

Once I finally calm down, I bring the pajama fabric up to my eyes and wipe the residual moisture.

Kaid catches my eye, noticing the motion's ease, and nods. He doesn't say anything, able to tell that I don't want to bring attention to it right now. As I move my arms more, it's becoming easier and easier, but I don't want to talk about it. I'm able to celebrate in my head, but the minute someone says something about it, I feel like shit. Somehow, Kaid and everyone else has noticed and done their best to not say anything, without needing to say anything in the first place.

"I love them," I tell Kaid, looking at everyone else, putting my love for them in the words as well as the pajamas, "Thank you."

"Of course, Clove," Kaid tells me, "I'll help you put them on after we're done, or we can call a nurse in if you'd prefer, before your infusion. I'm sure what you're wearing isn't that comfortable."

"Considering I've been stuck in it for three days and can't move," I say dryly, "It's not my preferred situation."

"Ha ha," he matches my tone. He grabs the pajamas and puts them back in the box haphazardly.

Zahra holds the DVDs out to me, and I grab them from her. I almost drop them, but manage to catch them.

I flip through the DVDs quickly, Friends: Season 1, and Pretty Little Liars: Season 1.

"I figured I'd give you a bit of variety," he explains, "I have my portable DVD player in my bag that you can borrow as long as you need. There's also a giftcard in there for you to pick some more."

I gape at him, not realizing how much thought he put into this gift. He definitely only had the pajamas as a gift before I was hospitalized, and then picked out some entertainment for me so I wouldn't be bored. He wanted to make damn sure that I would be as comfortable as possible as well.

"Thank you, Kaid," I tell him, full of sincerity. He smiles at me softly, mouthing "it was nothing" like he can tell exactly what I'm thinking.

"Who's present is last?" Adria asks from the phone, "Caitlyn or Zahra?"

"I want mine to be last," Zahra says, "So Caitlyn's next."

Kaid leans over and grabs a bag off the table, "here you go," he holds it next to me and I grab the tissue paper out one by one.

"Ooh!" I exclaim excitedly, seeing the black outline of the Little Black Classics editions by Penguin. I tend to collect the original Penguin editions, but I've mentioned wanting to start collecting these— as they're classic short stories and novellas to go along with the original Penguin Classics editions.

I toss the last piece of tissue paper out and see three black classics lined up neatly in the bag. Kaid puts the bag next to me so I can flip through them easier, and I do.

Caitlyn had picked out The Vampire, Wailing Ghosts, and The Tell Tale Heart. I excitedly pull them out and look at them, looking at the small details on the back of the book and inside them,

"I bought them before you were hospitalized, obviously," Caitlyn says softly, "But I remember you saying you wanted to start collecting these editions. Either way, since I know you can't read them now, and I know you don't like reading classics while in the hospital, I've sent audiobook copies of my books to your phone for you to listen to now."

My heart flutters. My friends know me so much better than I ever thought they did.

"Thank you, Caitlyn," I say softly, looking at the books, "I cannot wait to read these."

"My only request? If you hate my writing, don't tell me."

"I don't hate your writing, Caitlyn, I love your writing from what I've read so far."

"I told you," Adria singsongs to her girlfriend, making me smile.

Caitlyn sighs, and probably shakes her head at Adria. The two of them start bickering at each other jokingly, and in the process the phone ends up getting hung up.

Kaid shrugs and puts my phone back on the table for me. In my peripheral vision, I see Zahra sitting down in the chair and fidgeting with the handles.

"What's wrong, Zahra?" I ask softly, putting my hand on top of hers. She looks up at me, shocked that I'm able to move my arms and hands so smoothly. The proudest smile forms on her face and I almost start crying. I don't know why, but her approval has turned into what matters most to me.

"Kaid," she asks softly, making Kaid look up her her surprised. He tilts his head at her and hums in answer. "Can you leave for a few minutes?"

"Alright...?" he answers confused, but still nods. "I'll go ahead and get some snacks and take a bathroom break."

Once Kaid leaves the room, Zahra stands up shakily and goes over to the table where her present is laying, the only one still wrapped.

"Zahra." I tell her, stopping her in her tracks. "Are you okay? What's going on?"

"I'm alright, this is just something I need to do and I'm nervous."

"What?"

She ignores my question and puts the present on the table in front of me.

The present is rectangular— kind of book shaped— with a simple black and white polka dotted pattern on the paper.

I'm suddenly nervous to open the present. I'm not usually nervous opening presents, but based on Zahra's reaction and body language, this present feels like a lot more than I know of right now.

I tuck my finger underneath the paper and start unfolding it. The first thing I see is old, weathered book pages, which makes me even more confused.

I open the present the rest of the way, and find an old copy of *Sense and Sensibility*. A gorgeous, old, and worn version of *Sense and Sensibility*.

"It's gorgeous, Zahra," I say, my fingers skimming over the title of the book softly, "I love it, thank you."

"I'm glad, but there's more to it," she says, taking a deep breath.

"What?" I look up at her and grab her hand.

"This isn't just an old copy of *Sense and Sensibility*, Clove, this is so much more than that. This was my mom's copy of *Sense and Sensibility*." My breath hitches at her words, and my eyes trail back to the book. "This book was her pride and joy. She brought it with her everywhere, and she annotated the living hell out of it. She was almost buried with her, but at the last minute she decided she wanted to leave it here so it could be apart of her legacy."

"Zahra..." I say, unable to think or say much of anything else. "Why would you give this to me? N-not that I'm not appreciative, but... isn't this something that should stay in the family?"

"Well... hopefully one day you will be family." Zahra says, looking down at her shoes, a massive blush forming on both of our faces as I process her words, unable to make eye contact. "Mom would want it to be read, she'd want her knowledge spread. I feel like you'd appreciate it more than I would in the long run, and if there's anytime where I want to read it, I know where to find you."

Tears form in my eyes as I look between Zahra and the priceless gift she just gave me. As the tears fall, I quickly move the book onto the table instead of my lap so it doesn't get tear-stained. I don't want anything to happen to it. I want this book to be as pristine as it is now hundreds of years from now. In a matter of seconds, this book has become my most prized possession, over my wheelchair and mine and Kaid's apartment.

"Thank you," I tell her, reaching to give her a tight hug, "Thank you."

THIS IS one of the only times I've been alone since being admitted into the hospital. I'm in the middle of my last infusion, and now that I can move my hands and arms I'm going between scrolling on my phone and reading. I'm feeling pretty sick from the infusion, but I'm getting pretty used to it by now. I do know that once I get home I'm going to feel like shit, but I'm so ready to be feeling like shit in my own bed compared to this shitty hospital bed (although it's better than the ER one... but not by much).

A knock sounds on my door, and without looking up I say "Come in," figuring it was a nurse who was checking in on me.

"Clover?" I look up as the door opens and my eyes widen in surprise as I see Melody standing in my doorway.

"Prof-uh-Melody?' I stammer, struggling to find the right name to call her for a second in my shock.

She laughs, "You can call me Melody, you know that. Can I come in?"

"Oh yeah, of course," I motion for her to come in, and she

does. "My brain still hasn't quite gotten used to not having to call you 'Professor'."

She nods, "That makes sense."

She sits down next to my hospital bed, and we sit in an awkward silence until I blurt "What are you doing here?"

"Well," she says, twiddling her thumbs, "I wanted to talk to you in general after your presentation— which was amazing by the way, if Zahra didn't give you my notes on it— but when Zahra told me you were in the hospital, for your birthday nonetheless, I figured I'd come and visit you."

"Oh god," I say, overthinking everything I've done in the last month within the millisecond. "What'd I do?"

"Oh nothing," she laughs, "It's about the class trip to Chawton."

I gasp, "Jane Austen's house! I forgot about that!"

"I know you and Zahra are the ones who are most excited about going, so I wanted to make sure everything was accessible to you. I was gonna suggest having a meeting, but I brought everything so we can do it now."

"Sounds good to me," I nod. I spot a brown box tucked under Melody's arm, and as much as I want to ask what it is, I hold back.

"Oh!" she says, probably noticing me looking at the box, "I brought us some pastries to have while we talk, to celebrate your birthday and to make this long conversation more fun."

"Oh, thank you!" I exclaim, slowly pushing myself up on my bed as Melody puts the box down on the table next to me and opens it up. There are little cupcakes and cookies, and bars. My mouth starts watering at first glance.

"So, I'm not really worried about the train, we're taking a direct train. It was a bit more expensive in the long run, but I liked that I'll actually be able to relax this year instead of tracking when we'll be switching lines. So that'll be about five and a half hours. For the hotel, I've already taken the liberty of getting you and Zahra— since rooms will be shared between students— a room on the first floor with a roll in shower and plenty of space for your chair."

"That sounds good to me," I tell her, nodding.

"Yeah, but this is where it gets a bit more choppy. I reached out to some people at the house, and the first floor is accessible with a few bumps and dips along the way— which is to be expected with a historical house— but unfortunately the second floor isn't accessible. I mean, unless you get someone to lift you and the chair up the stairs, but I don't think that's going to be possible, unfortunately."

I nod, disappointed. There's nothing I can do about it, it's not like I *can* climb the stairs to see the top floor if I wanted to, but I'm still kicking myself.

If I had only come to England sooner. If I was only able to move my legs and go up stairs. If only I had gotten disabled later.

"Let me guess," Melody says softly, breaking me from my thoughts, "You're stuck in your mind in the world of 'what if's?'"

"How can you tell?" I ask, my eyes wide.

She laughs, "I've had my fair share of those, I know the look in an instant these days."

I smile slightly.

"You can't go upstairs, but the lovely folks at the Austen house have already figured out an alternative. There are 3D online tours of the upstairs— every part of the house, really— but they have set ups for people who can't go upstairs to be able to see and experience it as much as they can."

"That could work," I tell her, still disappointed but glad that there's another option.

"I know," she says, "I know you're disappointed, and I'm sorry. This is the best I could do, and I'm still waiting to hear from the Chawton House so I don't know how that's going to work either, but I understand if you don't want to come. I can exempt you from the paper, you've already done more than enough for this class..."

"W-wait what's saying I don't want to come? I mean, other than not being able to go upstairs in Jane Austen's house, and who knows what with the Chawton House... but that's not that big of a deal in the grand scheme of things." I say quickly, talking faster I can process my thoughts at the time.

"You still want to come?" Melody asks, looking relieved, "I'm so glad. I'm sure you and Zahra will have the best time!"

She gives me a big smile as she grabs a cupcake from the bakery box. I chuckle and grab a cookie as well.

"Happy birthday, Clover," she says holding her cupcake up for me to bump my cookie with in a cheers, "I'll see you in a week for our trip, it's going to be amazing."

You need to tell me where your prof got these from," Kaid says through a mouthful of brownie a few days later, "Cause they're incredible, like even three days after, they're still soft and moist."

I roll my eyes, "You know, considering it was my birthday, I should be the one eating the last pastry."

He looks at me, and raises an eyebrow, "You said you had everything you wanted from the box."

"My point still stands," I shrug.

It's been three days since Melody came and visited me in the hospital. I went home the day after, that is after all my nurses grabbed a pastry if they wanted. Melody was called 'pastry lady' whenever someone talked about her.

I've eaten so many of these pastries over the last few days, having one for every meal basically. As much as I love a good brownie, I decided to let Kaid have the last one.

"How're you feeling today?" he asks, changing the topic while wordlessly passing me a bite of the brownie. I roll my eyes, but in the end, I can't resist it.

"Feeling a bit better, I needed to sleep a ton to catch up

from the hospital and I think I finally got enough back to function-ish."

"Yeah, it's seriously crazy how much rest you lose going to the hospital. I mean, I wasn't the one getting prodded and looked at, but I lost so much sleep, it's ridiculous."

"Yeah, but I think I'm finally able to get out of bed and do something, I *want* to get out of bed and do something."

"Wanna order some takeout and watch tv in the living room?" he suggests.

"You know me so well," I laugh.

He laughs, and we make our way to the living room slowly. I'm still weak and weary from the hospital visit and my symptoms in general. Kaid's moving a bit faster, and instead of waiting for me on the couch, he grabs some snacks for us. By the time I get to the couch, he's already put the snack down and started pulling up CSI.

I chuckle as I lock my chair and transfer onto my spot on the couch. I curl up on the pillow next to me as Kaid makes himself a plate of snacks.

"Y'know," he says, eating a cracker, "People are always assuming that we're dating, and I find that weird. We aren't *that* close."

"People say that?" I ask confused, looking over at him,

"Apparently?" he raises an end of the word like a question, "I don't know for certain because nobody's actually asked me to my face."

"Oh, well then who the fuck cares?" I ask, exasperated, throwing my hands up in the air.

"I don't," he clarifies quickly, "People just like spreading rumors."

"Ugh," I groan, "People are the worst."

"They really are. I don't understand why."

"For real! Like seriously, don't people understand that

we're platonic and are always going to be? The one time we tried and thought it could work out, we very quickly realized it wouldn't!" I exclaim, throwing my hands up in the air, sigh, and grab a handful of popcorn to shove in my mouth.

"No seriously," Kaid agrees, nodding, "I love you so much, but we are *not* compatible romantically, and it'll never happen. Besides— YOU AND ZAHRA ARE DATING!"

I crack up, "I mean we don't really push our relationship into the world, but that still doesn't give people the right to assume."

"People will always assume that's the first thing you need to know about them." Kaid tells me seriously, putting a hand on my shoulder in a comforting way. I can't keep a straight face. "Either way, we're always going to be here for each other, and that's all that matters."

I smile at him and nod, "Yeah, that's the only thing that matters."

THREE EPISODES into our CSI binge, Kaid's phone goes off. I transfer into my chair to pause the TV and to go get some water, to give him privacy.

I refill my water, putting the jug back into the fridge and putting a few dishes away to waste time. I can still hear him talking faintly from the living room, so I procrastinate a little bit more.

I roll back into the living room with my water, and watch Kaid slowly put his phone onto the couch from his ear. He doesn't turn around or look at me as I come in and I start moving even quicker. I turn the corner and see the look of sheer grief and panic on his face. I drop everything I'm holding and transfer onto the couch as fast as I can.

"Kaid?" I ask as I scoot closer to him. He blinks, and turns his head, like he didn't even realize I was there.

"Clover?" he whispers, his voice breaking. I can immediately tell that something is wrong.

"Kaid," I say again, putting my hand on his shoulder and slowly start to rub the tension out of it. "What's wrong? Who just called?"

"It's Nonna Helen," he whimpers. I immediately remember our conversation where he told me about his absent parents, and how his Nonna Helen was the one who raised him. Nonna Helen is the person he cares about most in the world, and if something's happened to her... Kaid's definitely not doing well.

"Oh Kaid," I say softly, "What happened?"

"I don't know, she had a fall and was admitted to the hospital... and through the scans they found cancer... and she needs someone there, and nobody else is willing to go, so I'm going to go."

"Cancer?" My voice breaks at the word, and my heart breaks for her. "I'm so sorry."

I don't say anything else, and don't make him say anything else either. I scoot closer to him and wrap him up into a hug.

He latches onto me. I tuck his head into the crook of my neck, wrapping myself around him, trying to comfort him as much as I can.

He clings onto me like a monkey and I feel something wet hit my neck: Kaid's tears. I squeeze my eyes closed and pull him closer to me, trying to hold back my own tears.

KAID LEFT to go back home for Nonna Helen early the next morning, and it's so lonely in this apartment without him.

Luckily it's not going to be for much longer, since Zahra and I are leaving for our trip to Chawton tomorrow.

Zahra and I spent the day on FaceTime, packing out bags for the week-long trip. We talked a little bit, but spent most of the time in silence doing our own thing.

We've gotten to the point in our relationship where we love just being on FaceTime while doing our own thing, so that we're in each other's company regardless. Although we did decide to have a sleepover here tonight to make it easier for us to get to the train station tomorrow.

We're meeting Melody and the rest of the class at the train station at 7am. Since Zahra has a car and I don't, we decided to just spend the night here so she doesn't have to come out of her way to pick me up.

A knock sounds on the apartment door, and a smile goes on my face instinctively as I go to open the door for Zahra.

"Hey hon," she smiles at me as I open the door. She's leaning against her purple suitcase, and even in her pajamas she's absolutely beautiful.

"Hey," I say, scooting back to let her in. She follows and I shut the door. She puts her suitcase next to mine and we make our way to the couch, where I've already set up some snacks. Zahra agreed to get some as well, so she unpacks what she brought. Whatever we don't eat tonight, we're going to bring with us.

Zahra flops on the couch, grabbing one of my throw pillows and wrapping herself around it.

"What's wrong?" I ask, sitting on the couch next to her. I move to wrap my arms around her, but hesitate, not sure what she needs right now.

"I'm just emotional," she tells me, looking up at me, "It doesn't help that I'm on my period... but we're going to Jane

Austen's house, which was my mom's dream. Her dream that she never accomplished."

"Oh honey," I tell her gently, taking the pillow from her and tucking her in my arms. "We're bringing her with us in spirit, and going for her."

She sniffles, "Thank you." She looks up at me and wipes her eyes.

"Of course," I say, smiling down at her.

"You're so beautiful, you know that? I'm sorry if you don't like the word beautiful, but I feel like it fits people of every gender."

"I didn't think I'd like being called beautiful, but I like when you call me beautiful." I tell her, blushing.

Zahra untucks herself from my arms for a second before repositioning herself and tucking back into my arms. Now that we're face to face, she kisses my forehead gently.

My blush goes even deeper, and she chuckles. She leans down and kisses my lips softly.

I reciprocate, wrapping my arms around her neck. Her hands fly into my hair as she pulls me closer and kisses me deeper.

My heart rate picks up, but I ignore it as I kiss her back, trying my best to keep up.

We continue kissing, hands exploring the top half of each other's bodies. I don't know where my body ends and her body starts. I've never been kissed like this before, and I want to do it again and again.

Zahra breaks the kiss and catches her breath. I tuck my head into the crook of her neck and start kissing down the neck. Her breath catches and I grin, continuing my descent. I kiss her collarbone and she lets out a groan. I gasp, and she groans even louder.

"C-clover," she groans my name, tucking her head into my

neck. She kisses my neck, making me groan. We go back and forth a few times before I pull back, grabbing her face into my hands, pulling her lips to mine desperately.

The kiss sparks a flame in both of us, and we kiss each other passionately, both groaning. Zahra's tongue caresses mine and when I don't respond, she nibbles on my lip gently. I groan even louder, giving her access into my mouth.

Our tongues battle for dominance, as I pull her hair gently and get my hands caught in her gorgeous hair.

"Clove?" she pants, breaking the kiss.

"Hmm?" I groan.

"Will I hurt you if I lean you back so you're laying on the couch? I don't want to hurt you."

"You're not going to hurt me," I chuckle, twisting her hair and tucking it behind her ears.

"I'm worried."

"I'm not fragile," I tell her softly, "If you do something that hurts me, I'll tell you to stop."

"Sounds good to me," she says softly. Her eyes darken and she smirks at me as she pushes me onto the couch.

My back hits the couch and before I can blink, Zahra's on top of me. She smirks at me before smashing her mouth to mine.

I can barely keep up with her kisses, but she doesn't slow down to accommodate me. Even something so small makes my heart flutter.

She breaks the kiss, and smiles at me shyly. I can't help the blush from forming on my face, and she chuckles. She helps shift our bodies so we're cuddling on the couch, her being the big spoon to my little spoon.

32

My alarm goes off this morning and I'm wrapped around Zahra. There's no big or little spoons here, we're just completely wrapped up in each other's arms. Limbs are tangled, and I can't tell what's what.

Zahra groans and her hand flails out to try and turn my alarm off, but her hand hits the corner of the nightstand. After cuddling on the couch, and almost falling asleep a few times, we sleepily made our way back to my room where we spent the rest of the night cuddling in our sleep.

"Ow, fuck," she exclaims, shaking her hands a few times. I grab my phone and turn the alarm off for her, "Thanks."

"No problem," I say, sleep lacing my tone. I close my eyes, considering sleeping for a few more minutes. I'm so excited for our trip, but I want to stay in Zahra's arms for just a little bit longer...

Zahra's arms come around me and bring me into a gentle hug. I smile softly, wrapping my arms around her. We wordlessly stay curled up in each other's embrace for a few minutes before we have to stand up.

I groan as Zahra untangles herself from me and stands up.

I stretch and grapple around to make sure I'm not going to knock anything over before I sit up and transfer into my chair.

"I'm going to get dressed in the bathroom, and then we can brush our teeth together when I'm done." Zahra hollers from the bathroom before the door closes.

I chuckle, of course she's already figured out a schedule. I roll down the hall and into my room, going through my closet quickly to find something to wear.

I swipe through my clothes quickly, trying to decide if I care more about looking cute or being more comfortable through the five and a half hour train ride to Chawton.

Comfortable, always comfortable. I shake my head, I don't know what I was thinking. The answer is always going to be comfortable. It's not like my outfits for the rest of the trip are going to be much different anyways.

I grab a pair of linen pants and a t-shirt, and use my bed to help me stand up to get dressed. I sit down in my chair as I hear Zahra open the bathroom door.

"I love your outfit!" I exclaim, as I turn the corner into the bathroom and see her. She's wearing a gorgeous purple tye-dye sundress with black strappy sandals. I can't help gaping at her, in a trance of her beauty.

"You look stunning, hon," Zahra compliments me back, making me roll my eyes.

"I'm not wearing anything out of the ordinary," I tell her, blushing from the compliment regardless.

"Doesn't mean you don't look good," she smirks at me.

I blush, and pick up my toothbrush to distract myself.

"Jacob? Olivia? Ethan? Theo? Rose?" Melody— err Professor Kingston since we're at a school sanctioned event—

goes through her class list, making sure that everyone who said they'd be coming on this trip would be here. "Ah, Clover, Zahra, I'm glad you're here."

"We're so excited to be here, Professor!" Zahra exclaims. She rolls her suitcase and mine up next to me.

"Once the train gets here, I'm going to have you two get on first so you aren't crowded, then the rest of the class will get on. Then we have the entire trip to rest." She sighs, like she's already ready for the break so she can rest.

We nod, and she continues through the roster, making sure everyone's here with everything they need.

Zahra starts rolling the suitcases towards where the train is going to be coming in, and I roll behind her with our purses hanging off my handlebars.

Zahra pushes my suitcases against the corner and leans on one of them. I roll up and park my chair next to the suitcases, my back against the wall. I'm paranoid about someone being able to come up behind me and snatch the purses off the back of my chair. That, and I want to be able to hold Zahra's hand while we wait.

I put my hand out and Zahra grabs it, bringing it up to kiss gently before resting our hands on my armrest.

My phone buzzes and I grab it quickly. A text message from Kaid pops up on my lock screen, and I quickly open it.

It's a message in a group chat with me, him, and Zahra, so I nudge her gently and put the phone between us. She looks at it and nods, grabbing her phone almost as quickly as I did.

Kaid left almost four days ago, and we've barely heard anything from him. We've both texted him multiple times, worried, and he's finally gotten back to us.

KAID:

I'm alive

ME:

Finally! What's been going on, are you alright?

ZAHRA:

Oh hey, good to hear you're alive

KAID:

Wow, thanks ZaZa. I love you too.

ZAHRA:

Haha. I know you do.

Now tell us everything, we've been worried.

KAID:

It's been a long few days. I'm sorry I haven't reached out.

I swear I've been meaning to, but the wifi here is so spotty, and my schedule has been packed.

ME:

How's Nonna Helen?

KAID:

She's struggling, but she's stable for now. There's been a lot of medicine changes and things that they're able to do now that I'm here to support, which is good. But a lot of them aren't as well known or are new which makes me worry.

ZAHRA:

I'm glad you're there with her, I'm glad she has someone with her now.

ME:

Me too

KAID:

Yeah, it's been an adjustment for sure, but I think I'll be getting more adjusted soon

ME:

Don't forget, we're always here for you if you need us

ZAHRA:

Yeah, for sure. Reach out anytime, I'm sure one of us will be awake. If not both of us.

KAID:

Thank you guys, you're the best

The apartment's paid off through the year by mommy dearest, so Clover you don't have to worry about that for now. Also, Zahra, if you want to take my room… you're more than welcome to. I'm going to be here for a while. I know you hate your roommates.

ME:

That's a great idea, Kaid!

ZAHRA:

Are you sure?

KAID:

Of course I am! I'm definitely going to be here through the rest of the school year, and if there's a room open that you could be in instead of with your shitty roommates, I want you to have it.

ME:

Yeah! You seriously hate your roommates, and if you lived with me you wouldn't have to pay for your dorm anymore.

ZAHRA:

Are you sure?

KAID:

100%

ME:

For sure

ZAHRA:

Ok, if you're sure…

KAID:

Please take it

ME:

Yes please

ZAHRA:

Fine, if you insist. I'll start the process once we get back from Chawton

KAID:

Oh shit! I forgot you're in Chawton. Sorry to bother you on your trip.

ZAHRA:

You aren't a bother, we were worried about you.

ME:

And besides, we haven't left for Chawton yet. We're waiting for the train.

KAID:

Oh, well I hope you have fun then. I want to hear everything.

ZAHRA:

Don't worry, we're going to take pictures of everything

ME:

And I was going to do a recap call with Adria and Caitlyn when we get home, if you want to join that.

KAID:

Let me know when you end up doing that, if I can fit it into my schedule I'll definitely join.

The train rattles up to the stop, and I put my phone back

in my pocket. I roll my chair up towards the train, waiting for the doors to open.

The class pushes up behind me and Zahra, and I flinch a little. There's nothing Zahra can do about it, so she puts a hand on my shoulder reassuringly.

"Make way!" I hear Melody holler faintly, "Quit crowding the front, it's not going to get you in faster!"

She pushes through the students and finally gets to the front.

"Ah," she sighs, dusting off her clothes. She smiles at me and Zahra, before making her way to the train conductor.

"Hello," the attendant says, smiling softly at Melody. "Tickets?"

She fumbles for her phone, almost dropping it, and pulling up the tickets. "I have twenty-three tickets, since this is for a class trip. One of my students is in a wheelchair, do you mind if I have xem and xeir girlfriend get on first?"

They turn and glance at me, before turning back to Melody. "Of course— did you say xe?— I actually have a wheelchair ramp I can have my colleagues set up, and a car that would work best for xem. That is, if you don't mind having xem wait until everyone else gets on."

"Oh," Melody says, excitedly, "Yes, Clover uses xe/xem pronouns, and that sounds perfect. I'll go ahead and talk to xem now, and we can start getting everyone on our cars."

She turns around and makes her way to us, quickly explaining what they said, even though we heard them nod and make our way back to the corner we were sitting in before.

The rest of the students make their way onto the train with their luggage, excitedly chattering. Melody stands and counts everyone off, triple checking her numbers.

"Hi," the same attendant who talked to Melody comes up

to me and Zahra, "My name is Darcy, and I use they/them pronouns. I'm going to be helping you throughout your journey to and from Chawton."

"Hi," I wave, "I'm Clover, xe/xem, and this is my girlfriend Zahra, she/her."

"My coworkers are setting up the ramp so you can get onto the train easier. Do you mind if I take your bags now? I figured I'd put them in your car now, I've upgraded you and your professor to a private car, so no worries there." Darcy blushes and looks at their hands at the mention of Melody, but quickly moves past it, as to not bring attention to themself. "The ramp can be steep, so I figured you could help Clover out instead of worrying about the bags."

Zahra nods, "Good idea." She rolls our bags over to Darcy, who grabs them, nods, and starts making their way to the train.

We watch the other employees put the ramp in place, continuously adjusting the ramp position with a confused look on their faces.

Darcy comes back, getting ready to escort us to our seat probably, and sees the ramp.

"What the hell?" they exclaim, "What is going on here? Why is the ramp not built correctly?"

The employees murmur amongst themselves, looking at each other and trying now to make eye contact with Darcy.

"Someone answer me!" they yell, annoyance obvious in their tone. "God, do I have to do everything myself? They taught this in training, why were none of you idiots paying attention?"

One of the employees turns to his friend and mutters, "I never thought we'd need to."

"Of course you'd need to build the ramp!" Darcy yells, throwing their hands up into the air, "Wheelchair users are people too! They need to use the train too! You know what? As newly appointed manager, I'm sending you all back to training. Obviously you all need it."

The employees groan and holler in annoyance. I can't hold back the smirk that forms on my face and it grows even more when I see Melody standing on the train watching with a soft smile on her face.

Darcy groans and starts fixing the ramp. Adjusting it, tilting their head and groaning even louder once they realized that everything was done wrong from the start. They quickly disassemble the ramp, and reassemble it correctly this time. They test it multiple times for stability before coming to get us.

"I'm so sorry about the wait, and for my incredibly inept employee," they roll their eyes, "Follow me to your seats."

33

───────

"They're so cute together!" I gush to Zahra, making sure my voice is quiet so Melody and Darcy can't hear. The two of them are currently sitting next to each other, chattering while sharing some of Melody's snacks.

"I know," Zahra whispers back, sneakily taking some pictures of the two of them, "I'm going to have to show these at the wedding."

I snort, "You're one for thinking ahead, obviously."

She smacks my shoulder gently, and I chuckle. "Stop staring at them, they'll still be there if you blink."

"Ha ha," she deadpans.

"I'm telling the truth, I swear! How about you watch this with me?"

"What are you watching?"

"Youtube vlogs, I downloaded them before we left so they wouldn't lag."

"Smart, smart," she nods, leaning closer to me. She wraps an arm around my shoulders and tucks me into her chest. I take out one of my earbuds and pass it to her before adjusting myself in her arms.

Darcy stands up and makes their way out of the car, and Zahra immediately perks up. I pause the video and sit up, giving Zahra the opportunity to stand up and make her way over to Melody.

I adjust myself in my chair, and watch their interaction. Unfortunately for me right now, we chose a spot in the car just far enough away that we wouldn't be able to hear any of their conversations.

I watch Zahra put her hands over her mouth and try to to hold back a smile. Melody's smiling so hard. She has a twinkle in her eye that I've never seen before. She's talking with her hands so excitedly.

Zahra looks over towards the door, spots something that makes her eyes go wide and says something quickly to Melody before rushing back to me.

"So?" I say immediately, but she shushes me. She holds her pointer finger up and watches the door. Once it opens, she turns to me and leans in to kiss my cheek.

Darcy walks by to us and makes their way back to Melody. I nod, realizing what Zahra was doing. I turn to her and kiss her cheek before repeating myself.

"Melody's definitely got a crush on Darcy, and I promised her that I'd talk to Darcy when she goes back to check on the class. She hasn't told me all the details yet, but the two of them definitely have similar interests and are getting along well."

"I figured things were going well since I saw your reaction, but that's so great." I exclaim happily, "Do you think they're going to keep in touch after the trip?"

"I don't know, but I'm sure that Melody's going to realize that she's going to want to talk to them during the trip and will probably get their number on the trip home."

"Imagine if they started dating, that'd be so cute."

"Oh, I really hope so. They're so cute together."

About twenty minutes later, Melody sighs and stands up to leave the train car. On the way out, she winks at Zahra, who nods.

Zahra waits a few seconds before standing up and making their way to Darcy, who had stood up to let Melody out.

"Do you know if she's single?" I hear Darcy ask Zahra. The question makes me slap my hand over my mouth in shock, and to hold back my surprised laugh. Maybe this will work out after all.

Zahra nods, "She is, and I'm pretty sure she's interested... if you get what I'm saying."

I raise an eyebrow, not sure how Melody's gonna feel that Zahra told Darcy, but thankfully it doesn't end badly.

"I think I'm gonna ask her out on a date," they say after taking a deep breath and pulling their confidence together.

"Yay!" Zahra exclaims excitedly, bringing her hands to her face. "Trust me, you're going to do great, and Melody's going to be so excited!"

"Thanks," Darcy says, blush spreading on their cheeks. They don't look down or try to cover it, like most people instinctively.

"Did you hear that?" Zahra asks excitedly as she comes back to sit next to me.

"Yes! I'm so happy for those two. I can't wait to see how this goes." Now that I know that they're both interested in each other and a relationship, I'm more excited to see how this goes. I didn't have my hopes up before I knew about their relationship, I didn't want to be disappointed if it didn't work out.

We glance over at Melody and Darcy just in time to see them hug each other excitedly Seems like everything's going to turn out good for these two.

"So I have you down for nine rooms, and an accessible room. The accessible room is on the first floor, the rest are on the third." The concierge explains to Melody as she passes her the keys. She thanks her and turns back to the class.

"Alright, everyone, let's congregate in this area," Melody hollers to the class, gesturing to the right. Everyone follows her directions and Zahra and I linger in the back.

"I have your keys here, and the student agreement is on these papers I've written up. I expect to have them signed and given back to me when I come around for bed checks. Speaking of: you can do whatever you want or need to in the hotel up until ten o'clock. Bedtime is ten. You have to be in your room by ten, I don't care what you do as long as you aren't disruptive. I'll be heading around at ten to check and make sure everyone's in their rooms and to tape the doors. Breakfast in the morning starts at eight, goes till ten. Bus leaves at nine thirty, make sure to have eaten beforehand since you won't have the chance to eat until about two. Alright I'm going to go ahead and start handing out keys, any questions, you all have my number." Melody explains quickly, making sure to hit every point and look at students who she thinks needs the information most when it comes along.

She starts naming students for them to grab their keys and paperwork, and we're the last ones remaining after two minutes. Melody smiles at us, and walks over.

"Soooooo?" Zahra asks, wiggling her eyebrows suggestively at Melody, making all of us laugh.

"We're going to go out," she tells us, a smile unconsciously forming on her face, "Not putting any labels on yet, but we have a date planned and each other's numbers. We've barely been separated and we've been texting so much."

"Yes!" I pump a fist, unable to hold back my reaction.

"I'm so happy for you two!" Zahra tells her excitedly, reaching out to squeeze her arm.

"Thanks you two, especially for helping us out— I know you were wing- manning both sides. Darcy probably doesn't know, but I know you two so well."

I laugh, "In our defense, they did ask us for help, we didn't just push on them."

"Ach, I know you well enough to not have to worry about that," she waves me off, making Zahra laugh.

If you don't mind, I want to go up to my room and rest before I have to check rooms. So here's your key, and the paper I mentioned. Feel free to text me if you have any questions." Melody explains, rolling the paper up and putting it in my wheelchair's cupholder with the key.

"Well *you* feel free to text us if there's any updates with Darcy." Darcy tells Melody with lightness flitting through her tone.

Melody laughs, "Don't worry, I will. I'll see you guys around ten."

I SWIPE the key to the room, Zahra right behind me with the luggage, and open the door. I was expecting the door to be heavy and in the way, but it's only a bit heavy and stays open. I wheel in as far as I can, giving Zahra space to come in behind me with the luggage.

"Woah," she exclaims, looking around the room with wide eyes. She tucks our suitcases in the corner of the room and starts opening every cabinet and closet she can find. I turn around in my chair and start exploring the room.

There's a king sized bed with a nightstand on either side, plenty of room for a wheelchair to fit on both sides comfortably without worry of running into a wall or furniture. There's a media console with a tv facing the bed, and a desk. A wardrobe on each side of the room. All the furniture is a light toned wood against the off white walls.

"I've never seen an accessible shower before!" Zahra's voice echoes around the room as she hollers from the bathroom. I wheel over towards the door to see. "Is that what it's called? I'm not sure."

"I've heard people call them 'roll in showers' but I think you can use either." I tell her, turning the corner to go into the bathroom.

The bathroom is painted in the same off-white tone as the other room, but instead of carpet, the floor is tiled. Like Zahra said, the shower is a roll in, with a bench to transfer onto, and the water nozzle lowered so I can reach it.

I turn to find Zahra leaning against the double sinks, feeling the towels displayed on the floating shelves. She turns around and smiles at me, leaning forward with a sly grin on her face.

"So," she murmurs, "What side of the bed do you want?"

34

———

"Chawton is most known for both the Chawton House— which was owned by Jane Austen's brother Edward— and Jane Austen's house where she wrote her six novels. She wrote in both of these houses, but primarily she wrote in her own home. She wrote, edited, revised, and published all of them herself." Melody explains over the bus loudspeaker to the class. Me and Zahra, although in the back, are probably the only ones paying attention.

She continues explaining fun facts and telling us about what we're going to see for the rest of the drive. We arrive at Jane Austen's house first, around ten fifteen. Everyone gets off the bus, and the driver helps me with the lift so I can get off the bus.

Jane Austen's house is a small cottage on the outskirts of Chawton. I mean, small is an understatement, it's actually quite large. At first glance, it looks small, but as you drive closer you see that it's actually much bigger than you think.

Melody goes and collects the tickets and passes them out. She explains, "We're going to start inside, and then we can explore the garden. We won't have much time here, but that's fine because these gardens are pretty small in comparison to Chawton House's. We'll have more time there, and that's where we're going to have our lunch— don't forget, lunch is on you!"

She leads us inside, and my brain has left me. We've barely gone anywhere, we're in a hallway that Melody keeps calling 'the vestibule'. It makes sense that all of these have fancy names, because this was from quite a long time ago. I still find it slightly funny that a hallway is called a vestibule, though.

She leads us first into the drawing room, which is barely big enough to fit all of us in at once. The room has all sorts of pieces of furniture that Jane used, like the piano she practiced on every morning as well as her writing desk. Across the house are displays with her clothing.

Melody leads us through the rest of the main floor of the house, and every room is more fascinating than the last. It's so interesting to me to see how Jane Austen lived and wrote in comparison to how we live and write now.

The more we tour, the more I can't stop thinking about how I'm in the same room that Jane Austen was in. The fact that I'm sitting in her house, learning about her blows my mind.

"Alright so we're going to go ahead and head upstairs now," Melody tells the class, motioning for them to start heading up the stairs. We had talked before about me separating from the group and going through the virtual tour with one of the guides so I can still see and learn everything. I'm still slightly disappointed that I can't go upstairs, but there's nothing I can do about it.

"Aren't you going to go upstairs with the class?" I ask Zahra, noticing she's still standing beside me.

"I'm staying with you," she tells me, "I don't need to go upstairs, I'd rather go with you."

"Are you sure?" I ask, guilt seeping through my body. I don't want her to miss out on this like I am, especially since it's her mom's dream.

"Yeah, I'm sure. Honestly I prefer the virtual tour, because mom and I used to sit on the couch and do it together. It reminds me of her."

Her words bring a smile to my face, making me feel a bit better. I grab her hand and squeeze it once, turning to smile at her. She smiles back at me, giving my hand a squeeze too.

"Hello!" A cheery voice says from behind us. I turn my head to see, and can't, shaking my head as I turn my chair to face them as Zahra says 'Hi!".

"My name is Emma, and I'm going to be taking you through your virtual tour."

"It's nice to meet you," I tell her, "Thanks for going through this with us."

"It's not a problem at all! I love going through these tours, especially when I don't have to be standing and walking while doing it." She laughs and we can't resist laughing with her. "It's a nice day out, and I was thinking we could do our tour in the gardens."

"That sounds nice," Zahra says, and I nod in agreement. Emma smiles and starts guiding us towards the gardens, her tote bag with the house on it shifting slightly with every step she takes.

Once we get to the gardens, Emma finds an empty table and sits down. Zahra sits down across from her and I park my chair at the edge of the table in-between the two of them. Emma sets up her laptop in the middle of the table, making sure we can all see it before she starts her presentation.

She finishes her virtual tour moments before Melody and our classmates come into the gardens.

"You have fifteen minutes to explore the gardens and/or head back inside- be back on the bus at one o'clock!" she hollers as the class scatters in all directions.

"Thank you so much," I say turning back to Emma, "You did the tour so well, it felt like I was actually there, so thank you."

"That's so sweet," Emma gushes, holding a hand to her heart. "I'm so glad I was able to do your tour for you and make it immersive. I still feel really bad you weren't able to actually go upstairs, and there's nothing I can really do other than this, but I hope you'll accept this coupon to the gift shop."

She hands me a slip of paper that declares that it's worth 30% off your purchase at the Austen House Gift Shop. I smile, accepting it. I was already planning on going to the store, having a coupon is just a bonus.

"Thank you," I tell her.

"No, thank you," she tells me. "I wrote my number on the back if you ever have any questions. Have a good day."

We wave at her as she walks back towards the house.

ZAHRA and I make our way to the gift shop inside. I've been saving since I saw this trip in the syllabus for this gift shop in particular. The first time at Jane Austen's house is kind of a big deal to me, and I will be making my way back if I'm able to in the future.

The gift shop itself is small, but packed to the brim with items. Everything is organized meticulously, and I'm immediately overwhelmed in the best way possible. Zahra immediately slinks towards the book section to the left, and I start to the right, deciding to look at everything before deciding what to buy.

That plan quickly goes awry as I find the 'Chawton Cottage' collection that was made for Jane Austen's 250th birthday. My eyes go wide at the light blue and gold designs, and the variety of items available.

I immediately grab the trinket tray when I see there's only one available. I lay it on my lap gently as I make my way around the gift shop. I ignore the clothes, most of them being dresses based on Austen characters. I don't like wearing dresses. The shirts for the house aren't my favorite design, I know I can find better elsewhere.

I finally find the display for the character series, with artwork commissioned by the House staff just for this line and Austen products. There's a variety of items, but I ultimately decide on a mug with Jane and her characters on it. I do love having tea every now and then, and I didn't bring mugs with me when I moved.

As I continue through the little shop, my pile grows and grows. Stationery, books, and post cards are stacked on my mug and trinket tray. I check out before I can do another lap and spend even more money.

Zahra and I get back outside to the garden where we were sitting before.

"I wanna see what you got!" I exclaim excitedly, seeing a small bag I didn't notice before tucked under her arm. She smiles at me, putting the bag on the table in front of me.

"Firstly, I got this mug from the Chawton collection, I think that's what it's called at least. The blue and gold got me, it's just so pretty." She unwraps the mug and shows me a bit of the gorgeous mug. I laugh, reaching into my bag and unwrapping a little bit of the trinket tray I bought from the same collection.

"I also bought these cookies based on Marianne, with one of the wallpaper designs. I figured they'd be good with tea, and I liked the container," she shrugs, opening it and showing me the inside. "Want one?"

I shrug, "Why not." Zahra passes me the container and I unwrap the cookies from the plastic. I pass one to her and grab another for myself. I take a bite, "Hmm, they aren't bad actually."

"I like them," she shrugs, grabbing another. Once she finishes chewing, she reaches into her bag again and pulls out a copy of *Sense and Sensibility*.

"Wow, that's a gorgeous edition," I exclaim, eyes going wide as I look at the book closer. It has a dark teal cover with flowers and leaves on it, they look embroidered. The title and detailing are gold, and as she shifts the book I notice the pages are gold as well.

"Yeah," Zahra says, a twinge of sadness in her voice as she looks at it closer. "I feel like this is what mom would've liked, and frankly she wouldn't have gotten it for herself. So I decided to splurge on it for her, and add it to my collection."

I smile at her, putting my hand over hers in silent solidarity as Zahra gets lost in her thoughts for a few seconds. She knocks herself out of it, wipes a single tear from her eye, and puts everything back into her bag.

"So," she says, "I wanna change the subject. What'd you get?"

I smile at her, changing the subject like she requested.

"First, I got this notebook," I pull out a notebook with one of the wallpaper designs on it. "I got something that matches, but it's farther down..."

"Then I got the wallpaper editions of <u>Sense</u> and *Sensibility* — how could I not?— and *Emma*. I felt it was fitting to get *Emma*." I shrug, and Zahra laughs.

"If you hadn't, I would've gone back and gotten a copy for you," she tells me.

I laugh before continuing. "I got this mug with Jane and her characters— the sign in the shop said this art is exclusive to the Austen house. It was commissioned for the house and merch."

"Honestly it's kind of weird to think that a house has merch," Zahra muses, making me groan.

"I never thought of it that way, and now I'm going into an existential crisis." I put my head in my hands, trying to make sense of it. I ultimately don't come to any conclusions. I force the thoughts from my head, knowing I won't stop unless I do, and move on.

"Ah," I pull a box out, flipping it around trying to find a picture so I don't have to unbox it. "I got the green wallpaper design on the quill as well, I figured it'd be nice desk decor. Also I dabble in calligraphy sometimes."

"Ooh! That's really cool— I missed that section in the store."

"They had so many things with the wallpapers on it— things I didn't think would work, but do work exceptionally well.

"Ooh, that's cool."

I nod. "Last but certainly not least for me, I got this pack of postcards with the house on it. It just felt... right."

Zahra nods, "I understand," she says softly.

"Then I got this pack of postcards with each of Jane's books and details about each of them. I figured I'd give this to Melody at the end of the trip, as a little 'thank you' for all she's done for me this semester."

"I like that idea," Zahra tells me.

I put my things away, quickly realizing that we only have a few minutes left before we have to go back to the bus. There was only one more thing I wanted to do before we left, and there's just enough time to do it.

I pull my new copy of *Emma* out of my bag and open it. Zahra smiles gently at me before going back to her phone. I flip to the first page and start to read Jane Austen's work in her garden.

35

W e took the bus to Chawton House, which isn't really far from Austen House. On the ride, I put my purchases into my tote bag, keeping the books I bought on me so I can read in the gardens. Melody said we'd have much more free time to explore and get some food, so I definitely want to take some down time to rest my body and do some reading.

We get to the Chawton House, and as I get lowered off the bus, I lose my breath seeing the gardens and rolling hills that seem to go on forever.

"Did you see the gardens?" I ask Zahra excitedly as she puts her bag on the back of my chair and prepares to push me towards the house.

"No, I wasn't so high up," she explains.

"Oh, you're going to *love* it!" I tell her, "There are so many pretty flowers and places to sit and rest, and they go on forever!"

"They are!" Melody says from behind us, obviously hearing me talk about the gardens. "We have our tour first, but then we'll have about two hours to eat and explore! This is one of my favorite spots of the trip, it's so soothing and relaxing."

"That makes me even more excited!"

We make our way into the house and meet our tour guide, a lanky boy who seems shy as he makes small talk with Melody. Once he starts touring, though, his shyness goes away. He's animated, and passionate as he talks about the house's history and I can't stop smiling.

Like the Austen House, there are definitely some parts I can't access, but I don't mind. Being in my chair for the entire day, and having a mediocre night of sleep last night has made me so tired and sore. I'll gladly sit in the gardens and watch a virtual tour of the upstairs like we did before.

We venture through the first floor of the house, our tour guide pointing out Jane Austen's favorite places to sit, famous paintings and artwork hung throughout. The lavishness of this house and grounds that Edward inherited from distant relatives is kind of insane to think about. I mean, he inherited this ginormous house, and the grounds, *and* the Austen house where his sisters and parents lived.

"We're going to make our way upstairs now," I hear our guide say as he goes into a stairway that is definitely too narrow for me even if I was standing, let alone my wheelchair.

"Hey," Zahra pulls my chair to the side where there's a bench and sits next to me. "I was checking the site for the virtual visits, and it's down. I know you told Melody you'd do things on your own, but I was wondering if you wanted me to go on the rest of the tour and either film or FaceTime you so you can see it?"

"You would do that?" I ask, eyes wide in surprise.

"Of course," she shrugs, "I just feel bad leaving you alone."

"No, seriously, I could use the alone time— no offense—

and just want to rest in the gardens for a while before getting food."

"Great. I'll FaceTime you in a second and make my way to the front of the tour group so you can hear. Feel free to just mute, watch, and disassociate for a while."

"Thank you," I tell her, still in shock and awe.

"Of course," she repeats. She bends down to kiss my temple and I pull her into a kiss. "I'll see you in about an hour, alright?"

THE GARDENS at Chawton House are absolutely stunning and the silence is even more stunning. It's not completely silent, there are kids running around and having fun, and other visitors meandering around the grounds, but I found myself a little corner where I can watch people and rest without it being super loud. Compared to my class' boisterous nature, this is a breath of fresh air— literally.

My phone starts vibrating and I pull it out, accepting the call from Zahra as I put my trusty headphones on. These have been with me for years, and are my equivalent of a comfort water bottle. I prop my phone up against my water bottle, and listen to the tour with the sounds of the gardens surrounding me.

Zahra ends the call once the tour ends, and I put on the soundtrack of my favorite *Sense and Sensibility* adaptation. I pull out the book I brought and open it up, and let myself relax as I get lost in a story I could be lost in forever.

I look up as Zahra walks up to me, bags in hand. I smile at her, closing my book and putting it down, not bothering with a bookmark since I've read it a million times.

"How was the rest of the tour?" I ask her. She hung up

after the tour technically ended, but there was probably more outside and on the way to the gardens.

"The guide didn't say much more, so you weren't missing much. But I did stop at the gift shop on the way here, and I got you some things."

"What? You didn't have to do that!"

"I felt bad that you had to sit out so much of today, that and I wanted to."

"Well, I needed the down time— the tour was perfectly good from here."

"Just open the package," she tells me, pushing the bag across the table at me and sitting down next to me.

"Fine," I roll my eyes and grab the bag. I reach in and feel a book, and decide to look at that last. I feel two small things and pull them out.

The first is a circle sticker with a beautiful watercolor illustration of the house on it.

"This is beautiful," I tell her, my finger brushing over the sticker and feeling the texture. It's raised and slightly bumpy like watercolor paper is. Zahra smiles and grabs another from her purse, holding it up with a chuckle.

"I think I'm going to put this on my laptop," she explains, brushing her hand over it like I did. "For my mom, but also to remember this amazing trip."

"I love that," I tell her, smiling. I reach into the bag and grab the next thing. A print with the expanded version of the art from the sticker. "Wow, the detail on this is even more than I could've imagined."

"I knew you'd say that!" Zahra laughs, "I thought you'd like the print version to hang above your desk, to inspire you."

There is, in fact, an empty spot on the wall above my desk that would be perfect for this print. I nod excitedly, imagining how much better that wall's going to look once the print is there.

I pull the book out and gasp as I read the title: '*Jane and Me: My Austen Heritage*' by Caroline Jane Knight (Jane Austen's fifth great niece).

"I didn't know a book like this existed," I say breathlessly, immediately flipping it over and flipping through the pages.

"Yeah," Zahra says excitedly. "It's exclusive to Chawton House— the minute I saw it, I knew you needed it. She grew up here!"

"No way!" I exclaim, "That's so cool!"

"Obviously in a different wing than we toured, but it's still so cool."

"Yeah!" I exclaim, still in awe and flipping through the pages. "Thank you, babe."

"Of course," she says immediately. I lean over and kiss her once before tucking my arms around her back into a big hug. She tucks her head into the crease of my shoulder and wraps her arms around me.

I take a deep exhale as she kisses my neck gently once. We stay in each other's arms for almost a minute, taking in all the comfort we need from each other and reveling in the silence.

"I passed the cafe on the way here," Zahra tells me as the two of us meander around the gardens slowly. "We have about an hour and fifteen minutes, I think?"

"Let's get food now," I suggest, thinking that it'll give my body more time to digest before getting back on the bus. And hopefully there won't be a ton of our classmates eating right now.

Zahra nods, and gestures in the direction of the cafe.

"I thought-?" I gesture in the other direction, confused. Zahra interrupts, "This way's faster, and more scenic and private."

"You know me too well," I shake my head, smiling at her. She smiles back, bending down to peck my lips once, like she couldn't resist.

I turn the corner into the little alleyway that she pointed at, and immediately gasp. The path is slim, a bit wider than a usual sidewalk, but definitely not able to have two way traffic. There's walls covered in greenery on either side, going at least ten feet up, making the space intimate and secluded.

I wheel through slowly, taking my time to look at every flower and vine on the wall. My hand reaches out to gently brush the petals of a daisy that's right at my eye level. I cup the flower in my palm, smiling at the feeling of the flower. I've never been into botany, but I think I might need to try some-time, because these flowers are making me so happy and I'd love to have some in the apartment.

"And, there's my new profile picture for you," I hear Zahra mutter to herself. I jump, dropping the flower. I forgot she was there, and as I turn around, she's swiping through her camera roll.

"Have you been taking pictures this whole time?"

"Yes," she shrugs, nonchalantly.

"I-uh... I..."

"You're pretty and I need a contact picture for you. A new lock screen wouldn't hurt."

"Zahra!"

"Trust me, you look beautiful. You aren't going to convince me to delete these, I've already sent them to the group chat."

My phone buzzes at that very second, proving her point

even more. I groan, and shake my head, turning back to the greenery and making my way down the alleyway quicker than before.

I get to the end and turn around, deciding to take pictures of Zahra as well. I pull my phone out, ignoring the notifications, and open my camera.

Zahra crouches down to look at a flower closer and I smile at her. She grasps the buttercup in her hand gently, bringing it up to her nose to sniff. My thumb hits the shutter button basically every time she moves, unable to stop myself from capturing these beautiful moments for me to look back on for eternity.

She sees me and smirks, knowing exactly what I'm doing. I shrug, "We're even."

She laughs, making her way back to me. She gently moves my chair so my back is to the wall of flowers and she matches the position, holding her phone up and taking a few selfies.

She kisses my cheek, and my smile grows even more. I turn my head to meet hers, meeting her lips with mine.

The kiss is sweet and chaste, both of us feeling shy to kiss in public even if we're in a hidden alleyway. I kiss her longer, making sure she has the chance to get that picture. I realize we don't have many pictures together, and I want to change that from now on.

"I changed my mind," she says slightly as she pulls back from our kiss, "I think I want one of those to be my lock screen."

"I want them too," I tell her, "We don't take enough pictures together."

"Well, I'm going to change that from now on," she tells me, "I put those in the group chat, don't worry your pretty little head about that."

At her words, she kisses the top of my head, smiling into it. She grabs the back of my chair, tapping the handlebars twice, silently asking if she can push. Once I nod, and move my hands off the wheels, she starts pushing me towards the cafe.

36

———

The Chawton House cafe is a cute bodega-style building and even though the building is old, they still added a ramp and a button to open the door. I can't help but smile, even though the building is historical they still made the decision to add these modifications so everyone can go in.

Zahra pushes me up the ramp, and opens the door for me. I lean forward, taking extra care to not run over her toes as I push my wheels over the curb. Thankfully the inside of the cafe is spacious, so I have space to get all the way in without hitting anyone or anything.

Zahra tucks in behind me and closes the door as I make my way up to the line, stopping behind the last person about three people behind the register. I look up at the menu, skimming through it, trying to decide what I want to eat. Zahra hugs me from behind, arms wrapping around my chest and head resting on top of mine as she reads the menu as well. She's been getting more and more touchy as we've been getting closer, and I love it so much.

"What can I get for you?" the clerk asks, notepad at the ready. I look at the menu again, quickly deciding between two things. "Can I get the brie and bacon toastie, a water, and a fruit scone?" She nods, writing down the order and ringing me up. I tap my card and after it processes, I make my way to the end of the bar. I turn towards the other side of the cafe, looking at the available tables and trying to decide which one to sit at.

I make my way to the far wall, it's harder to get to now, but in the long run I know that people will run into me less. I move a chair and replace it with my wheelchair, locking my wheels so they don't move, and start people watching.

Like I had hoped, most of the tables and chairs were empty, the few only occupied with other visitors. I fidget with my phone as I wait for Zahra.

"Alright," I hear Zahra say, coming up to my side and starting to place plates on the table. There are two drinks, a bowl and three plates. Hopefully it's good, because we've got a lot of food between the two of us.

"This one's yours, I think," she passes me a plate with my toastie on it. She passes me my bottled water and a small plate with my scone. Everything's fresh and steaming. It all smells delicious.

"What'd you get?" I ask, leaning forward to see her plates too. I pick up my sandwich to take a bite, but it's too hot and I burn the tips of my fingers slightly.

"I got the bacon, lettuce, and tomato sandwich. I also got the loaded hot chocolate and salted caramel ice cream. I'm willing to share if you are, I want to try everything."

"Ooh yeah!" I exclaim. I grab a spoon and hold it over Zahra's ice cream in a silent question. She nods and I take a small bite, immediately moaning as the cold dessert hits my lips. The ice cream is the perfect combination of sweet and salty, and I immediately love it.

Zahra immediately takes a bite of the ice cream, and reacts similarly to me. We pass the spoon back and forth, eating all the ice cream as the rest of our meals cool down to an appropriate eating temperature.

"Hey, isn't that Melody?" I ask, gesturing to the cafe entrance. I take the last bite of my toastie, savoring the delicious brie and bacon flavor exploding in my mouth,

"Oh, I think it is!" Zahra says, leaning forward. I lean forward too, wondering what's got her so interested. Melody's texting someone, I realize, and she has a small smile on her face. "I hope she's texting Darcy."

"Me too!" I exclaim, remembering the sweet person from the train. "They really are perfect together."

"They really are," she sighs happily, putting her chin in her hands. "I'm so happy for her, Melody really deserves someone like Darcy after all she's been through."

"Yeah," I say softly. I don't know much about Melody's past, but based on the hints she's thrown our way, it was pretty hard. "She deserves a love like ours."

Zahra looks up at me, eyes wide. "Yeah," she says softly, "She does."

Melody orders her food, and looks around the sitting area as she waits. She sees us, and a smile forms on her face. We both gesture for her to come sit with us, knowing that she wouldn't if we didn't make it obvious we wanted her there.

She nods at us, going back to her phone responding to something that (hopefully) Darcy sent. She grabs her food, and makes her way over to us, her smile growing as she gets closer.

"How are the gardens for you two?" she asks, taking the chair I moved earlier to make space for my wheelchair.

"Good," I smile, going along with her original conversation. It's only a matter of time before Zahra changes it to Darcy, though. "We had a little photoshoot, and Zahra got me a few presents."

"Oh that's so sweet!" Melody exclaims, "If you don't mind me asking, what'd she get you?"

"I don't mind you asking," Zahra answers, waving her off, "I figured you'd be interested in them too."

Melody and I laugh, knowing she's right. I pull the bag off the back of my chair and pass it to Melody to look through.

"Wait, how have I never seen this before?" she exclaims, pulling the book out.

"Right?!" I almost yell in excitement. I blink and lower my tone, "I had no idea it existed, it looks so good!"

"I think I might need to go back to the gift shop and get it for myself. I never went in there before, worried that I'd spend a lot. I might have to risk it today."

"Don't worry," Zahra jokes, "This store is smaller than the last one, you'll only spend a small fortune in comparison to a regular fortune."

I can't hold back my laugh at that. Zahra's absolutely right about that, I had to hold back a *lot* in the last gift shop. I didn't go to this one, but I know it probably would've been about the same.

"Oh!" I exclaim, remembering the gift I got for Melody. "I got you something at the Austen House."

"Me?" Melody points to herself, confusion and excitement littering her expression.

"Yeah!"

"Thank you," she says shyly, a blush forming over her cheeks.

"Of course!" I exclaim. She's done so much for me, especially over this semester. I didn't want to let that go unsaid. I reach into my bag and grab the pack of postcards I picked out, passing them to Melody.

"Oh these are so cool!" she exclaims excitedly as she opens the packaging and flips through them giddily. I smile at her, glad that she loves the gift as much as I thought she would. "I'm going to have to implement these into my presentations next semester, and they'll make such cool wall decor in my office!"

"That's what I was thinking too!" I say delightedly. I hear Zahra chuckle at our excitement over postcards, but I ignore her for the time being.

"Thank you," Melody repeats, reaching over and bringing me into a side hug. I happily reciprocate.

"No, thank *you*." I tell her, "You've made this semester so seamless for me and have been a great friend and resource for me."

"I hope we can stay in touch after this semester."

"I'm a classics major, specifically studying Austen. I'm sure I'll be around," I deadpan, making Zahra and Melody guffaw.

"Then you're more than welcome to hang out in my classroom or office if you need somewhere to rest between classes or need somewhere to work." Melody offers, "And I'll be sure to send you my teacher's assistant applications once they come in. Usually there's a long process, but I have the power to waive that for you."

"You don't have to do that," I exclaim, waving my hands, "I'll gladly go through the regular channels, I want to do this!"

"Trust me, you don't want to do the paperwork."

"Oh, it's a lot of paperwork? Yeah, never mind, I'll take your offer, thank you." I say, laughing.

"I thought that's what you'd say." She laughs.

"So," Zahra says, changing the topic as I thought she'd inevitably do. "Were you texting Darcy just now? How're you two doing together?"

Melody blushes a super deep red and hides her face in her hands. Zahra and I chuckle, understanding how she's feeling.

"Yeah, we've been texting nonstop since we got off the train. Planning our date, planning dates for the future, how we're going to do the long distance thing…"

"I mean, it's not really long distance, right?" I ask.

"Darcy lives in Newcastle as well, but with their work they're sent to wherever for a few days to a week at a time."

"Oh that makes sense," I nod, "Sorry, continue."

She laughs, "That's pretty much it, honestly. It's been a lot of getting to know each other and being flirty."

"Yes!" Zahra exclaims excitedly, "I'm so happy that you two are going to be together."

"Me too," I add. "I can't believe you two are getting together, it's going to be so good for you."

"I hope they continue to visit you at work sometime," Zahra says, "Imagine how cute it'd be if they showed up with coffee and pastries for you between classes."

Melody smiles and looks at her phone. "I'm sure they would, honestly, but their schedule is just so busy they can barely get coffee and pastries for themselves at a decent coffee shop. Let alone getting coffee and pastries for me. They're always complaining about how shit the coffee and pastries they get from work are."

"You should go and surprise them at work sometime with good coffee and pastries." I suggest using Zahra's idea and flipping it on the head.

"Ooh, I'll definitely have to consider that," she says, switching apps and typing the suggestion down. "I've had a running list of dates, gifts, and surprises I think Darcy would like ever since we've started talking."

Zahra and I both swoon as Melody thinks of something else and adds it to the list.

37

———

The last two days of our trip were free days, and Zahra and I opted to stay at the hotel and rest. I brought my kindle and spent my days reading by the pool. After I listened to Caitlyn's book in the hospital, I've been in the mood to read more from her and Adria, so I've got most of them downloaded. They're the perfect poolside reads to relax with while everyone else was out exploring Chawton.

Zahra, being the overachiever she is, spent her days by my side working on the paper Melody assigned for after the trip. There's nothing saying you can't write it on the actual trip, but I'm pretty sure it's frowned upon. I needed the rest anyway.

Now we're waiting for the train back to Newcastle, our luggage surrounding us.

"Is this giving you deja vu, or just me?" I ask Zahra, sarcasm laced in my tone.

She huffs a dry laugh and responds in the same tone as me, "No, no, I've never been at a train station surrounded by luggage waiting for Darcy."

I can't resist laughing at that, and Zahra joins me. We laugh for almost a full minute, losing our breath quickly, but not stopping. I calm down finally, but when I look up at Zahra it just sets me off again, which sets her off again. It's a brutal cycle, but one I wouldn't want to be stuck in with anyone else.

"All aboard!" A conductor— not Darcy, Zahra and I immediately notice— yells from the open train doors. He stands off to the side and holds the door open for the rambunctious class to go through.

Zahra and I stay back, knowing the routine by now. We definitely don't want to be stuck in front of, or surrounded by the class, so we keep our distance. We don't bother moving towards the train until Melody is the only person remaining.

Melody stands by the conductor, helping Zahra with our luggage and with my chair. She grabs one of the suitcases from Zahra, and guides us to our car.

"Melody," Darcy says softly, a fond look on their face as she enters the train car.

"Darcy," Melody responds in the same fond tone, almost dropping my suitcase as she goes to give it back to Zahra. She just takes it, silently moving them to the other side of the car to give them privacy. I follow.

Zahra puts our suitcases in the over-seat storage, before sitting down next to me. Darcy prepared a seat for me and my chair before we got here, and I'm so thankful for them. I'm so glad I don't have to ask for myself for once. I'd do it a million times, but it's so nice for someone to put me first for once. Thinking of me and my needs, because even though I'm in a wheelchair and have different needs than most other people, I still am a person with feelings.

I transfer into the train seat after locking my wheelchair. Zahra immediately puts the divider between us away, and scoots over to wrap an arm around me. I cuddle into her, immediately relaxing into her embrace and feeling all my feelings slip away. It feels like I'm high, in the best possible way.

She kisses the side of my forehead as she brings me closer. I nuzzle into her side, and I feel her smile against my forehead. She silently passes me an earbud as she sets her phone up in front of us to watch *New Girl*. I put the earbud in, and let myself get lost in the world of Jess, Nick, Schmidt, and Winston for a few hours.

"CANDY?" Melody asks, breaking me out of my daze. I look up, and she's holding out a plastic bag full of fun sized candies. "Don't tell the rest of the class," she adds quickly.

"Where'd that even come from?" Zahra asks, grabbing a pack of Skittles. "I thought you said you wouldn't provide any snacks for the class?"

"Well these didn't come from me," she admits. "Darcy bought them for me. I told them in passing that I prefer fun size candy, especially on long trips. They surprised me with this just now, and I figured you guys would like some."

"Thank you," I say, grabbing a two pack of starbursts and unwrap it: orange and yellow. I smile as I unwrap the orange one, those have always been my favorites. "So you two are talking more?"

"Yeah, we're going on a date to a boba shop next week, and going to see one of their favorite movies in theaters." Melody tells us, a blush forming on her face, but not letting it show.

"That's sweet," I swoon.

"Who chose?" Zahra asks.

"We both did. I found the screening for the movie after

they mentioned it was their favorite. Then they suggested the boba shop so we could hang out and actually talk afterwards."

"That's so sweet," I tell her, holding my hand to my chest. "I need to plan a date for us, actually." I look over at Zahra, raising an eyebrow at her.

"Don't worry about it," she says, "I love planning our dates, and you don't need to feel like you owe me just because you struggle to plan them."

"But I feel bad," I say, fiddling with my fingers.

"Don't," Both Melody and Zahra say at the same time. Zahra motions for Melody to go first, and she nods.

"It took me a while to gain my confidence," Melody tells me, looking down at her hands as she fidgets with the plastic bag she's holding. "Especially being trans, my self confidence was at an all-time low. As I got to know myself better, my confidence grew. But especially as I started dating again, I struggled finding people who understood me... but eventually I found my people and felt comfortable and confident enough to plan something they'd love. But that takes time, so it's okay that you aren't ready now. You'll get there in time."

She sniffles, looking up at the ceiling for a second before looking back at us. There's water in her eyes, but she doesn't move to wipe it, and I don't point it out. Hearing more about Melody's past was hard for us, but it definitely made me feel better.

"Well, what I was going to say isn't nearly as... umm... emotional, but that's alright." Zahra says after an awkward silence and eye contact. "I was going to say; you don't need to plan dates if you aren't ready. If you want to start, I'd love to plan some with you as you become more confident. We can get through this together."

I turn to face her, and I can't resist smiling. She pecks my lips gently, and I can taste the sweet sickly flavor of her Skittles and my Starbursts mixing. I kiss her back, conveying all the feelings I can't say into the kiss. I know she understands what I'm saying.

Melody softly clears her throat and I jump back from the kiss, immediately apologizing over and over again.

"Stop apologizing," Melody says, laughing softly, "I understand what it's like to be in your position, trust me, Me and Darcy are definitely in the same stage right now."

Zahra and I both laugh, and I avoid eye contact with either of them.

38

———————

Zahra spent the last few days in her dorm room, and I miss living with someone else. Yes, living alone is nice, but there's just something about living with your best friend that makes the experience so much better and easier, especially as a disabled person.

She's spent the last few days packing and terminating her housing contract, as I've gotten things set up for her here. I've moved most of Kaid's things into boxes for now, things that Zahra won't be needing while she's living here. I know Kaid's probably going to come back and pick those up so they're all organized and ready for him whenever that day comes.

A knock sounds, and I laugh as I go check the peephole and open it for Zahra. "You're living here now, you don't need to knock. Hell, you didn't need to knock in the first place, you've had a key for months." I remember her telling me that Kaid gave her a spare key to use when I was in the hospital, so she could come and grab us necessities without having to go to the hospital first.

She laughs, "True, but the keys are pretty far in my pockets."

Her hands are full, and I quickly grab what I can stack on my lap before scooting back and letting Zahra come in with a big cart full of those IKEA bags and luggage.

"Besides," she tells me, shrugging, "I wanted to do it all in one trip."

"You got everything here in one trip?" My eyes widen as I look at the overflowing cart, "Impressive."

"Right?"

I take the boxes off my lap and put them on the kitchen island, not sure where they're supposed to go just yet. I read the labels "toiletries" and "nightstand", nodding as I grab the top box and make my way to the bathroom.

"Feel free to start unloading!" I holler over my shoulder as I get into the hallway. "When you need a break, I have some water bottles chilling in the fridge, and your favorite snicker-doodle cookies!"

"You're the best, you know that?"

"I try," I singsong.

A few moments later, I hear a beep before music starts playing loudly throughout the apartment. I laugh as Zahra hollers "This is what I need!" over the music.

I unload the first box, not super particular with where I'm putting things, I know Zahra will fix it to her liking later anyways. I open the bathroom door, about to go out into the hallway when Zahra's massive cart comes barreling through. I can't resist a laugh, it's a good thing I waited a split second before going out there.

"Sorry babe," she says, noticing me. She leans down and pecks my lips. I can't resist grabbing her by the back of the neck and deepening the kiss.

"I'm so happy you're here," I tell her against her lips.

"I'm so happy I'm here too. Especially with you."

"WE SHOULD GO ON A DATE," Zahra suggests a few weeks later as we're watching *New Girl* on the couch.

"We've been hanging out almost nonstop since you moved in," I point out.

"Yeah, but we've barely left the house together."

"We went to the grocery store a few times."

"The grocery store doesn't count as a date," she raises an eyebrow at me and I nod.

"Fine, fine, you're right. Let's go on a date. What do you have in mind?"

"I have the perfect idea..."

"A FIELD?" I ask, confused, as Zahra shifts her car into park. Zahra wouldn't let me help her plan the date, no matter how much I bugged her. Hell, she wouldn't even tell me any details. It seemed like whatever she was planning was important to her. So as much as I'm confused about why we're in a field, I'm going to go in with an open mind and respect what Zahra's going to share.

"A field," she nods, not saying more. I shake my head at her words, and get out of the car. I shakily walk to the trunk, where my chair is already waiting for me.

By the time I get there, Zahra's already pulled it out of the truck and is halfway through putting it together. She quickly finishes, putting the cushion on with a flourish before helping me sit.

"Thanks," I say softly, adjusting my grip on the wheels.

"Of course," Zahra replies, kissing my cheek.

"Are you going to tell us why we're going to a field now?" I ask her, as we start making our way into the field.

"Almost."

We continue going through the field, slower than we would usually because of the grass. We keep going, feeling like there's no end, but eventually Zahra stops us next to a bench.

"Here we are," she says, holding her arms out. She sits on the bench, and motions for me to transfer and sit next to her.

I move to lock my chair, but shrug, no bothering since I know it'll stay stuck in the grass. I transfer onto the bench seamlessly, Zahra parked the chair at the perfect angle for me to do so.

"So," I say, resting my arm on top of the bench, gently draping it over Zahra's shoulder. I bring her closer to me and ask, "Wanna tell me why you drug my wheelchair through a field?" I say it lightly, but know there's something about this field she needs to get to slowly.

"It's one of my favorite places," she says softly, bending down and grabbing some grass from the field. As she brings them up, my breath hitches as I realize it's not grass. They're four leaf clovers. She's found a field of four leaf clovers.

"I used to come here all the time and just sit with my thoughts," she continues, "Especially after Mom died, I spent all my days on this bench staring into the distance. I know it doesn't look like much, but it means the world to me."

"It's beautiful," I tell her truthfully, "I bet the sunrises and sunsets are stunning over those hills," I motion towards the hills in the distance.

"I've seen many," she says plainly. I turn to face her, but don't say anything, letting her wrangle her thoughts before continuing. "Y'know, my mom and I used to come out here? It was her spot first, but when I was struggling in school she'd bring me out here. Then it became *our* place. We'd come together, say nothing, and just stare in the distance. We'd come out feeling lighter every time."

She bends down to grab more four leaf clovers to fidget with.

"I don't think my dad knew about it," she chuckles, as if recalling a memory. "I don't know what my mom would tell him— or even if— he asked where we were going, but there was a point after her death where he couldn't find me. He called the police after three days."

She laughs wryly, and I bring her closer in our side hug. I know she struggled with mourning after her mom's death, but I didn't realize it was *that* bad. Sitting on this bench for three days straight, with no food or water.

"Obviously my dad made me go to therapy after that, and it did help somewhat... but this is my first time back since then."

"It's your first time back since then?" I repeat her words, unable to take the shock out of my tone in time. "You didn't have to come with me!" That's probably an obvious statement, but I had to say it. She needs to hear it.

"Yeah," she shrugs, "But it felt right, and I've been treating that very specific feeling as my mom gently nudging me in the right direction, so I tend to follow them. Besides, I spent those three days staring at all these four leaf clovers, begging for the universe to send me a miracle or a good luck charm."

She turns to look at me fully, grabbing one of my clammy hands in hers.

"Clover, I think you're my good luck charm. Everything seems to have shifted in my favor since I've met you, and I haven't felt this happy in so long."

My breath hitches and tears immediately start forming in my eyes and falling down my cheeks. I blink, trying to make it better, but it just makes it worse. I can't help but chuckle.

"That was meant to be happy," Zahra says, voice breaking. I look at her, and she's crying too. I chuckle again and bring my hand up to her face, shakily trying to brush her tears off her cheeks. She does the same thing to me.

"I love you," I say before I can process my thoughts. My eyes go wide, and hers do to. Before I can say anything— or stutter— Zahra caresses my cheek gently as she says "I love you too."

I smile shakily at her, bringing her into a soft kiss as more tears fall down my face. She pulls back from the kiss, her hand moving up my face gently to wipe my tears.

"Thank you," I tell her softly after I calm down a little bit.

"Why the fuck are you thanking *me*? I'm the one who should be thanking you, you've helped me out so much more than you'll ever realize."

I wrap her up into a hug, unable to hold back the tears again. My chest heaves as I sob into Zahra's shoulder and her grasp tightens on my back as she struggles to hold back her tears as well.

"Thank you," I repeat again, not expecting or wanting a response. I just need to thank her for everything she's done for me.

"Oh here," she says, looking down at the pile of clovers in her hands. She grabs it and holds it up, showing me. This whole time I thought it was just a pile of clovers she was fidgeting with, turns out she was weaving them together and making me a flower crown.

I gasp as she lifts it to my head gently and puts it on it. I lean back against the bench carefully, trying my best to not mess the crown up. I know it's a bunch of weeds, basically, but at the moment it feels like my most prized possession.

"My hands just make them at this point, making them helps me relax." Zahra tells me, as she leans down to grab more clovers to start a new one. "My mom taught me when we first started coming here because I struggled to sit still... you should've seen how many crowns I finished after those three days. I barely remember any of it."

"Oh I can imagine," I say, watching her hands nimbly weave the clovers together, not letting any of the leaves touch each other or dent. She makes these so fast, she has to have been surrounded by them in hordes by the time she was found.

"The police probably thought I was mad," she laughs, "Especially by that point, I was incredibly depressed and surrounded by flower crowns? They were probably about to throw me into the psych ward— it's amazing I got through with only a therapist once a week."

"They didn't think you were mad," I reassure her, "You were grieving your mom. Everyone does weird things while they're grieving."

She shrugs, "Sure." It doesn't sound like she believes me, but I take it as good enough for now.

She continues, "At least I was able to make my cousin's birthday party awesome. My aunt took all of them and added faux flowers between the leaves before giving them to all of Ellie's friends. They had the best time playing princesses."

"That's so sweet," I say, mesmerized by her putting the clovers together into these beautiful crowns.

"I'm going home to visit this weekend," she tells me, "Aunt Michelle suggested I invite you."

"Do you want me to come with you?" I ask, not caring what her aunt wants. I want Zahra to want this.

"I mean, it'd be nice, but it'd be weird introducing my family to my girlfriend without mom there."

"Yeah," I shrug, "Everything family related is going to be awkward for a bit without her there."

"You're right," she tells me, finishing up the flower crown and putting it on herself. "I think I want you to go."

"Then I'll go," I say. "Easy as that. Tell me when and where, and I'll be there."

She smiles at me gently, "Thank you. I was planning to leave at nine thirty Saturday morning."

"Sounds good to me."

39

"RaRa!" A high pitched voice yells in excitement. A blur flies by me and attaches itself to Zahra's leg. The toddler is two or three years old with matted light brown hair. Zahra laughs and puts her bag down, hugging her back with the same enthusiasm.

She picks her up into the air, spinning around as she yells and laughs joyously. I grab Zahra's abandoned bag, tossing it onto the back of my chair as the girl chatters endlessly to Zahra.

"Ellie!" I hear someone holler from the house, "Are they here?"

"Yeah, Mommy!" Ellie hollers back loudly, making Zahra wince, then laugh.

That must've been Zahra's Aunt Michelle, I think as I make my way up the driveway towards the house.

"Who's that?" Ellie whisper-shouts at Zahra as I finally make it into the house. Thankfully there were only two small stairs I could get my chair over easily enough without assistance.

"She still hasn't *quite* grasped the concept of whispering,"

Zahra's Aunt Michelle (I think) shares with me. "Can I take your bags? I have a room all set up and ready for you."

"Yes, please," I tell her, gesturing to the back of my chair where our weekend bags are hanging. She smiles at me, grabs the bags and makes her way farther into the house.

"This is my partner," Zahra whisper-shouts to Ellie, matching her volume. She puts her hand over her mouth for extra emphasis, making me smile.

"Your partner? Is that like a girlfriend?" Ellie asks, tilting her head adorably at Zahra, and losing the whisper.

"Yeah, except that Clover is nonbinary— that means the xe doesn't like being called a girl or a boy."

"Ohh," she nods, thinking about it. "That makes sense."

Zahra stands up to her full height and shoots me a thumbs up as Ellie toddles towards me.

"Hi," she tells me, looking up at me with curiosity riddling her gaze.

"Hi Ellie," I say, I'm Clover."

"I like your name!" she exclaims excitedly, "Four leaf clovers are my favorite flower!"

"Are they?" I say excitedly, leaning down so I can try to be at her level more. I hold my hand over my mouth like I'm about to tell her a secret and tell her, "They're my favorite too."

She gasps, holding a hand over her mouth excitedly. She turns around and excitedly runs farther into the house, hollering for her mom.

I laugh, watching her until she turns a corner.

"She's a little ball of energy, isn't she?" I ask Zahra, as she comes over and starts pushing me towards the main part of the house.

"She is, but I love her," Zahra tells me, as we turn a corner into a beautiful kitchen. Zahra sits at the table, and Ellie's watching tv in the next room over. Michelle's making some food on the stove, and glancing over at Ellie every few seconds.

"I had Zahra tell me about your food needs and general preferences, so you should be good on that front, but I hope you like ravioli," she tells me as she puts the noodles in the pot with the sauce.

"Ravioli sounds great," I tell her, as I roll up to the table to sit next to Zahra. Her hands are resting on the table, so I grab one in mine.

"I'm her Aunt Michelle, by the way, you're more than welcome to call me Michelle or Aunt Michelle, or anything really," she introduces herself and waves at me from over the kitchen counter.

"Hi, I'm Clover, it's nice to meet you." I introduce myself to her, also waving.

There's a muted bark, and scratching sounds. I turn around and see a beautiful black and tan Rottweiler sitting outside on their back porch, begging to be let back inside.

"Oh, I forgot to ask you earlier so I let him outside before you got here," Michelle says, shaking her head, annoyed at herself for forgetting. "Aldo is really sweet, but I wasn't sure how you felt about dogs. Usually, I'm not going to lie, I wouldn't care but I was worried about your chair. I don't mind leaving him outside or away from you while you're here."

"He really is the sweetest dog ever," Zahra pipes up, "I know he can look scary, but I feel like those dogs are always the sweetest."

"I'm fine letting him in," I tell them, "I love dogs, and I'll be fine as long as he doesn't jump." I shrug.

"He usually doesn't, but I'll keep an eye on him," Zahra reassures me. Aunt Michelle moves from the stove towards the door, but Zahra waves her off, "I've got it, don't worry."

"Thanks RaRa," she says gratefully, using Ellie's nickname for her.

Zahra opens the door, letting Aldo come into the house. He barks once, low and happily, and immediately sits on his haunches as best as he can with his butt wiggling in excitement.

Zahra laughs, and starts petting, and his butt starts shaking even more. He's so excited as Zahra pets him, sometimes getting off his haunches, but always going back to his sitting position. He tries to lick her hands excitedly, and I can't hold back my laugh.

He tilts his head as he hears my laugh, like he didn't realize there was someone else in here. He stands up and comes over to me, sniffing my chair before sitting next to me and sniffing my hands.

He's a lot bigger than I thought he was. I know Rottweilers are large dogs, but I've never seen one in person before, and I sorely underestimated their size. He's about two feet standing up, a bit taller once he sits. He sits next to my chair, and is taller than my armrest.

I hold my hands out to him, willing them not to shake like they tend to do randomly. Aldo sniffs it gently, close but not touching my hand with his nose. He then nudges my hand and starts licking it all over.

I laugh as I start petting him on his head, since it's in my reach and my back can't take leaning down right now. His butt wiggles like it did with Zahra, and he tries to lick my hand and arm excitedly as I pet him from his head down to his shoulder.

"Aldo!" I hear Ellie exclaim from the other room. She rushes in, bee-lining towards the dog. I flinch back a little bit, mainly from the tone of her voice, but also in worry for her. I know Aldo wouldn't hurt her, there's no way Michelle would let him in the house if there was even a slight chance of that, but there's still some worry in the back of my head.

Aldo is her height, possibly taller when sitting, and Ellie doesn't even hesitate to wrap her arms around Aldo's shoulder and give him a big hug. The dog doesn't even flinch, his butt wiggling even more than before. He licks her neck and shoulder as Ellie squeals in happiness.

"RaRa! CloClo!" I hear Ellie yell before the knob shakes and she starts banging on the door. "Wake up! We're going to the apple orchard today!"

I groan, stretching as much as I can. It's not that much, considering I'm basically wrapped around Zahra, but it's enough for me. She groans as well, stretching before kissing me softly and quickly.

"Good morning," she mumbles, trying to direct it at me, but actually directing it at her pillow. She groans as Ellie bangs on the door again, and I know she's thankful she thought to lock our door last night.

"Come on! Let's go!" Ellie yells, and Aldo barks twice. I groan as well, wanting to smash my head into the pillow and fall back asleep. I know that's not going to be able to happen.

"We'll be out in a few minutes once we get ready," I raise my voice so Ellie can hear through the door.

"Ok!" Ellie exclaims happily, "Get ready fast! Mommy made pancakes!"

"Mmm pancakes," Zahra groans.

"Mhm," I mumble, kissing her temple, "Let's go get ready so they can be warm."

"Aunt Michelle makes the best pancakes."

I get out of bed and into my chair, wheeling over to my

suitcase and grabbing my clothes for the day and what I'll need while I'm in the bathroom. I stack it all on my lap, telling Zahra I'm getting ready in the bathroom, and opening the door.

I start wheeling towards the bathroom and am about to enter when I hear, "CloClo!"

"One second!" I tell her as I go into the bathroom and put my things onto the counter. I wheel into the kitchen where Ellie's sitting at the table, eating some fruit. Aunt Michelle's making pancakes at the stove. I lock my chair as I get to Ellie's side.

"What's up?" I ask her, smiling at her. She smiles back at me and scrambles to stand on her chair. My arms immediately jolt and I move to grab her hips so she doesn't fall.

"Hug!" she says excitedly as she holds her arms out and wraps them around me. I wrap my arms around her, hugging her back, my heart melting for this three year old.

"Thank you!" she exclaims before sitting back down and continuing to watch her cartoons while eating.

I make my way back to the bathroom, and as I turn around to close the door, I find that Aldo's followed me and is sitting in front of the door. I blink and wheel back towards him. He quickly stands up and rushes towards me as I make the slightest motion.

I shake my head as I pet him, immediately feeling better (even thought I didn't realize I wasn't feeling the best). He licks my arm as I pet him, and it seems like he never wants to stop.

"Aldo!" Aunt Michelle calls for him as she turns the corner and sees us. He immediately stops and goes over to her. She absentmindedly pets his ears as she addresses me.

"Sorry about him," she tells me. "He loves pets, and will beg for them from everyone, anytime. Go ahead and get ready for the day, then we can have pancakes before we go.

IT'S the perfect fall day out, and even though it's Saturday, it isn't that busy at the apple orchard. There are plenty of people around, but not enough that we're squished. We can do what we want to do with one or two families around, but that's it.

"Do you like red apples more, or green apples?" I ask everyone, but primarily Ellie, while looking at the maps. The map has all the orchards labeled with either a green apple or a red apple, and numbers that specify the type of apple more in depth.

"Umm..." Ellie thinks about it for a second before excitedly exclaiming "Red!"

"I like red too!" I tell her. She claps and tugs my arm because she wants to see the map. I put the map down so she can lean on my armrest and look at it too. Zahra props her head on top of mine as she looks at the map too.

"So do we want to get apples first, or go shoot some apples out of a canon?" Zahra asks, looking between me and Aunt Michelle.

"There's a cannon?" I ask rhetorically, surprised that an apple orchard has a canon you can shoot apples out of.

"Yes, there's a cannon!" Zahra tells us, "according to the map it's pretty close to us, and it should be wheelchair accessible."

"Then let's go to the cannon first." Aunt Michelle says, making the decision for us. She has Aldo on a leash, since this is pretty much all outdoors he can come with us.

We make our way to the cannon, and we're in the queue within five minutes. We go up past the sign and go into the second line, labeled handicap entrance. An employee guides us through the building, around the market, and into an elevator. We go up to the second floor and the elevator opens to show the balcony with three cannons.

"Woah!" Ellie exclaims and I agree. I've never seen anything like this before, this is going to be so fun. There's also a shorter one on the end that's closed off and labeled 'accessible lane: please see associate to open'.

The associate who helped us unlocks the rope blocking the accessible cannon and letting us through.

"I paid for half an hour," Aunt Michelle tells us, taking a seat with Aldo at the bench. There's a large barrel of apples of all kinds to the side of the cannon, and there's multiple targets at different distances from the cannon.

Ellie rushes up excitedly as Zahra quickly reads the instructions and thanks the employee before showing Ellie how to use the cannon. I smile as I park my chair next to Michelle to watch.

Aldo nudges my hand and I smile at him softly as I pat his head and ears.

"I wanted to tell you," Aunt Michelle tells me, "Zahra's been through a lot, especially after her mom passed, and I was really worried about her going to college." Her voice breaks, and she looks down at Aldo, her hand petting his back to distract herself. "She's doing so much better now... and she's been so much better since she met you, so I just wanted to thank you. I didn't think I'd get this emotional, I'm sorry."

I sniffle, trying to hold back my tears. "I'm glad I could help. She's been really helping me too, more than you could ever know."

She smiles at me, tears in her eyes, and I smile back with tears in mine. She holds an arm out, silently asking for a hug and I nod, leaning into her embrace. We sit with our arms on each other's shoulders, watching Ellie and Zahra shoot apples out of cannons in silence.

"Your turn, Clover," Zahra comes over to me and Michelle with Ellie. I roll over to the cannon and grab an apple, tossing it up and down in my hands as I inspect the canon.

I put the apple in, and aim, shooting the apple out of the cannon towards the targets. I hit one of the targets, not in the middle, but close enough that I call it good enough.

"Yay CloClo!" Ellie exclaims from next to me, watching the apples go flying. "You hit the target!"

"I wonder..." I mutter to myself as I put another apple in the cannon. I shoot the next apple, not worrying about the aim. I fiddle with the trigger, and shrug mentally.

I grab an apple and put it in the cannon. I grab five more apples and put them in the cannon as well, filling the barrel up to the brim. There's nothing that says I can't shoot the cannon like a machine gun, so I might as well try.

I aim the cannon and put my finger on the trigger. I take a deep breath and press, and the first apple shoots from the cannon. I keep a hold on the trigger, and the apples keep shooting out of the cannon. I laugh happily as I shift the cannon from side to side trying to hit the cannons next to ours.

"Woah!" Ellie exclaims, "It went like bambambambam-bam!" She mimics a machine gun, making the sound effect. "Let's do it again!"

"Do you want to help me load the apples?" I ask her.

"Yeah!" Ellie says happily, grabbing as many apples as she can hold in her little arms. She comes back over, excitedly loading the cannon and making machine gun sounds.

"Alright, let's do this!" I exclaim, bringing Ellie to stand in front of my chair. I put my hands on the trigger, and Ellie puts her hand over mine. We count down from three before pushing the trigger and holding down on it.

"That was so much fun!" Ellie exclaims once all the apples are shot, she turns around and hugs me quickly before rushing back to her mom and Zahra asking if they saw that.

"You're so good with kids," Zahra tells me softly as she takes over pushing my chair again. I smile to myself softly, feeling good. I've never really dealt with kids before, so I'm just glad it turned out well. Although Ellie made it easy, she's the cutest and best kid I've ever seen.

"I tried my best," I shrug, watching Aunt Michelle and Ellie lead the way toward the orchards.

"Thank you for coming with me this weekend," she tells me vulnerably.

"Of course," I tell her, "I don't mind it one bit, I love getting to know your family and meeting another side of you."

I can't see her, but I can imagine she has a soft smile on her face.

"WHAT DO WE RECKON?" Aunt Michelle says, "Do we think one bag is enough? I feel like one bag is more than enough, we might not even be able to eat all these apples."

"We can take some off your hands," I tell her, "We all like apples, and I'm sure we can find some fun recipes for them."

"Ooh I love a good apple pie," Zahra says, "We should make an apple pie when we get home."

"Too bad Kaid isn't here, I'm sure he'd love that."

"One bag it is," Michelle nods, and pays for it as well as a few more things she found at the market on the way to the checkout.

We make our way to the first orchard, where we enter and immediately turn around and leave.

"Too green," Ellie declares, guiding us to the next aisle, where she refuses because they were too yellow. The next, too red. Eventually, though, we get to an aisle that Ellie approves of and we start picking apples.

I hang back a bit, watching the three of them pick apples together. I snap a few pictures for Zahra before heading into the aisle.

I immediately stop and grab an apple, twisting it so it comes off the tree. I take a bite, gauging the sweetness, and as I eat the apple I think about what I should make with them. Apple pie is a must, maybe a crumble or cake as well.

"I've already gotten twenty seven apples, CloClo!" Ellie tells me excitedly as she rushes over, picking like four more and stacking them in her arms.

"Wow!" I exclaim, eyes wide. I know kids move fast, but she seriously has a ton of energy and will to fill this bag of apples as fast as possible. I should pick some more before there isn't any space anymore.

Zahra and I pick apples on the right side of the aisle, in each other's company but enjoying the silence. Zahra's got Aldo on his leash, and every few seconds she checks to make sure that he isn't eating something as he isn't eating something as he sniffs the ground. He doesn't, but she's still paranoid. I would be too.

"Should we get another bag?" I ask, looking at the bag that Michelle's holding. We make our way over to her, and give her the apples we picked. "It doesn't hold as many apples as I thought it would. And I'm really craving an apple pie."

"Yeah, I think we should go get one for ourselves," Zahra decides. "I found this recipes for apple cake I want to try, plus apples are a good snack for in-between classes."

"Hey, we're going to get another bag, and explore the market," I tell Michelle, tapping her arm to get her attention.

"Here, since we're almost done, we can play with Aldo while we wait for you," she holds her hand out and Zahra passes the leash to her. I pet him quickly before Zahra and I turn around and go back to the market.

"Ooh these peaches look amazing," I say, unable to resist grabbing a few. Zahra nods excitedly, grabbing some more fruits that the orchard has grown.

I grab peaches and grapes, and Zahra grabs some pears and plums. We wander the market, trying not to grab too many things before we get to the checkout. We purchase another apple bag and quickly get back to the orchard.

"You're back!" Ellie exclaims excitedly, "I picked the bestest apples for you!"

My heart melts again as I look at the perfect apples sitting in a pile next to her. "Thank you," I exclaim, holding the bag open for her to start loading the apples into it.

"She spent so long comparing apples, making sure you two got the best ones," Aunt Michelle tells us. "It kept her distracted pretty much the entire time you were gone."

I smile at them, suddenly feeling this gut feeling in my chest. I don't want to leave, Michelle and Ellie and Aldo feel like my family, just like they're Zahra's family. I don't want to leave.

The bag of apples fills up quickly, and we make our way back to Aunt Michelle's house. Conversations happen around me, but I can't seem to fully concentrate on them and everything.

Saying goodbye to them was hard, for both of us, but Zahra took it hard. She had been staying with her aunt instead of her dad after her mom's death and Aunt Michelle had basically turned into a second mom for her. Her dad was never really in the picture to begin with, and they tried living together for a bit, but it didn't end very well.

We open our apartment door, and don't say anything as we go in and deposit our bags in the living room. I feel empty as I transfer onto my bed and lay down.

40

"Thank you for visiting my family with me," Zahra tells me a few days later, for what feels like the millionth time.

"You don't need to thank me," I tell her gently.

"Yes, I do. There are so many other things you could've been doing with your weekend! Like studying for finals!"

"I have next weekend to study as well!" I shrug, "I loved visiting your family with you, it felt like a breath of fresh air. I didn't have to worry about school, or studying, or finals."

"Yeah, but you were worried about meeting them, and probably about Aldo too," she exclaims, throwing her hands up into the air.

"It's okay," I say sweetly, grabbing her hands in mind, "I was worried for a little bit, but it wasn't that much. Once I got through that first hour, I was fine."

"That's a good point, I'm just so stressed and my brain keeps telling me that I forced you... but I know I didn't, but I feel like I did." Tears form in her eyes and she sniffles. I let one of her hands go so she can wipe them, and she immediately puts her hand back on top of ours.

I lean forward and kiss her nose and then under each of her eyes. She sniffles again, and I can't help but lean my forehead against hers and close my eyes.

"It's okay," I say softly, slowly giving her eskimo kisses. "I understand your brain trying to trick you, and mess with you, but trust me when I say: I will always communicate with you. I will always tell you the truth."

"Thank you," she says, letting out a deep breath. She opens her eyes and looks at me as all of the tears that have built up fall from her eyes. I wipe them with the pads of my fingers.

"I promise," I whisper against her lips as I lean in and kiss her.

The kiss is soft, and she presses closer to me. I can taste her tears on my lips and she can probably taste mine too.

She leans closer and wraps her arms around me, and I wrap mine around her. I melt into her, and her kiss, as it gets deeper and deeper. I press closer to her as I probe her lips with my tongue, asking for her to open. She opens her mouth and our tongues dance together.

A key inserts into the lock at our apartment door and I don't hear it until the door opens. I break apart from the kiss, as I hear the door open. I look at Zahra with wide eyes.

She looks at me confused for a second before the door creaks again, and she looks at me with wide eyes. I frantically look around, not looking over the side of the couch, looking for anything to use against this intruder if necessary.

"Hello?" A voice calls out. I pause, confused. "Clover? Zahra? I'm home."

I look at Zahra confused and slowly lift my head up over the couch to find Kaid.

"Kaid? What are you doing here?" I ask, the second I see

him standing in the doorway of our apartment, with a suitcase.

"Kaid?" Zahra mouths at me, and I nod at her. She shrugs and pokes her head over the side of the couch. "Hey, long time no see."

"Please tell me I didn't just interrupt something…" he asks, raising an eyebrow at us.

A blush immediately forms on my face and I can't look either of them in the eye.

"What are you doing here, Kaid?" I ask, changing the subject.

"Oh, I'm coming to get my things and to transfer ownership of the apartment to you," he tells us. "The landlord reached out because he hadn't seen me in awhile, and so I told him that I was going to switch ownership of the apartment to you if you were ok with it."

"I don't have a job right now, but I do want to keep staying here," I say softly.

"Don't worry, I can help for the first few months until you're comfortable."

"I want to stay here with you," Zahra tells me softly, "I can get a job at school and help pay, if you'll have me, that is."

"Of course!" I exclaim, "I'd love to have you here, was that even a question?"

"I figured you'd be ok with it, but I wanted to make sure before I signed the papers," Kaid said. "He said that if I didn't come this weekend he'd put the apartment up for sale, that bastard."

"Seriously?" Zahra exclaims, "Are we sure we want to live here with the landlord pulling shit like that?"

"There's no way I'm going to be able to find a place— that's wheelchair accessible at that— in our price range." I point out.

"Shit, you're right."

"In his defense, I have been kind of avoiding coming back here." Kaid says, rubbing the back of his head with his hand.

"Is everything alright with Nonna Helen?" I have to ask, even though I'm scared to hear the answer.

"She's still kicking, but we're not in the clear yet. I have Faye and Bethy with her now, but I'm just praying that she'll be alive by the time I get home. If I lose her without being home, I don't know how I'll cope."

His voice cracks at that last word, and I immediately push off the back of the couch and transfer into the chair, going over to his side as quick as I can.

My legs are going to kill me for this... My body screams at me as I stand up shakily in front of Kaid, holding my arms out for a hug. He looks up at me with watery eyes, and immediately pulls me into a hug.

I haven't hugged someone like this in so long, *and* I haven't seen Kaid in so long. Tears form in my eyes as Kaid sobs into my shoulder, and I hug him even closer. I close my eyes, begging my tears to not fall. They don't listen. My tears fall into the crook of his shoulder, and I hiccup. My hand shakily strokes his back and twists his hair in my hand, trying to distract myself.

"Umm..." Zahra says from behind us. I hear something open and then close before she says, "We made pie yesterday, if you want some?"

I chuckle into Kaid's neck and he doesn't react other than a sniffle for a few seconds. I lift my head, worried, but he starts full on belly laughing. He lets go from the hug, still holding onto my shoulders so I don't fall, and helps me back into my chair.

I can't help but laugh too, as Kaid makes his way into the kitchen, finally calming down from his laugh attack.

"Pie sounds good," he tells Zahra, who puts the pie on the kitchen island. He turns to grab the utensils, but Zahra stops him, already holding some up for him to choose from. He chuckles, and grabs what he needs.

I roll into the kitchen behind him, wanting some pie too, and when Kaid turns around he almost trips over me. There definitely isn't any room for the three of us on this side of the kitchen.

He laughs, "Sorry Clove, do you mind backing up and giving me some space?"

"How bout *you* give me some space?" I throw his words right back at him before I can tell my brain to stop. He freezes for a second, and I regret the words.

He laughs, "Oh how I've missed your sense of humor," he says to himself, but I hear it anyway. He leans down and kisses the top of my forehead. "Go back to the couch, I'll make you a plate. I better see your legs up when I get there," he waggles a finger at me in faux aggression and I have to bite back a smile.

I do as he says, and wheel back to the couch, transferring onto the couch and making sure to pull my legs up. I grope for the remote, finding it deep in the couch cushions, and turn on *New Girl*.

I don't know if Kaid's had time to catch up on *New Girl*, but Zahra and I have been texting him updates since we've started. It'll be easy enough to update him if he's behind. I pull it up on the tv as he and Zahra come back to the couch, and sit next to me.

Kaid sits in-between me and Zahra, claiming that he deserves to because he's missed us. I don't complain as he picks my feet up and puts them in his lap. He passes me my plate with pie and vanilla ice cream piled high and my mouth starts watering.

I dig my fork into the pie and ice cream and take a bite. I

had a plate yesterday, but somehow it managed to be even better today. I smile as I take a second bite, even bigger than the first one.

Kaid groans as he takes the first bite from his pie. His eyes roll back, and his head hits the back of the couch. It's a bit of a dramatic reaction for some pie and ice cream, but I'm glad he's appreciating it.

I hit play on the show before taking another bite of pie. I finish my plate off after a few minutes and put it on the side table. I lean back, adjusting my body in an attempt to get comfortable, but nothing works.

I grumble as I turn this way and that way, any direction I can in an attempt to get comfortable. Nothing works, and I give up wanting to cross my arms and flip off the world.

That won't work, hell *nothing* I do is going to help me right now. Trust me, I'd do anything, I *have* done everything in an attempt to sate the pain but nothing helps.

Kaid looks at me, noting my struggles and starts massaging my feet gently. It doesn't do much to help with the pain, but it helps me relax and I'll take that if I can't get anything else.

"How are your legs?" he whispers to me, "I'm sure standing up probably hurt them, but I appreciate you standing up for that hug... it really helped me."

I smile at him softly, my eyelids getting heavy as he massages me, "I'm glad."

"I can start Monday, yeah," I tell Janice, the owner of *Lights and Ledgers*, my favorite bookstore in Newcastle. Once Kaid told me he was going to transfer ownership of his apartment to me and Zahra, we both went looking for jobs.

Thankfully my first choice was doing interviews and I got the job.

"Great, thank you so much again for the opportunity. I'll see you on Monday," I tell her after she tells me more details. I hang up the phone after we say our goodbyes and turn to Zahra and Kaid excitedly.

"You got the job?" he asks excitedly, overhearing my phone call.

"Yeah!" I tell them, putting my phone down on the table. "I start on Monday, and I'm so excited."

"As you should be!" Zahra pipes up, "You've worked hard for this, and I'm glad you've gotten your dream job basically."

I nod, "I'm so excited," I repeat again.

"I'm so happy for you!" Kaid tells me, giving me a hug, "What do we need to do before Monday?"

"Do you have an outfit, or should we go shopping for a new one? Do you have a bag and lunch box?" Zahra thinks, listing off a few things.

"Well..." I think, "I was thinking I'd use my school lunch box and bag, since I'll be primarily going straight to work from school."

"Do you need an outfit, though?" Kaid asks, "That's the most important piece."

"Is it?" I ask, "I already got through the interview and got the job."

"That first impression post interview matters." Kaid tells me, "Just wear something cute."

"Like what? I'm terrible at outfits, it's impossible for me to find things I like."

"Well since you're working at a bookstore, how about we find you some nice slacks and some cute bookish t-shirts and/or earrings?" Zahra suggests, "I'll go with you. I know some good places we can go, and we can make a day out of it."

I groan, knowing that she's right, but I don't want to go shopping. I try to avoid it at all costs. I don't know how to shop well, and being nonbinary makes it even harder.

"Fine," I tell her, putting my head on the counter dramatically.

"I'll come with you too," Kaid offers, "Then you'll have both of our options; maybe that'll help a bit?"

I shrug, "I don't know, I just hate shopping and I don't know the first place to start here."

"That's what we're here for," Zahra says, "Kaid and I will help you find exactly what you need."

"I already have an idea," Kaid shrugs, "Going for the perfect in-between gender confusion look."

"Yeah?" I look up from the counter at him.

"I'm thinking slacks, a bookish t-shirt and cardigan over," he tells me, "A classic library/bookseller look."

"Sounds good to me," I say.

"Go ahead and get dressed," Zahra says, "Let's go now before we all get busy and before Kaid leaves tomorrow."

"Can we get food too?"

"Of course," Zahra reassures me, able to tell how stressed I am about this. Food will make everything better. Food *should* make everything better.

I go to my room and get dressed in a simple pair of jeans and a t-shirt. I'm going to have to change in and out of these multiple times, so I wanted to make this as easy as possible for me.

"First stop, I think, should be <u>Primark</u>," Kaid says as Zahra and I get into the front of the car. Zahra's driving us in her car today, with me in the passenger seat and Kaid in the back. My wheelchair is folded up snugly in the back hatch.

"Primark's a good idea," Zahra agrees. "I like that idea, do the boring things first then go to the fun stuff."

"Primark isn't boring!" Kaid interjects, faux annoyance in his tone. "I love Primark! Don't you, Clover?"

"I've never been," I shrug, not putting myself on either side of the argument.

"Primark itself isn't boring," Zahra admits, "We're looking for pants and cardigans here, that's not the most interesting shopping compared to going to Bookishly for t-shirts and earrings."

"Ok, yeah, sorry Kaid. I'm on Zahra's side on this one." I tell him, shrugging.

"Yeah, I know you're right," he grumbles, crossing his arms and leaning back against the seat.

We pull into the Primark parking lot thirty minutes later, and Kaid gets out of the car first to put my chair together before Zahra or I have the chance to.

By the time Zahra gets out of the car after turning everything off, Kaid's already closed the back hatch and wheeled the chair to my door.

I open the car door and transfer into the chair seamlessly, feeling extra grateful for the people in my life who care for me so deeply.

"I can do xeir chair next time," I hear Zahra tell Kaid as we make our way towards the store.

"No," he says simply, making me laugh. I hold my palm over my mouth, trying not to interrupt them.

"I'm xeir girlfriend, I feel like this counts as girlfriend duties!"

"Don't pull the girlfriend card on me," Kaid retorts, "I was here first and I'm xeir best friend."

"And I'm xeir girlfriend, I think that's a bit of a level up compared to best friend."

"I think they both count as about the same," Kaid reasons, "Can I please do it today? I haven't been here to help in a few months, I feel bad."

Zahra immediately relents, "If you really feel that bad, fine, you can. But just know that doesn't mean you rank above me in favorite person status."

Kaid takes his hands off my chair for a second to hold them up. "Don't worry about that, there's only one person I need to be number one for... and as much as I love you two, I know I'm not your number ones."

"Damn right," Zahra says as she goes to open the door to the store. Having three people in our little outing does make getting around much easier.

Zahra and Kaid switch positions as we get into the store, and Kaid leads the way towards the pants.

"I'm assuming you want men's pants, cause they're overall better than women's. Feel free to correct me, though, I don't mind finding women's pants." Kaid explains.

"No, no you're definitely right," I wave him off, "Men's pants for the win."

"I've never tried them," Zahra says, "Do you think I'd like them?"

"They're generally longer so you'll have to roll them up, but they have much larger pockets and tend to be more comfortable— at least in my opinion." I explain.

"I might try on a pair if I see one I like," she muses, "The prices here are good enough that I don't mind buying something to try out— I'd only be out fifteen or twenty bucks if I didn't like them."

"Or you could just return them...?" Kaid says, turning to

shoot Zahra an incredulous look, "Then you'd be out nothing."

Zahra doesn't respond.

We make it to the section Kaid was looking for and start going through the racks.

There's an incredibly wide selection of pants available, there's sweats, and cargos, and plenty of different slacks options.

"I'm thinking black is a good place to start, at least until we know what you like," Kaid muses from behind me, flipping through the pants on display in front of me. "Are you liking these?"

"Yeah," I tell him, and gesture to the pants on the other side of the aisle, "Or these ones."

"Let's try both," he shrugs, flipping through the other rack now. "What's your size?"

I tell him, and he grabs a pair of pants from each rack for me to try on. The two of us make our way towards the dressing room, and Kaid stops multiple times, grabbing more pants for me to try on.

"Kaid, I don't need that many pairs of pants," I try to tell him, but he shrugs me off. "I don't have the energy to try on that many pairs of pants."

"Then don't try all of them on," he shrugs, "I'm just trying to give you options."

I shake my head and stop trying, knowing that nothing I say will make him stop grabbing pants.

I look for Zahra, and find her on the other side of the walkway, looking at skirts and dresses for herself. I guess the pants didn't work out for her. I'm sure she'll find something she likes over there, and we'll find her later.

"Okay," Kaid announces a few seconds later, "Let's go ahead and try some of these on."

We go into the dressing rooms and the attendant unlocks the wheelchair accessible room for me. The door is super wide and I glide into the room with ease. The room is also super wide on the inside, and I'm able to spin around in a few circles.

Back in the states, wheelchair accessible dressing rooms were barely bigger than regular stalls and I usually couldn't fit in them, having to guess on sizing and try on at home.

One time I went to a store and they had a larger accessible dressing room, and was told I couldn't use it because they were using it as storage. They refused to take whatever shit they had in there until we got a manager.

I sigh as Kaid comes into the room and puts my pants on the bench beside me.

"I'll be sitting out here," he tells me, "Feel free to show me the pants as you try them on."

I do my best to smile at him, but the second the door closes, a deep breath escapes me.

I turn to look at the pants in front of me and sigh again. I love Kaid, I really do, but he really didn't have to pick out this many pairs of pants.

I go through them quickly, trying to see what's most gender neutral and what suits me best.

Sweatpants, sweatpants, cargo pants, jeans, fancy slacks, uber fancy slacks... they're all here. I put the sweatpants and jeans to the side, I have enough of those already— and grab the cargo pants to start out with.

I put the pants on and stare at myself in the mirror. Another sigh escapes me as my brain tries to convince me that I'm not a man and shouldn't be wearing these pants.

My brain pulls this kind of shit whenever I put on anything, and I've done pretty well in ignoring it, but when I try on new things it gets worse. My brain has never liked clothes, and I've never really felt confident in them.

I turn around and open the door before my brain can throw anything else hateful at me.

Kaid stands up and puts his phone in his pocket the second the door creaks open.

"Those look so good on you!" he exclaims, as he comes closer to see. He walks around me, making sure it looks good from all sides, and nods to himself as he finishes.

"Have you sat in them yet?"

"No," I realized, and slowly make my way back to my chair. I sit down and adjust the pants as needed.

"And they pass the sit test!" Kaid exclaims excitedly, making me laugh, "These go in the *yes pile* don't you think?"

I nod and he ushers me back into the room to try on the rest of the pants.

WE COME out of the store with two pairs of pants and a grey cardigan. Kaid and I decided on getting the cargo pants, and a pair of slacks that worked well with the wheelchair. The fancier pair looked good, but were so uncomfortable when I sat in them so we immediately discarded them.

Zahra, while we were pants shopping, had found some cute things for herself as well as a cardigan for me. She found me a light grey short cardigan for me to wear as the weather gets chillier. It fits me perfectly, and she claims it will work with the outfit perfectly. I'm doubtful, it feels a bit too feminine for me, but we'll see. If all else fails, I know it will fit her well as well.

We drive to <u>Bookishly</u>, a store that Kaid claims I will love and will have everything we need. I instantly believed him, cause why wouldn't a store called <u>Bookishly</u> have everything I could ever need and more?

The store is a decent size, and I get even more excited as we pull up and park in one of the handicap spots in the front. Like before, Kaid jumps out of the car faster than Zahra can park it to set my chair up.

We get into the store and I immediately get distracted by the display they have at the front of the store celebrating Jane Austen's 250th birthday.

There's posters, mugs, tote bags, books, and so much more celebrating Austen on this small table. I pick up the copy of <u>Sense of Sensibility</u>, immediately falling in love with it.

"Nope," Kaid takes the book from my hand, putting it back on the display. "We're here to look for shirts, not books, let's go."

"What did you think was going to happen? We're in a bookstore!" I exclaim as he rolls me away from the table and towards the back of the store to find shirts.

"Ooh!" I immediately notice a Jane Austen shirt and veer towards it, "Look Kaid, it's a tatted up Jane Austen!" I grab the shirt in my size and hold it up to him.

He laughs and immediately grabs it out of my hold. He drapes it over his arm, and I assume that means we're buying it. He flips through the rack and laughs even harder as he finds even more.

"Look look," he shows me, "There's Brontë and Shakespeare too!"

"This is great," I snicker as I look closer at the Austen design, finding the word 'love' stamped across her knuckles.

"Let's move on from this one rack, you two," Zahra pushes us away from the rack and towards the next.

Nothing intrigues me quite as much as the tatted up Austen shirt, but there are still plenty of good options to choose from. There are plenty of shirts for different genres, and tropes that are popular. I almost grab one that says 'ask me about queer literature' but realize that if someone did ask, I really only know of Adria and Caitlyn's books... *I really need to get on that.*

I end up grabbing two more shirts and call it a day. One says 'read banned books' and the other says 'Amazon sucks, buy from small bookstores'. The latter one felt appropriate considering I work for a small bookstore now.

We get to the checkout and Kaid pays, ignoring all my insistence to pay. He claims he has more than enough money to spare, and wants to spoil me before he has to leave again. I reluctantly let him.

41

———

"How'd your first day of work go?" I ask Zahra, as she comes into the apartment. We both had our first days of work today, her at the university library and me and *Lights and Ledgers*.

"It was good, but I'm exhausted," she basically falls onto one of the seats at the counter. I'm also exhausted, we both had classes this morning and went directly to work afterwards.

I decided to wear the slacks we bought with the banned books shirt and cardigan. Zahra was right, the cardigan worked perfectly with the outfit and even though it felt feminine it worked well.

"I need some comfort food," she groans.

"I was thinking the same thing," I rest my chin on the counter, looking at her. She smiles at me, and can't resist smiling back. "I was thinking maybe grilled cheese."

"Ooh," Zahra looks up at me with wide eyes, "That sounds good— especially with some tomato soup!"

"I don't know if we have everything we need, at least to make it super good, so I think I'm going to put in a grocery store order."

"Add ice cream too, I need some of that today."

I nod, pulling the grocery app on my phone. I add the American cheese on, the squares wrapped in plastic— it's the only way to have grilled cheese— tomato soup, ice cream, and a few more things I see along the way that we need.

"It'll be here in an hour," I tell her, reading off my phone. She nods and stands up, making her way back to her room to change out of her clothes. I stretch in my chair and go back to my room to do the same thing.

"So for your final," Melody explains to the class, "You should be through your book at this point and working on your paper. I'll be checking in with everyone during your work time."

Melody's final was to read one of Austen's works that you hadn't read before and to do a paper on it. For the actual final's week, there's a small test you need to fill out. We've been working on the reading and paper since we finished our reflection papers from the trip.

I decided to read *Emma*— mainly because of our tour guide and that beautiful copy I bought from the Austen House. I've finished reading and am almost done with my paper. Zahra's reading *Pride and Prejudice*, and I've been helping her with her paper.

As usual, Melody starts her rounds of the classroom with us. She pulls out a chair and sits down next to me.

"So Clover," she says, "I know we talked about this briefly before, but are you still interested in potentially being my TA next semester?"

I look at her, eyes wide, "I'd love that!" I forgot about that suggestion, but that'll be such a great addition to my resume.

It'll also give me more time with Melody, I've been wanting to pick her mind all semester, especially considering she has my dream job.

"Oh great," she says, "I didn't have anyone else apply— at least that got past the initial screenings— so the spot's yours. I'll email you more information soon, but I wanted to make sure we're on the same page here."

"We're definitely on the same page!" I exclaim excitedly, "I'm so excited to be your TA— I want to be you when I grow up."

Melody melts, and I swear tears form in her eyes, but she hugs me before they can fall. I hug her back, squeezing her tightly like she does to me.

She pulls back, looking at her notepad to make sure she didn't forget anything.

"Ah, and don't worry, I negotiated to make your pay a bit higher than the average TA— you deserve it."

"I didn't realize this was a paid position," I mutter to myself, and Melody chuckles as she hears it.

"Bonus," she pokes fun at me and I laugh. "So how's your projects going?" She directs the question at both me and Zahra.

"I'm pushing through *Pride and Prejudice*," Zahra tells her, "Clover's been helping me through it, since I've been struggling. We've been writing parts of the paper as I read, but it's been going well."

"*Pride and Prejudice* can be a hard read," she sympathizes, "Especially since I know you don't read many classics to begin with."

Zahra nods, "I feel like the more I'm reading, the easier it gets."

"Good, good, that was my hope."

"Mine too," I tell Zahra softly, squeezing her hand, pride seeping through me.

"You're a good teacher, Clover," Melody tells me, making my eyes go wide in shock, not expecting the compliment. "I can't wait to see how we can improve your skills. I know it's going to be great."

I blush at the compliment, and feel proud of myself at the same time. Zahra squeezes my hand, like I did to her, and I can't help but smile.

"And how's *Emma*?"

"Going good, I finished reading the book last week, and I'm almost finished with the paper."

She nods, "Good job, you two. I'm going to miss having you both in the back of my classes.

Dear Mom and Dad,

A few months ago, I never thought I'd be thriving the way I am here in Newcastle. And for that, I want to thank you for pushing me to go. Because I know for a fact I was a stubborn ass, and I don't thank you enough.

I've made two incredible friends (one of whom has become my girlfriend) Zahra, and Kaid. I can't imagine my life without them. Zahra and I are living in an off-campus apartment together. It's completely wheelchair accessible and we both have jobs we love to help pay for our necessities. I'm working at this incredible small bookstore Lights and Ledgers, which is run by a wheelchair user so everything is accessible. I'm also starting work as a teacher's assistant next semester for my favorite professor Melody Kingston. Her and I have gotten close as well.

I've really made myself a little found family here in Newcastle, and I wouldn't have it any other way.

My first semester here is drawing to a close, and I'm going to be coming home soon to visit. I wanted to send this card ahead of time because I realized I haven't reached out as much as I should've. I deeply apologize for that, and I promise to do better in the future.

Inclosed is a picture of me, Zahra, and Kaid. I hope it brings a smile to your face like it always does mine.

I'll see you soon. I love you.

Your child,

Clover

ACKNOWLEDGMENTS

Firstly, to my parents. Like Clover, I was diagnosed with FND randomly and woke up one day without the ability to move my legs. Talk about terrifying. Without my parents, I never would've gotten a diagnosis, a team of doctors on my side who want to help, and most of all I wouldn't have gotten my creativity back. There was a long time where I was stuck, unsure of what to do with my life after it basically imploded my junior year of high school. Without my parents, and my closest friends I never would've been able to bounce back and take my life back and rewrite my story.

To my best friends; Cory, Toby, and Ria. You three motivate me everyday, even if you don't know it. Knowing that I can wake up in the morning (or in the middle of the night... thanks insomnia) and that you'll be there for me... it means more than you could ever know. If something happens, I know that you'll drop everything for me. I lost a lot of friends after I got diagnosed with FND, and you guys stuck with me through the good, the bad, and the ugly. So, thank you.

Thank you to Caitlin, Kaitlyn, Christina and Wonderful Duo PR for helping me with ARCs and pulling together a Street Team. Thank you for being on top of everything and answering all of my random questions.

Thank you to my Street Team, current and future. The support you have for me and my book is mind boggling, and I appreciate you guys so much (even though I struggle to express it sometimes). Thank you for marketing the hell out of this book and getting the word out.

Thank you to my group of beta readers; Charlie, Cyenna, and Cassandra. Your comments and recommendations have helped shape this book into what it is. It wouldn't be the same without you.

Thank you to my sensitivity readers, Jess and Gretch (@happilyeveraccessible). Having you two comb through my manuscript has made me feel so much better about publishing. Also, thank you for always pushing for books with disabled main characters; my TBR has grown exponentially but I don't mind.

Thank you to my editor, Anna. You came through and polished everything so it was shiny and perfect for the readers, and I truly appreciate it. Also, thank you (again) for asking about Clover's pronouns and clarification. It might seem like a small thing to you, but to me it means the entire world. And I'll probably never shut up about it (sorry not sorry).

To my stunning artists, Addie and Kye (and anyone who's drawn character art for this book). Thank you for capturing the essence of Kaid, Clover, and Zahra so well. I'm still in awe every time I look at it, and I'm so glad your art is immortalized in this book.

Thank you to any ARC readers. Thank you for reading and for spreading the word and writing reviews.

Last, but certainly not least, thank you, reader. Thank you for taking a chance on my book, and reading all the way to the end. It means the world to me. I hope you'll consider writing a review on your preferred bookish platform, they truly help spread the word of my book.

ABOUT THE AUTHOR

Hannah Phillips is a young author. She reads and writes books about people in love, and people with disabilities. Her book, Nightly Dreams is available now. She hopes you have a good day reading all of the good books.

You can find her...
@hannahphillipstheauthor on Instagram
@whatshannahthinking on Instagram (bookstagram)

https://hannahphillipsauthor.weebly.com/